MW00790587

Her Last Lie

TANYA STONE FBI MYSTERY THRILLER

TIKIRI HERATH

Rebel Diva
ACADEMY PRESS

The use of any part of this publication, reproduced, transmitted in any form or by any means electronic, mechanical, photocopying, recording, or otherwise or stored in a retrieval system without prior written consent of the publisher—or in the case of photocopying or other reprographic copying, a license from the Canadian Copyright Licensing Agency—is an infringement of the copyright law.

Data mining or use of this work in any manner for the purposes of training artificial intelligence technologies of any kind is expressly prohibited.

All rights reserved.

This is a work of fiction. Names, characters, businesses, places, events, and incidents are either the products of the author's imagination or used in a fictitious manner. Any resemblance to actual persons, living or dead, or actual events, situations, and customs is purely coincidental.

HER LAST LIE

Tanya Stone FBI K9 Mystery Thriller Series

www.TikiriHerath.com

Copyright © Tikiri Herath 2023

Library & Archives Canada Cataloging in Publication

E-book ISBN: 978-1-990234-19-4

Paperback ISBN: 978-1-990234-20-0

Hardback ISBN: 978-1-990234-21-7

Audio book ISBN: 978-1-990234-22-4

Large Print ISBN: 978-1-990234-49-1

Author: Tikiri Herath

Publisher Imprint: Rebel Diva Academy Press

Copy Editor: Stephanie Parent

Back Cover Headshot: Aura McKay

A Gift For You

T hank you for picking up my book.

There's a twisty bonus epiloge for this novel. Learn the surprising turn of events at Crescent Bay four months after the events in this story.

Revelation on the Pier!

You'll find the secret link to the bonus story at the end of this book.

Enjoy the read.

Best wishes,

Tikiri

＊━━━━＊

There is no explicit sex, heavy cursing, or graphic violence in my books. There is, however, a closed circle of suspects, many twists and turns, fast-paced action, and nail-biting suspense.

NO DOG IS EVER HARMED IN MY BOOKS. But the villains always are...

Tropes you'll find in this mystery thriller series include: female protagonist, women sleuths, detective, police officers, police procedural, crime, murder, kidnapping, missing people, creepy cabins, serial killers, dark secrets, small towns, plot twists, shocking endings, revenge, vigilante justice, family lies, intrigue, suspense, and psychological terror.

The Red Heeled Rebels Universe

The Red Heeled Rebels universe of mystery thrillers, featuring your favorite kick-ass female characters.

❖━━❖

Tanya Stone FBI K9 Mystery Thrillers

Thriller series starring Red Heeled Rebel and FBI Special Agent Tanya Stone, and her loyal German Shepherd K9, Max. These are serial killer thrillers set in Black Rock, a small upscale resort town on the coast of Washington state.

Her Deadly End

Her Cold Blood

Her Last Lie

Her Secret Crime

Her Perfect Murder

Her Grisly Grave

www.TikiriHerath.com/Thrillers

Asha Kade Private Detective Murder Mysteries
Murder mystery thrillers, featuring the Red Heeled Rebels, Asha Kade and Katy McCafferty. Asha and Katy receive one million dollars for their favorite children's charity from a secret benefactor's estate every time they solve a cold case.
Merciless Legacy
Merciless Games
Merciless Crimes
Merciless Lies
Merciless Past
Merciless Deaths
www.TikiriHerath.com/Mysteries

Red Heeled Rebels International Mystery & Crime - The Origin Story
The award-winning origin story of the Red Heeled Rebels characters. Learn how a rag-tag group of trafficked orphans from different places united to fight for their freedom and their lives and became a found family.

The Girl Who Crossed the Line
The Girl Who Ran Away
The Girl Who Made Them Pay
The Girl Who Fought to Kill
The Girl Who Broke Free
The Girl Who Knew Their Names
The Girl Who Never Forgot
www.TikiriHerath.com/RedHeeledRebels
This series is now complete.

Tikiri's novels and nonfiction books are available in e-book, paperback, and hardback editions, on all good bookstores around the world.

These books are also available in libraries everywhere. Just ask your friendly local librarian or your local bookstore to order a copy via Ingram Spark.

www.TikiriHerath.com

Happy reading.

HER LAST LIE

AGENT TANYA STONE FBI K9 MYSTERY THRILLER

A naked female body smashes against the rough ocean waves, fifty yards from the rocky shore.

FBI Special Agent Tanya Stone jumps in to retrieve the dead woman before the tide pulls the body into the ocean. But an eerie dread ripples through her as she approaches the floating corpse.

The victim's head is missing....

A sinister cloud looms over this upscale seaside town.

A twisted secret of deadly rituals is about to explode into the open. It will upend the perfect lives of the wealthy locals. They don't know a serial killer with a chilling track record is hiding in plain sight, waiting for their next kill.

With Max, her K9 partner, Tanya races against the clock to expose lies and double identities and catch the killer before they strike again.
But will she become the killer's next prey?

Blood Wine Kill

"You will kill tonight, my dear."

Her voice was soft, but I heard her.

I turned and stared at the dagger.

The Star of Death.

It lay innocently in her beautiful white-gloved hand, but I had seen that blade slash through human flesh and bone.

My stomach lurched.

The Queen, as she called herself, glided up to me across the marble floor. Her arctic-blue eyes bored into mine. But I couldn't look away.

The woman never walked. She floated with sinewy grace, her pose regal, her face stern.

She was clad in a stunning Victorian ballgown of crimson satin. Her ruby studded tiara glittered under the crystal chandeliers that dangled from the cathedral ceiling of the ballroom.

She was one of the most mesmerizing people I'd met, but her sylphlike movements reminded me of a King cobra stalking its prey.

My shoulders tightened. A bead of sweat trickled down my back. Only one thought swirled through my troubled mind.

Can I kill tonight?

My blood pounded in my ears. I barely heard the murmurs around me.

They were beautiful people, dressed in luxurious Rocco gowns and fancy tuxedos which harkened back to an era that no longer existed. Hollywood stars and starlets from LA. Venture capitalists and hedge fund managers from Silicon Valley. Celebrities and social media influencers from all over. They were drinking vintage red wine from crystal glasses, waiting for the ceremony to begin.

The Queen was so close to me, I could smell her fragrance.

She got it from an exclusive boutique on Manhattan's Billionaire's Row. I know because she took me there last summer in her private jet and told me I could have anything I wanted for my twentieth birthday. She hadn't batted an eyelid when I pointed at the sapphire-studded eau de parfum from Switzerland that cost seven thousand dollars.

She bought me that day.

After that, there was no turning back.

The Queen thrust the precious dagger toward my chest.

The knife's tip grazed the French lace of my bodice. One twist of her wrist, and she could slash my chest in half.

Her lips quivered with anticipation, and her eyes blazed like luminous lasers that could incinerate me in one hot second.

"Take it," she whispered, her beautifully painted mouth curving into a coaxing smile.

My throat went dry. I could feel the others' eyes on me from all corners of the hall, staring, judging, mocking.

I spotted the man in the black tuxedo and top hat by the fireplace, a condescending sneer on his face. It was like he couldn't wait to see me fail.

I was sure his snooty girlfriend was fluttering nearby, swishing around in her golden gown, boring everyone with a recounting of the last yachting trip she made to the Bahamas.

Or wherever.

A warm flush crept up my neck.

I hate them.

With trembling fingers, I touched the carved hilt of the dagger. The handle felt cold against my skin. Like death itself.

I pulled back.

"I chose you because you're special." The Queen's face was inches from mine, her perfume intoxicating my senses. "Because you're the only one in this room who can do this."

My head spun.

"I want to…," I whispered, "but I'm not ready."

Every fiber in my body screamed at me to walk away.

But I couldn't.

"This will be yours tonight," she said.

I glanced down at her hand. On her other gloved palm was a dazzling diamond bracelet, the red vial pendant glowing, beckoning me to pick it up.

That wasn't a ruby.

"Do you really want them to win?" she hissed in my ear.

I glanced over her shoulder. The top-hatted man's arrogant smirk had widened. He had seen me hesitate.

Something dark stirred inside of me. I could feel the slow boil of my blood swelling inside my veins. My heart quickened.

No. I can't let them have the last say.

I curled my fingers around the dagger. Its power surged up my arm like a lightning strike. I could have sworn the knife was alive.

"Good girl," she whispered.

I stared at the ominous red stains on the blade. That wasn't rust.

"I never wash after my kills," said the Queen.

With those last words, she swirled around and stepped away from me, sweeping the marble floor with her majestic ballgown.

She headed toward the man in the top hat to tell him the news. His smirk vanished. This time, I smiled.

Today is the day I take my power back.

"Wine?"

I turned to see a server in a crisp black shirt and pants next to my elbow, a silver tray in her hand. That used to be my job, once. Not anymore.

I picked up a glass and brought the crystal close to my lips, smelling the human blood mixed in with the Château Margot.

A shiver ran up my spine.

Each glass got only a few drops, as per tradition, but the scent lingered. Maybe it was my imagination, but I savored every drop.

The Queen is right. I'll show them who I really am.

The trumpet call from the corner of the hall startled everyone. The room hushed to an expectant silence, and all eyes turned on me.

The Queen had taken a seat in her plush velvet throne. Next to her, a golden-haired harpist played a haunting song that would have made me cry any other day.

Not today.

I straightened my shoulders and lifted my head high.

My heart pounded inside my chest. My hands were wet with sweat, but I clutched the dagger even tighter.

I rotated and gazed at the stage set across from the Queen's dais. It was decorated with elaborate lights and exotic flowers, fit for a lavish wedding. A shrouded object took center stage, draped in a white cloth.

My throat constricted. The air felt heavy, like a thick fog had rolled in from the ocean and settled inside the ballroom.

A young man in a crisp footman's uniform hastened up to the platform and pulled away the cloth with a flourish.

Shocked gasps escaped the onlookers at the sight of the naked girl tied to the cross. Even if you had seen this scene a hundred times, it was always unexpected.

The air in the room had become warmer, and the tension thicker.

The girl on the cross raised her head. Her face contorted in horror as she realized the ceremony was about to begin.

I walked toward the podium, the dagger in my hand steeling my heart.

I could feel the eyes of the man in the top hat and his nasty girlfriend on my back. I could almost hear them snicker as they wondered if I was strong enough. I clenched my jaw.

I'll show you.

The girl on the cross struggled as I approached the podium, but she looked broken, like the life had already drained from her. The bloodletting rite had begun at noon. It was her blood we were drinking.

I was ten feet from the platform now. Behind me, a low chant rose from the crowd, melding with the harp's melodic harmony.

I climbed the steps carefully, one by one, onto the stage. I couldn't trip and fall. Not in front of them.

The singing got louder, echoing through the hall.

The girl on the cross cried out. They hadn't drugged her enough, but that was inconsequential now. I walked over to her, my head spinning.

Must be the wine.

I stood for a moment and observed the terrified young woman. She was about my age. Her skin looked baby soft and white as snow under the sparkling chandeliers. Her features were sharp, but pretty. A lot like mine. We could have been twins.

I raised the dagger in the air.

My hand trembled.

The chanting got louder.

I swept the knife down.

A bone-chilling scream cut through the hall, shredding my nerves.

The dagger fell from my hand. I crumpled to the floor.

And the world went black.

Day One

FBI SPECIAL AGENT TANYA STONE

Chapter One

"Someone's following us."

FBI Agent Tanya Stone glanced at her rearview mirror again.

They were on a quiet road that hugged the shoreline, on their way to a small seaside town she hadn't even known existed until this day.

"A white sedan with tinted windows. It's been weaving in and out behind us for five miles now."

She pressed on the Jeep's gas pedal.

In the passenger seat next to her, Deputy Shawn Fox had been fidgeting nervously ever since they started this trip. He twisted around and glanced at the rear window.

"Down, boy," he said to the massive German Shepherd sitting on his haunches in the back. "Move over so I can see, would you, Max?"

With a grunt, Max laid his head down on the seat.

"It's probably a family heading to Crescent Bay for the weekend," said Fox, turning back around. "There's only one road into town. If the weather was nicer, we'd hit a lot more traffic."

Tanya checked her rearview mirror again.

"Something tells me that isn't a family on vacation. They slowed down when I slowed, and they sped up when I sped up. I swear they're tailing us."

"Sometimes you talk so paranoid, it's like we're in a war zone or something." Fox clasped and unclasped his hands, his mind on more personal concerns. "Why would anyone follow us, anyway? We're not here on official business."

Tanya didn't respond.

As far as her fellow passenger knew, she was a contractor for the Black Rock police precinct—just another colleague at the office. What Deputy Fox didn't know was she was also an undercover federal agent sent to scope out a bloodthirsty crime ring on the West Coast.

Law-abiding citizens had been targeted. Normal people had gone missing. Bodies had washed up along the seashore.

Since the incidents had occurred across years and in disparate counties, and the local police departments were severely under-resourced, no one had connected the dots. That was, until a keen-eyed analyst in the federal bureau realized something was amiss.

Whoever the culprits were, they were getting away with multiple murders. And they knew Tanya had come to hunt them down.

The FBI headquarters in Seattle paid Tanya's salary. They had also trained Max in the K9 program. But as far as Fox and anyone else in Black Rock knew, she was just a war vet, happy to have a quiet civilian job with this small town's police force.

The flash of the white vehicle came from her mirror again. Tanya's stomach tightened. If there was one thing she had learned during her combat days in Ukraine, it was to trust her instincts.

Something isn't right.

She took stock.

To her left were the steel tracks made for the commercial coal trains that came down from Seattle. The dark blue Pacific Ocean lay beyond the tracks.

The sea wasn't in a good mood that day.

Angry swells crashed against the rocky shoreline, spraying a fine mist in the air as they slammed on barnacle-encrusted black boulders. The clouds loomed low and gray, as if they disapproved of the stormy seas below.

A handful of brave souls were scattered along the wet beach, snapping photos of the high waves.

"Storm watchers," muttered Fox, shaking his head. "Then they complain about tax hikes. It's because we have to save idiots like these all the time. None of them look like they can swim."

Tanya glanced at her rearview mirror again, then at her passenger. "No one knows we're coming here, right?"

Fox shot her a confused look. "This is a personal trip. I told you we have to keep this private."

"Don't worry, I've kept my mouth shut, but I was wondering if—"

"You better have."

What gratitude.

Tanya tried not to snap back.

"Look, I'm doing this to help you. I only agreed to come to stop you from pestering me, Fox. The least you could—"

"I wasn't pestering you...."

Fox's voice halted and his shoulders dropped, as if he was reminded why he was on this lonely road with a colleague he didn't know very well.

"I'm sorry," he said in a defeated voice. "There was literally no one else I could ask. Especially someone with skills like yours and Max's. I need your help."

Tanya didn't reply or take her eyes off the road. She was more worried about the strange car behind them than her colleague's ungracious attitude.

How do I lose this tail?

She glanced up as they passed a road sign.

Welcome to Crescent Bay. Population 10,000. Enjoy the breathtaking views of our coastal city.

"I thought this town was closed off," said Fox. "Didn't expect them to be advertising their views."

"It's a small town, and that's good news," said Tanya. "It shouldn't be too hard to find your sister, if she's here."

Fox let out a heavy sigh. His shoulders drooped some more. "Sure hope she's okay—"

"There!" Tanya sat up and grabbed the steering wheel with both hands. "The car's back again. Right behind us."

The powerful blast of a train's horn made her jump.

She snapped her head back. A coal train was heading north, its engine chugging slowly, looking like an orange monster lumbering along the shore.

She glanced up at her rearview mirror. The car behind them had slowed down, like it didn't want to be seen.

Her heart beat a tick faster. An idea was forming in her head.

They had just passed the storm watchers on the beach. The train was getting closer, but it was still several thousand yards away.

Tanya jumped on the gas.

They hurtled forward.

Fox clutched his seat. "Hey! What are you doing?"

The Jeep's engine roared, and its tires squealed on the asphalt.

Tanya glanced behind her one more time. She had a one-minute window before the train passed its braking distance.

"Hold on!" she shouted.

Chapter Two

T anya yanked the steering wheel to the left and gunned toward the tracks.

Fox shrieked. "No!"

The train blasted its horn.

The Jeep bucked like an enraged horse across the tracks, its engine screeching.

The train let out another angry blast.

Tanya gripped her steering wheel and put all her weight on the accelerator. The Jeep cleared the tracks and took air. Fox screamed and Max whined, but she kept her eyes dead straight ahead.

The Jeep landed on the beach with a thunderous crash, its suspension bouncing up and down.

Tanya heard a furious yell behind her, but her focus was on the enormous boulder in front of them. She turned a hard right and slammed on the brakes, coming to a halt ten feet from the ocean waves.

Behind them, the infuriated train engineer leaned into the horn again, its deafening blast slicing through the cold morning air.

Tanya's heart was pounding too hard to hear the irate cussing coming from the locomotive.

"What the hell do you think you're doing?" Fox turned to her, his face pale and his hands shaking. Beads of sweat covered his brow. "You nearly *killed* us."

A gigantic wave rolled in and slammed against the nearby rock, spraying a salty mist all over the Jeep.

Tanya didn't have time to explain.

She put the gear in reverse, took her foot off the brake, and tapped the gas pedal. The longer the Jeep stood on the sand, the deeper it would sink in. They couldn't hang out here.

Thankful her vehicle was built for rough terrain, she turned it sideways and pushed it forward, parallel to the shore.

Keep driving. Let's see if that car will follow us now.

The train thundered beside them, wagon after wagon, like an angry dragon.

Fox wiped his forehead with trembling hands.

"You're completely nuts. You know that? I have a wife and a kid. I can't risk my life. We came here to find Eva, not play crazy off-road games."

"Relax. This is a shortcut."

"Through the beach? While a storm's heading this way? Are you completely insane?"

"Keep your shirt on. I was trying to—"

"Help!"

The panicked cry came from behind them. Max got to his feet and started barking at the back window.

"What in heaven's name was that?" said Fox, sitting up.

Tanya stopped the Jeep and swiveled around. The storm watchers on the beach were jumping up and down like they had spotted a whale.

"Hey!"

"Someone help!"

She narrowed her eyes. "What are they shouting about?"

"A bunch of crazies." Fox shook his head. "Can we please get back on the road and drive like normal people? I'm regretting asking you to come with me."

The last of the train wagons passed. The engineer up front blasted the horn furiously one more time, as if to make a point.

Tanya peeked through the side window to see what happened to the car that had been following them.

She froze.

Parked behind the train tracks right above them was an unmarked Crown Victoria, its red and blue lights flashing. Even from where she was, Tanya could see the officer inside glaring at them.

Fox slumped in his seat and let out an angry sigh.

"What are you going to tell our chief now, huh? When we get arrested for reckless driving?"

The panicked voices behind them grew louder. The storm watchers were rushing toward them. No, they had seen the squad car by the tracks.

"Help!"

"Somebody do something!"

"Call nine-one-one!"

Chapter Three

A woman darted over and thumped her fist on the back of the Jeep.

"Hey! There's a girl in the sea! She's drowning!"

Tanya opened her door and leaped out, barely noticing Max jumping out after her.

Fox stumbled out of the vehicle.

"Oh, my God. Eva! Maybe it's Eva!"

The sound of a car door banging came from above. From the corner of her eyes, Tanya spotted a slightly overweight man in a brown sheriff's deputy uniform scramble across the tracks.

She didn't wait.

She raced over to where the storm watchers had been standing before, with Max and Fox at her heels. The small crowd followed, their hands on their heads, their faces pale in horror.

Though neither Tanya nor Fox were in their uniforms or carried their badges, the crowd seemed relieved to see them rush into action. One man pointed a shaky finger to a rocky outcrop thirty yards from the shoreline.

"We saw someone over there. It was a girl, I think."

Tanya could hear the huffing and puffing of the deputy trying to catch up with them.

"There she is!" cried a woman, jumping up and down, arms flailing. "Do something!"

"The tide's gonna take her away!" yelled another.

Tanya squinted into the distance and spotted the outline of a human bobbing up and down on the rough ocean waves. Fox stared at it, as if paralyzed in fear.

"Eva? Is it Eva?"

"Hang on," said Tanya. "I'll get her."

She ripped off her jacket and kicked off her boots. Without thinking, she darted into the cold ocean and dove in, head first.

The freezing water hit her like a sledgehammer, but she kicked her legs and propelled herself forward. When she turned to take a breath, she spotted a furry brown head paddling a few feet behind her.

Her heart jumped to her mouth.

She wanted to scream at Max to get back to the shore, but she'd only swallow salt water and drown if she panicked now.

Her pup was young and strong, but he didn't weigh much more than a teenage girl. He also wasn't the best swimmer in doggy school. But he had a heart of gold and didn't hesitate to jump in when someone called for help.

Tanya turned her head and swallowed a lungful of air.

"Max, get back!" she yelled, though she wasn't sure he could hear her.

He kept paddling, trying to match her speed.

If anything happens to him....

With one eye on her dog, and another on the human blob floating among the waves, Tanya pushed through, trying to focus on her task.

Kick. Reach. Pull back. Turn. Breathe.
Kick. Reach. Pull back....

Her clothes were completely wet now. They hung heavily on her body, which slowed her down, but she wasn't about to stop.

From the shore, she could hear the faint shouts of the storm watchers. She didn't have time to consider what Fox or the local deputy were up to, but she prayed they were calling for an ambulance.

A tornado whirled inside her head as she swam over to the woman adrift among the waves.

It can't be Fox's sister. That would be a weird coincidence. Whoever it is, I've got to get her away from the rocks.

The water calmed once she passed twenty yards into the sea. She turned to glance at Max, who was still paddling furiously, his furry snout in the air.

She stopped and treaded water so he could catch up. She was taking stock of her position when she realized there was something seriously wrong with the person she was about to rescue.

The woman, if it was a woman, was bobbing up and down at the whim of the currents. Something about the way the body moved felt wrong.

Tanya dove back in, kicking her feet and rocketing forward.

It was only when she approached the drifting body that she realized what had bothered her.

It was a naked woman.

Her head was missing.

Chapter Four

"Twenty-five years on the job. Never seen anything like this."

The local deputy stared at the body lying on the beach like he couldn't believe his eyes.

The storm watchers bunched up behind him, as if they were afraid the corpse would somehow come alive as a headless zombie.

The woman who had spotted the body in the ocean was sitting against a rock, cradling her knees. Next to her, a man was retching like he had a nasty bout of food poisoning.

Tanya couldn't blame them. She had been fighting nausea ever since she saw the crudely dismembered woman floating in front of her.

She sat on a rock a few feet away from everyone else, stroking Max's ears. They were both still panting hard from their unexpected excursion, and Tanya was still coming to terms with what she had pulled out of the stormy seas.

Fox had almost fainted when she had brought the body to the shore. But the woman wasn't his sister. That, Tanya knew for certain.

The victim had amber-colored skin and showed the first signs of wrinkling on the back of her hand.

Whoever killed her had stripped her down before throwing her headless body into the water. The only item she had on was a bracelet that had been wrapped around her wrist so tightly that even the rough waves hadn't ripped it off.

But it wasn't any piece of jewelry.

Even Tanya's untrained eyes knew this bracelet must have cost a fortune. The translucent gemstones on it had to be diamonds, and the blood-red prism embedded in the pendant must be a rare ruby.

Every fiber in Tanya's body was consumed by fatigue, but a melancholy sadness was creeping through her exhaustion.

That woman had been someone's daughter. Maybe someone's sister, someone's girlfriend, maybe even someone's mother.

Tanya touched the sunflower pendant on her neck. It was her mother's necklace. She had worn it the day the Russian militia had stormed into her home in her Ukrainian village and assassinated her in a hail of gunfire.

Tanya had only been eighteen.

According to Ukrainian folklore, the sunflower represented peace, but that hadn't helped her mom. Still, Tanya had slipped it off her mother's bloodied neck and kept it as a talisman ever since.

She clutched the pendant now, calling on her dead mother to help her find whoever committed this brutal crime.

Max turned to her and whined. He licked her cheek as if to say, *What's going on, Mom?*

"It's pretty horrific, bud," she said in a soft voice, stroking his furry head and wiping away the salt water. "Really sad."

If the dead woman had merely been in the wrong place at the wrong time, that ruby diamond bracelet wouldn't be on her wrist. The killer would have taken it. Whoever mutilated her had extremely malicious intent.

The perpetrator was someone the woman had known. Someone who had wanted her to suffer.

Tanya swallowed something bitter.

She had seen horror in war. Once, she had stumbled across a mass grave in Ukraine after the militia had left swathes of her childhood country on fire. She fought back those memories every sleepless night, when her PTSD flared up. Only pills helped her get rest. And knowing Max was always by her side to defend her.

Even without a dark past, finding a headless body discarded in the ocean would give anyone nightmares for the rest of their life.

"Had to be a hacksaw," proclaimed the local deputy to his small audience as he bumbled around the mutilated body.

"Maybe a chainsaw. But look at this mess... Whoever it was didn't know how to use it properly, that's for sure."

He had called dispatch from his shoulder radio and was waiting for reinforcement, but didn't seem to know what to do in the meantime.

Max turned his snout up and howled into the wind, the husky in him coming out. Tanya leaned over and loosened his collar, which had got tangled up during the swim.

"You did a good job, but don't ever surprise me like that again, okay?"

Max shook his head with vigor, splattering seawater droplets all over her face. Tanya scrunched her eyes.

"Wait for my command *before* you jump in," she said. "If you keep running into action like that, I'll have to send you back to K9 school, and you won't like that, bud."

But Max wasn't paying attention to her any more. He was on all fours, his ears pricked, and his eyes narrowed.

Something had caught his attention.

The wind had picked up since Tanya had swum back to the shore. It was coming from the woods toward the ocean now, rustling Tanya's hair and Max's fur.

Max sniffed the air.

"What is it, bud?"

Tanya scanned the horizon. With all that had happened, she had almost forgotten why she had ended up on the beach in the first place.

Is the person who was following us out there?

Chapter Five

Tanya surveyed the local deputy's unmarked vehicle parked across from the train tracks.

The emergency lights were still flashing. The car was a dirty white, and its windows were tinted. The driver's side panel had a large dent, like something had T-boned it recently.

Her eyes narrowed.

Was it the deputy? Had he been tailing them?

I was driving at the limit. At least, until I shook him off. If I had been speeding, why didn't he just turn on his siren and hand me a ticket, like a normal cop?

She glanced at the city sign further down the road.

Crescent Bay was a small but wealthy town, populated by retired celebrities, Silicon Valley millionaires, and anyone who could afford to buy a second or third mansion in an exclusive enclave on the West Coast.

Her stomach tightened.

This place unnerved her. She'd felt this way even before she had found out a headless body was floating in the nearby sea.

Something dark and dangerous underpinned this area, but she couldn't pinpoint it. It was a gut feeling, an intuition that told her to turn around and head back to Black Rock.

But she couldn't do that. She had promised Fox she'd help him find his missing sister, and Tanya always kept her promises.

Max barked in the direction of the tracks.

Tanya scanned the horizon, but there was no train to be seen or heard. And the road was quiet.

Max jumped off the rock, sniffed the air, then put his nose to the ground. With no warning, he headed in a straight line toward the tracks.

Tanya's heart quickened. She scrambled off the rock and ran after him.

"Wait up, bud."

Max stayed on his trail. Tanya's eyes darted back and forth, trying to figure out what was pulling him forward.

Her Glock was in the Jeep's glove compartment. For a moment, she wondered if she should run back and grab it, but Max was scurrying ahead with that determined look on his face, the one he got when he had caught a scent he couldn't let go.

He jumped on the tracks and headed in the direction of where the train had disappeared only moments ago.

Tanya jogged after him, scanning the tracks, the road, and the woods on the other side. Other than the wind rustling the leaves, there was no sign of anyone.

She heard footsteps from behind.

Tanya whipped around to see Fox coming after her, with the local deputy trailing behind him.

"Hey, where are you off to?" hollered the deputy, panting hard, stumbling across the tracks. "I need you people to make a statement. You can't run away."

"We're not running away," said Tanya. "My dog's picked up a scent—"

"Oh, my goodness."

Fox was pointing at something behind her, a horrified expression on his face.

"What the heck is that?"

Tanya whirled around to see Max sniffing at what looked like a football by the bushes.

"Max!" She rushed toward her pup. "Don't touch that."

Max looked up and wagged his tail as if to say, *Look what I found, Mom*.

Tanya grabbed him by the collar and pulled him away, trying not to retch.

"For all things holy," said the deputy, his hands on his face, staring at Max's gruesome find. "How did that ever get up here?"

Tanya looked away. There were some things even she couldn't stomach.

Fox gagged. "They gouged her eyes out."

He doubled over and vomited onto the train tracks.

Chapter Six

"Deputy Madden!"

Tanya, Fox, and the local officer spun around.

A Marine was marching up to them. At least, that's what he looked like, but he was dressed in a brown uniform and had a gold sheriff's star pinned to his lapel.

The man was built like a concrete pillar. It was hard to see his expression because his eyes were covered with shades, the dark wraparound kind that special forces wear in the field.

"What the hell's going on here, Madden?" barked the sheriff.

Max, who had been sitting quietly by Tanya's feet, got up, his ears alert, and his eyes on the newcomer. Tanya bent down and grabbed his collar. The last thing she needed was for her dog to attack the local sheriff.

The deputy gave his boss an awkward salute.

"Er... morning, sir."

The sheriff didn't salute back.

"N... nasty business, s... sir," stuttered Deputy Madden.

"I can see that," spat the sheriff. "Stop stammering and brief me, Deputy."

Tanya's back went up. Next to her, she saw Fox stiffen too. They wouldn't get along with the sheriff.

Madden's face reddened.

"I er, was, er, patrolling as usual, and saw these folks on the beach. Waiting to take storm pictures, I guess. But they started to, I mean, they spotted someone drowning out there."

A light flush crept up Deputy Madden's neck, as if he was uncomfortable being in the spotlight.

"This, er, lady here was at the scene." He pointed vaguely in Tanya's direction. "By the time I got down, she had already jumped in. Swam all the way and got a hold of the body, er, and pulled it to the shore. That's where we left her, I mean, the victim."

The sheriff turned to Tanya.

Tanya kept her face stoic and her body straight, like the soldier she was. But she knew how raggedy she must have looked. Her pants and T-shirt clung to places she didn't want them to, and her hair was wet and knotted like she had tumbled through a typhoon.

The sheriff gave her nod as if to acknowledge what she had done.

Tanya frowned. The deputy must have seen her jump the tracks illegally, but he hadn't mentioned that complication to his boss. Was he keeping that for later?

As an undercover agent, the last thing she needed was to get into trouble with local law enforcement. She also knew an early apology usually went far to avoid inquisitive questions—questions she didn't want to answer.

She stepped forward, but Fox tapped her arm discreetly.

"Don't tell them who we are," he whispered. "Please."

Tanya gave him a surprised look, but understood. They were in Crescent Bay for Fox's sake. This was his private quest to find his missing sister.

But neither officer had seen their quick exchange.

The sheriff was speaking to his deputy. "So, you found the victim in the ocean without the head?"

"Yes, sir. But after some searching, I tracked down the, er, other remains already."

Really? thought Tanya. *You mean, my K9 found the head.*

Max whined, as if he understood. Tanya scratched his ears, willing him to stay silent.

Fox was right. This incident, however horrifying, had nothing to do with them. They did their duty as good citizens, and now it was time to find Eva.

Madden turned and pointed at the woman's dismembered head lying by the bushes next to the tracks.

"There it is, sir."

The sheriff stared at the grisly object, seemingly undaunted by the sight. "How in heaven's name did that get up here?"

"Maybe the train hit her?" said Madden, scratching his chin. "Lopped her head off. The engineer never even saw it. But someone found her and threw her corpse into the sea. Sick thing to do, but there we are. I mean, there are psychos everywhere."

The sheriff put his hands on his hips. Despite his dark glasses, Tanya could imagine what was going through his mind.

What an asinine suggestion.

"That's an interesting theory," he said, finally.

So, the sheriff knows how to be diplomatic, thought Tanya.

"I er, already called the ME," continued Madden, seemingly unaware of what others were thinking of his idea. "Hatchet and

Jackson said they'll come to cordon off the area so we can secure the remains until Dr. Chen arrives."

The sheriff nodded. "Hatchet and Jackson were right behind me. They're down with the body now."

Tanya looked past him and spotted the three squad cars parked by the train tracks, their emergency lights flashing. Down at the beach, one officer was questioning the storm watchers while another stood over the headless corpse, guarding her.

The sheriff stepped away.

"Get that bagged right away, Madden."

"Will do, sir."

The sheriff turned to Tanya and Fox. "Haven't seen you folks before. You from out of town?"

"Here for the weekend," said Fox, before Tanya could answer. "We thought a getaway without the kids and some fresh ocean air would do us good."

The sheriff shook his head. "What a way to start your holiday."

He spun on his heels like one would at a military parade and marched down to the beach to join the rest of his team.

The deputy let out a relieved sigh.

"Tough boss?" said Fox.

Madden made a face.

"It's not every day I wish I worked for a bigger precinct. A forensics team would take care of this, but I guess it's my job today."

"You're lucky it's not a hot and muggy summer day," said Tanya.

With a resigned sigh, Madden pulled out a pair of gloves and a plastic bag from his utility belt. "I guess that's why it doesn't smell so bad, but your dog seems to have a stronger stomach than any of us."

Tanya turned to see Max sniffing the bushes by the head.

"This is why I get paid the big bucks, folks," said Madden as he took a tentative step towards the severed head.

"Shouldn't you be taking a few pictures before you bag the evidence?" said Tanya.

The deputy stared at her. He opened his mouth as if to say something but closed it, and instead, pulled out his phone.

Fox and Tanya exchanged a discreet side glance.

Madden had to win an award for being the most incompetent officer on the West Coast, thought Tanya. It was hard not to help him or give him proper instructions for the job.

Tanya turned to her pup. "You're going to photo bomb, bud."

Max turned around, tail wagging.

"Geez," said Fox, squinting at something the dog had in his jaws. "What did he bite into now?"

Tanya got on her haunches and gestured to Max. "Come over, bud."

Max trotted over, seemingly proud to have discovered one more thing. He stood in front of her, wagging his tail, as if waiting for his reward.

Tanya peered into his jaws and frowned. "It's a piece of paper." She turned to the deputy. "Do you have a spare glove?"

Madden pulled out a thin plastic pair and handed it to her, looking glad she was the one touching whatever it was, and not him.

Using the gloves, Tanya pried the paper out of Max's jaws and unraveled it.

Fox leaned over her shoulder and squinted. "Are those *blood* stains?"

"A lab would have to confirm, but I think you're right," said Tanya, smoothening the paper. "It's a note."

She read it out loud.
"Last witness still alive."

Chapter Seven

"**Y**ou lied to your wife?"

Tanya took her eyes off the road for a second and turned to Fox.

"I didn't want her to worry," said Fox.

The deep lines on his forehead told Tanya he was doing enough worrying for all of them.

"Zoe and my sister were good friends in school," he said. "They grew up together. If Zoe hears that Eva's disappeared, she'll panic. She thinks Eva's traveling overseas for work."

Tanya scrunched her forehead. Something in Fox's story didn't add up.

She turned her attention back to the road. Rain droplets started to fall and the Jeep's automatic wipers turned on.

They had been driving for ten minutes now, away from the crime scene and toward the town. The Jeep's GPS told them Crescent Bay didn't have much of a center. Neither was it a proper town. It was an aggregate of upscale suburbs with luxury villas sprinkled along the coast.

After assisting Deputy Madden in bagging the evidence, Tanya and Fox had got back inside the Jeep.

Tanya had been anxious to get away before the sheriff questioned how and why her vehicle had come down to the beach. But the team had their hands so full managing the crime scene, that no one seemed to notice them pull away.

"So what does Zoe think you're up to this weekend?" said Tanya, increasing the wipers' speed.

"I told her there's a martial arts training event in Seattle. I said you recommended it to me."

"Great." Tanya shook her head. "You've implicated me in your lies. Thank you, Fox."

"It's complicated." He sighed. "My wife's not... anyway, it's not something I want to talk about right now."

"Why didn't you just tell her you're coming to Crescent Bay to solve a cold case?"

"Because Zoe knows the chief. One call to the station and she'll find out I'm not on the roster this weekend."

"Does Jack know where you are?"

Fox shot her a sheepish look. "I told him you're teaching the martial arts class in Seattle. He wanted to come for training too, but thankfully, he had a mountain of paperwork."

"Why didn't you tell him?" It was the one thing that had nagged her since Fox asked her to help find his sister. "As chief, Jack has resources and connections. He could pull in the State Patrol for a proper search."

Tanya reached for her phone on the dash.

"It's not too late to call—"

"No!" Fox's hands shook like he had momentarily lost control of them. "You can't tell anyone about Eva. Not my wife. Not Jack. Not the local cops. No one."

Tanya raised a brow. His outburst had been so strong, she wasn't sure what to think.

What's he hiding?

"Tell me why we can't ask for help."

Fox shifted in his seat. "You won't understand."

As if he remembered something, he pulled his wallet out of his jacket and flipped it open. Tanya glimpsed his wedding photo in the transparent pocket inside. Fox touched Zoe's face and stared at the picture for a long time.

Tanya was dying to find out what was going through his mind, but didn't want to intrude on this private moment.

Fox snapped his wallet shut and shoved it back into his pocket. He turned away from her and gazed out of the window.

In the back seat, Max let out a heavy sigh, like he couldn't wait for this trip to end. Tanya raised her eyes to the rearview mirror and glanced at her pup. He'd had a busy morning.

Her mind whirled.

A dead woman in the sea and a bloody note by her severed head. *Last witness still alive.* What if that had something to do with Eva?

She gave a side glance at Fox. The bags under his eyes were more pronounced and his skin was blotchy, like he had been crying in secret. The man was going through hell.

"You need a nap," she said, feeling for him. "We'll get you to your hotel room first thing."

"I'm not going to sleep. Not until we find Eva."

"A hot shower, at least. You found a fancy spot to stay for the night. Might as well take advantage of it and get the rest you need."

"I booked that place because it's the only clue I have."

"Clue?"

"The last time Eva called, I saw the Crescent Bay hotel in the background."

"How long ago was that?"

"Exactly a year ago."

Tanya's brows shot up.

A year ago?

"Eva video calls me at noon on her birthday every year," said Fox. "She's done that for nine years, on the dot. Except this year. She was supposed to call last Monday."

"Are you two close?"

"She ran away from home when she was sixteen and I'm the only one she'll talk to. She never tells me where she is, but I can always count on that call on her birthday." Fox let out a heavy sigh. "I spend my entire year looking forward to that one phone call from her."

"What did she say the last time you spoke?"

"The usual. She asks me how I'm doing. Asks about Zoe and our son. After ten minutes, I sing happy birthday to her. Then, she blows us a kiss and hangs up. She hates anyone asking questions about her life, so I stopped doing that a long time ago."

"Maybe she's busy with work," said Tanya. "What does she do?"

Fox shifted in his seat again.

Why is he so secretive about her?

"Maybe she'll call you soon," said Tanya.

He shook his head. "Something's happened. I don't know what it is, but she's in trouble. I just know it. She never misses that call."

His face scrunched up like he was trying to hold back tears. "Do you know what it's like to lose someone you love?"

Tanya kept her eyes in front.

"I lost my brother," she said in a low voice. "He was sixteen. Two years younger than me."

Fox's brow furrowed. "What happened to him?"

"The Russian militia stormed into our house, shot my mother, and took him away."

"My goodness."

"They held him in a torture camp for political prisoners. But when the camp was liberated, they never found his body. It was like he never existed."

"Did you find out what happened?"

"Some say he escaped, and he's hiding somewhere. He's twenty-nine if he's still alive. Part of me wants to believe it, but another part of me knows the truth will crush me one day."

Tanya swallowed hard.

"I should have stopped those men that day. I'll never forget it till the day I die."

"But you were barely an adult yourself." Fox rubbed his face. "I'm so sorry. I didn't know."

Tanya shrugged. "I didn't have the typical American suburban childhood. Anyone will think I'm crazy to talk about war, militia gangs, torture camps—"

A police siren cut her off. Tanya frowned at the rearview mirror.

"Hey, that's Deputy Madden's unmarked car. I'd recognize that dented Crown Vic any day."

"Probably rushing back to the precinct," said Fox.

Tanya pulled to the side of the road to let Madden pass. To her surprise, the squad car came to a stop, inches from the Jeep's back bumper.

Fox twisted around, his brow furrowed. "What does he want with us now?"

They watched as Madden got out and strolled over to the driver's side of the Jeep, a hand over his head to keep the rain away.

Tanya lowered her window.

"Everything all right, Deputy?"

"The sheriff wants to see you both at the station."

Tanya and Fox exchanged puzzled glances.

"We gave our statements," said Tanya.

Madden leaned closer toward her open window.

"Sheriff wants to know what you were doing at the beach when we found the dead body."

He paused. Tanya thought she caught a glint in his eye.

"He sent me to bring you two in."

Chapter Eight

Deputy Madden escorted Tanya and Fox to the back of the local precinct.

It was like the deputy had forgotten how they had coached him by the tracks only minutes ago. He hadn't even read them their Miranda rights or explained why they were being detained.

A female officer brought Tanya's bag in from the Jeep and took Tanya to the toilets so she could change into something dry.

Deputy Kathy Hatchet said very little and treated her like a suspect in a murder investigation. After a few attempts, Tanya gave up trying to get information from her.

Without a word, the deputies ushered Tanya and Fox with Max inside a windowless interrogation room and shut the door behind them.

"Let me handle this," said Fox, once they were alone.

"There's nothing to handle," Tanya hissed, shifting in her uncomfortable steel chair. "They have our IDs and will find out soon enough who we really are."

"We'll cross that bridge when we get to it."

"They may have information, especially if there's a connection between the victim and your sister."

Fox's face turned pale. "There's no connection!"

Realizing what she had implied, Tanya softened her voice. "We need them on our side."

He shot her an exasperated look. "I told you. No one needs to know about Eva."

"You know they can keep us in custody for up to twenty-four hours?"

Fox turned away from her, his face sour. A nerve in his neck had begun to throb. He looked like a man on the verge of exploding at the slightest provocation.

Tanya threw her hands in the air and looked down at Max. Max thumped his tail and rested his snout on her thigh. She scratched his ears, wondering how she ended up in this place.

What a crazy trip.

It was a long hour later when Sheriff Adams stormed inside the room. Madden followed his boss in, but hovered by the door like he didn't want to be here.

Adams held a manila folder under his arm and a dangerous expression on his face. He threw the file on the table and glowered at Tanya and Fox.

"If you're a couple on holiday, I'm the King of England."

Tanya glared at him. The man didn't take his shades off even when inside.

A small-town cop on a big power trip.

She wasn't sure who she was mad at the most. Sheriff Adams or Fox.

Adams leaned across the table, his imposing physique towering over them.

Max growled.

"Who are you really?" said the sheriff.

Tanya summoned every ounce of patience inside of her. Then, she sat back and crossed her arms, waiting for Fox to "handle" it.

He was hiding something about his sister's disappearance, something he didn't want anyone to find out. Even her.

Maybe he'll open up under pressure.

But Fox shuffled his feet and didn't say a word.

What's got into him? Doesn't he want to get out so we can look for Eva?

"Crescent Bay is a small, quiet town," said Adams. "This is where retirees and wealthy business owners come to get away from everything. You two are too young to be retirees, and you sure don't look like a wealthy couple on holiday, if you'd pardon me for saying so."

The naked bulb hanging from the bare ceiling flashed on his sunglasses. Fox stared back, his face sullen.

"What is your business in town?" said Adams.

"No comment," snarled Fox.

Madden stood by the door looking uncomfortable. He was trying hard not to make eye contact, pretending to examine something on the wall.

The sheriff gave a frustrated hiss. "We have free accommodation here for you tonight, if you don't talk."

A flash of anger spiraled up Tanya's spine. Being locked up in a jail cell was not how she wanted to spend her weekend.

I've had enough of these games.

Tanya leaned across the table to respond to Sheriff Adams.

A swift kick on her shins from under the table stopped her. She whipped around to Fox, who was studiously ignoring her and glaring at the sheriff instead. She stopped herself from punching him just in time.

"I have a murder victim on my hands," Adams continued, oblivious to the hostility between his two suspects. "A brutally mutilated one at that. I suggest you answer my questions."

"We came here to get away from the city and enjoy some ocean air," said Fox. "We have rooms booked at the Crescent Bay hotel for two nights if you want to check."

"Believe me, we will."

"We know our rights." Fox's voice hardened. "You'd better have a good justification if you're going to keep us. If you don't, let us go."

The sheriff crossed his arms.

"This town hasn't had a murder, let alone a major crime, in the past decade. I'm proud of our track record. It's a safe town where people know they will never have to worry about their security."

"What does that have to do with us?" said Tanya.

"Forgive me for being suspicious, but it strikes me as a little too coincidental when two strangers arrive in town and spot a dismembered homicide victim floating in the ocean."

"The storm watchers saw her first," said Tanya. "I dove in to grab the body before the tide took her away. If we had anything to do with it, I wouldn't have risked my and my dog's life."

She wished the man would take off his glasses so she could see his expression better. Right now, it felt like she was talking to a brick wall.

Fox nodded. "You're wasting your time."

The sheriff flipped open the manila folder. Tanya stared at her driver's license and her Jeep keys, which Madden had confiscated when he had brought them in.

"You two are residents of Black Rock, not Seattle," said the sheriff.

He turned to Tanya. "You're a martial arts trainer." He looked at Fox. "And you, sir, are Deputy Shawn Fox of the Black Rock precinct. You both work for Chief Jack Bold."

Fox glowered.

Tanya stopped herself from saying, *I told you.*

"Why are you playing games with me?" The sheriff's voice had become weary.

Fox pushed his chair back and stood up to face him. Adams didn't blink, but Madden straightened up, suddenly paying attention.

"I don't think you heard me the first time," said Fox, "so I will say it again. If you're going to arrest us, do so. Otherwise, let us go."

With a heavy sigh, the sheriff picked up the manila folder and turned to Madden.

"Take them to the back. Maybe a few hours marinating in the tank will help them talk."

Adams looked down at Max, who was still bristling by Tanya's feet. Seeing him look his way, Max barked.

"Call the pound to pick up the dog."

Chapter Nine

Tanya kicked her chair back and got up, her face red in fury.

"No one's separating my dog from me."

"You're giving me no choice." Adams shrugged. "You weren't forthcoming about who you are or why you're here. You should have at least informed me about your presence in my county. As a courtesy."

He turned to Fox.

"I'll be calling your boss to lodge a formal complaint."

Fox's face flushed a deep red.

"Hold on," said Tanya, putting her hand up. She turned to her colleague. "Do you really want to play this losing game?"

Fox didn't answer, but she could see his anger had turned into a mix of dread and dismay.

Tanya faced the sheriff.

"We came to Crescent Bay for a personal matter." She paused. "We're looking for Fox's missing sister."

Sheriff Adams's eyebrows shot up.

Tanya braced for furious words from Fox, but he remained silent. His shoulders had drooped, and his face was pale. He looked like a man defeated.

The sheriff looked at him.

"Why on earth were you ready to spend the night in jail, Deputy Fox?"

Fox looked away. His Adams's apple bobbed up and down as he swallowed hard. When he spoke, it was in such a low whisper, Tanya had to strain to hear.

"My sister has a criminal record."

Tanya raised a brow. "What for?"

"She used to belong to the Hells Angels."

"What else haven't you told me about her?"

Fox let out a heavy sigh.

"She was a drug mule for the gangsters. She was just a teen. She slipped up, got caught, and spent time in juvenile prison. The other members got away scot-free."

He looked up, the worry lines on his forehead deepening.

"She texted me on her birthday last week. It was a strange message."

Tanya's brow furrowed. "You told me you didn't hear from her."

"I said she didn't call like usual."

His voice was unusually brusque. Noticing her stare at him, he blinked and looked away.

Defensive, thought Tanya.

"Look," said Fox. "I just don't like talking about my sister, okay?"

"Can I see the text?" said Tanya.

Fox fumbled in his pocket and pulled his phone out. He scrolled through the messages, clicked on one and read it out aloud.

"Can't talk. Got new gig. Don't try to reach me."

Adams frowned. "What kind of gig?"

Fox lifted his chin and turned to the sheriff.

"I'm scared she's returned to the gang. I just want to find her and get her away from these creeps." He swallowed. "If the gangsters don't kill her, jail time will. That's why I couldn't let anyone know."

No one spoke. Those words hung in the air for a moment. Then, to Tanya's surprise, Max got up, trotted over to Fox, and licked his hand.

Like someone had pricked a balloon, the tension cleared, and the air in the room lightened.

The sheriff pulled up a chair and sat on it heavily.

"We're not talking about a minor, are we?" His voice had softened considerably.

"She's twenty-five now," said Fox. "If they try her again, it will be as an adult. That could mean life."

"When did she go missing?" said Adams.

"She was supposed to call a week ago, but didn't. Instead, I got this weird text." Fox wiped the sweat from his forehead. "Do you have a Hells Angels chapter here?"

Adams and Madden exchanged a quick glance.

Tanya caught that look.

She knew the reach and power that crime organization had across the country. In some counties, the Hells Angels had more authority than the local law enforcement officers. In others, the local officers *were* the gangsters.

"If I found one in my town," growled the sheriff, "I'd pack them up and kick them out like the rats they are."

That didn't seem to make Fox feel any better. His shoulders stooped even more.

"I can't have her get caught in the crosshairs."

"If Eva's being held against her will," said Tanya, "she can ask for leniency. If she helps with insider information, the courts will treat her better than you think. The worst-case scenario you're ruminating about isn't going to happen."

Fox didn't reply, his face scrunched in worry.

"What makes you think she's in Crescent Bay?" said Adams.

Fox laid his cell phone on the table and clicked on a video call.

"This was when she called a year ago. See that building in the background? If I zoom on it, I can make out the words on top. That's Crescent Bay Hotel."

Tanya leaned across the table to get a better look. She heard Deputy Madden walk over and stand next to her, breathing down her neck.

Fox turned the video off and clicked open another one.

"This was the call we had two years ago," he said in a hoarse whisper. "I save every one of them because I'm scared it will be the last conversation I'll have with her."

Everyone leaned in to see, their heads almost touching.

"Hey, I know this place," said Madden, jabbing the screen. "That's just up the hill. It's where all the big houses are."

It was the first time he had spoken.

Tanya picked up the phone and replayed the video. There was something about it that seemed familiar. She zoomed in on Eva's profile.

The sheriff leaned back in his chair. "I'll get my team on this, Deputy Fox, and we'll see if we can find any clues of her whereabouts."

Tanya gasped.

All eyes turned on her. She placed the cell on the table.

"I've seen this before."

Adams peered at the screen. "What are we looking at?"

HER LAST LIE

On her wrist, Eva had a thin diamond bracelet with a red prism-shaped pendant. It was partially concealed by her sleeve, but it was unmistakable.

Tanya pointed at the fancy bracelet.

"This is the same one I saw on the dead woman's hand."

Chapter Ten

A stunned silence fell in the room.

Sheriff Adams whipped around to Deputy Madden. "Show me the pics you took of the crime scene just now."

Madden rummaged through his pockets while everyone waited impatiently. It took him a minute to find his phone and unlock it, before pulling up the photo app.

With an impatient hiss, Adams plucked the cell from his hands and scrolled through the images. Tanya wondered how he could see with those shades on, especially under the somber yellow light of the interrogation room.

"What's this?" The sheriff frowned. "These are..." He trailed off and looked up at Madden, whose face flushed.

"This one's blurry." Adams tapped the phone. "This one's at a bad angle. Come on, we can do better than this."

Madden's face reddened.

The sheriff handed him back his phone, as if realizing there were strangers present.

"Where's the body right now, Deputy?"

"At Dr. Chen's, sir."

"Head down and take more photos. We need every angle of the victim, and especially of this piece of jewelry. Make sure you have the image in focus before you take the photo."

Madden snapped to attention. "Right away, sir."

He whirled around and slipped out of the room.

The sheriff turned to Fox.

"I understand your concern for your sister's criminal record, but right now, I think we need to worry about her safety."

A sharp cry came from Fox. He swallowed it quickly.

Max licked his hand again like he understood something terrible was going on. Fox ruffled the dog's head absentmindedly.

Sometimes, Tanya thought, her pup had more emotional intelligence than any human she knew. She was glad he was here because she had no idea how to placate her coworker.

She put a tentative hand on Fox's shoulder.

"I promise you, I'll do everything I can to find her."

Fox scrunched his face.

"Eva's my only sibling. Do you know why she ran away from home the first time?"

Neither Adams nor Tanya spoke.

"I found out years later that our next-door neighbor had been molesting her. He was a registered pedophile, but no one told us. I was her big brother. I was supposed to watch out for her, and I didn't."

"You were a kid," said Tanya. "You can't blame yourself."

"She was so messed up, she kept running away. Then at sixteen, she left and never came back. That was the year the Hells Angels lured her in."

"When was the last time you saw her?" asked Adams.

"Last year. On her birthday video call."

Fox lifted his tear-stained face to them.

"Every year, Zoe and I plead with her to come home. We tell her we can take care of her. She can go to college, find a job, start a fresh life, you know? But that never happened."

Sheriff Adams picked up Fox's phone and started scrolling through the videos.

"We'll check our databases for missing person's reports. We'll share her picture with townsfolk in case they spotted her, and I'll get my team to scour every inch of the county."

Tanya watched the sheriff, glad he was saying all the right things, but wondered why he still had his shades on. It gave her an uncomfortable feeling that he was hiding something. And usually, her instincts were right.

Can we trust this man? Did I make a big mistake by telling him why we came?

Adams played an older video and frowned.

"I recognize this area. It's up the hill. Most of the homes up there are walled off and guarded by private security."

He brought the phone closer to his nose. "The house she's standing in front of is Patel's."

Fox looked up. "Who's Patel?"

"Retired physician turned philanthropist. He lives alone in this big house. Donates generously to local charities, and doubles them every year, so the town adores him, and our council loves him. The man's untouchable."

The sheriff made a face like he bit into something bitter.

Tanya didn't have enough fingers on her hands to count the times she had discovered dirty skeletons in the cellars of supposedly respectable citizens. Their charity work usually masked the stink that rose from their dank basements.

"You don't like the man, do you?" she said.

"I think he has a shady past," said Adams. "He just appeared one day, and set up house. But I have no evidence for my suspicions, just a gut feel. Believe you me, I dug deep. But if I mention my doubts in public, the entire town will skewer me for defamation."

Tanya pulled her jacket off her chair.

"I'm going to have a word with this Patel. Let's go, Fox."

"Not so fast, cowboy," said the sheriff, raising a hand. "This is a delicate business."

"Delicate?" said Tanya. "If he knows something or is possibly involved in something nasty, we need to shake it out of him."

"He's going to clam up, speed dial his team of highly paid attorneys, and scoot out of the country by the time we get to his front door."

"You're the town's top cop, Sheriff Adams. You go talk to him."

"That's the problem. Patel gets along with everyone in town, except for one."

Tanya stared at him.

"I guess that would be you?"

Sheriff Adams looked away, like he was embarrassed.

Tanya spotted the slight purple bruising next to his right eye underneath those shades. It was a momentary glimpse which had disappeared as soon as he had turned around. But now, she was sure.

Sheriff Adams was covering something up.

Chapter Eleven

"Remember the note left by the head?" Adams's face turned a shade dark.

"Last witness still alive?" said Tanya.

"What does that even mean?" said Fox, his voice plaintive.

"If I have to guess," said Adams, "it's a threat they will kill again."

Fox dropped his head in his hands. Tanya took a deep breath in to settle her nerves.

"That also means we don't have a lot of time," she said.

The sheriff turned to her.

"I'll circulate these images of Eva ASAP to see if anyone has spotted her in town. Deputy Kathy Hatchet has worked with Patel on charity events. I'll get her over to his place right now."

"Maybe Patel will open up to us," said Tanya. "Fox and I have been trained. Plus, we're outsiders. We're not a threat."

Adams shook his head. "Bad idea."

"With all due respect, Sheriff. Your deputy couldn't even take proper photos of a crime scene."

"Madden's a good man." Adams pursed his lips. "Not the sharpest knife but he's willing, able, and keen. He steps in to do jobs no one else wants to."

"He bumbled around the corpse and stepped on evidence by the beach," said Tanya, trying hard to keep the caustic tone out of her voice. "I wouldn't trust him to take care of a kitten."

Plus, I'm not sure yet, but I think he was following us when we came into town.

Tanya didn't share this last piece of information because it would make her sound paranoid. The revelation of Fox's missing sister and her criminal past were enough to rattle a small-town sheriff as it was.

Adams turned to her, his glasses glinting under the light.

"You can't come in here and badmouth my employees." He got up with a frustrated hiss. "I'll send Deputy Hatchet with Turner to Patel's residence and see if they can squeeze anything out of him. She's the best for the job."

He flipped open the manila folder and let the identification cards and the Jeep's keys slide to the table.

"Let's get one thing perfectly clear. This is my investigation. Understood?"

Neither Tanya nor Fox replied.

Adams marched toward the entrance, but stopped at the threshold and whirled back.

"I could charge you with obstruction of justice, but I'm giving you the benefit of the doubt as fellow law enforcement professionals. I'd like you, in turn, to respect my jurisdiction."

Tanya kept her face stoic, but Fox nodded.

"I appreciate your help, but I won't sit on my hands, Sheriff," said Fox. "I'm not going to stop looking for Eva."

"I'd advise you to not interfere with my team under any circumstance, whatsoever. If that happens, I will charge you and you will find yourselves locked up. Don't test my patience."

With that, Adams stepped out of the room. Through the open doorway, Tanya heard him yell at his assistant.

"Get me Chief Jack Bold from Black Rock on the line ASAP."

His voice faded as he stomped through the corridor toward the office area.

Fox whirled around to Tanya and opened his mouth, but she raised her hands in defense.

"We didn't have a choice. It was either us spending the night in jail or telling the truth. Getting locked up won't help your sister."

Fox looked at her with bloodshot eyes.

"What are we going to do now?"

Tanya narrowed her eyes. "The tables have turned."

"What do you mean?"

She picked up her driver's license and car keys.

"We'll be doing the following from now on." She whistled to her pup. "Let's go, Max. We have work to do."

Chapter Twelve

"I see them."

Fox pointed at the squad car with the sheriff's decal on the side. It was several yards ahead of them, crawling through the upscale suburbs of Crescent Bay.

Tanya slowed down and drove as stealthily as she could, so the two deputies wouldn't realize they were being shadowed.

She was the fox now, and they were the rabbit.

Only moments ago, Sheriff Adams had stepped into his office and slammed the door shut before they could overhear what he was saying to their boss. A junior officer had marched over and asked them to leave.

With Max and Fox in tow, Tanya had picked up her Jeep and driven it out of the impound lot at the back of the precinct building.

"Gotcha," she'd said, as she saw what she had hoped to see.

"What?" Fox had said, turning around.

Tanya had spotted a squad car pull out to the main road. In the driver's seat was Deputy Kathy Hatchet—the same officer who had taken her to the washrooms so she could change into dry clothes.

Tanya didn't know if they were on a wild goose chase, but they weren't in the best position to demand information from the sheriff or his team.

She kept her eyes on the cruiser ahead.

Deputy Kathy Hatchet drove through the winding roads of Black Rock lined with whitewashed walls on either side.

Tanya followed, trying not to get distracted by the spectacular ocean vistas that came to view at every turn. The sound of waves crashing on the shoreline came from beyond the cliff. The rain had stopped, but the ocean was still raging.

While the labyrinth of streets made it harder to keep the vehicle up front in their line of vision, it also meant the deputies wouldn't spot them as easily.

Closer to the top of the hill, they passed a park with benches, picnic tables, and a lookout platform. Next to the viewing platform was a billboard, smaller than one you'd see on the highway.

"What's he doing making an appearance at a local fundraiser?" said Fox.

Tanya glanced through her side window.

The man on the billboard wore a black tuxedo and top hat, and was standing alone in the middle of a lavish ballroom. One look at his pearly white teeth, chiseled features, and tanned skin, and Tanya was sure the image had been computer generated.

No human can look that good.

"Creepy," said Tanya, turning back toward the road. "Something about him looks vaguely familiar though."

"It's Felipe Fernando."

"Actor? Musician?" Tanya shrugged. "I don't keep up with the tabloids."

"He played Detective Gonzales in *The Killing Room*. Even won an Oscar for it. What would someone like him be doing in a small town in the middle of nowhere?"

"Money," said Tanya. "They probably pay him very well for a brief appearance."

She had little interest in the mainstream entertainment industry, which she felt was plastic at best. She was sure she had never seen the actor before on screen, but she couldn't shake the feeling she had seen him in real life.

Focus.

The squad car up front took another curve up the hill. Tanya stalked them, maintaining her distance. Fox pulled up the latest video call with his sister and started rolling it frame by frame.

The police vehicle up ahead revved loudly as it headed up a steep slope toward a white gate.

Fox looked up and gave a start.

"What in heaven's name?" he said, pointing at the large gray structure overhanging on top.

Tanya raised her eyes briefly to the stone facade looming over them.

On the summit of the hill, behind the house with the long white gate, was what looked like a stone castle with high turrets. A streaming red flag hoisted on the pointy spire fluttered in the wind. It stood alone, isolated from the rest of the modern houses around it.

"A medieval castle," she said. "How eccentric."

"Spooky."

Tanya turned back to the road. Fox was right. Something about that place gave her the creeps.

Fox focused on the video calls, zooming into the backgrounds to see if he recognized any of it. He gasped. Tanya shot him a quick side glance.

"Look at this. You can spot the bottom half of that castle-like building," said Fox, pointing at his phone though Tanya couldn't see. "Eva was here. There's no doubt about that."

"Seems like we've arrived at our destination," said Tanya.

The police car up front had come to a complete stop.

Tanya pulled into a side street and parked in front of a hidden driveway. Keeping the engine running, she plucked a pair of binoculars from the glove compartment and peered through her side window.

Deputy Hatchet was out of the car and was hovering by an intercom panel on the wall. The gate opened before she got back in her car.

Tanya and Fox watched silently as the cruiser rolled through the gates.

"That's someone's *house*?" said Fox.

"A luxury compound," said Tanya. "That's the owner's mansion in the middle. Those smaller buildings are probably staff quarters or guest houses."

"What was Eva doing here?" Fox rubbed his tired forehead. "Is she still in there? Why did she come here, of all places?"

Tanya had no answers.

She surveyed the grounds before the gates closed on them, but it was hard to see what was inside that whitewashed wall.

"Can we get in?" said Fox, squinting through the window.

Tanya turned the Jeep around and drove slowly along the wall, her eyes scanning for people.

"Let's do a recon first."

Other than a few cameras on the gates of a handful of houses, she didn't see too much surveillance equipment on the properties. No one was out and about.

"It's a quiet neighborhood all right," she muttered under her breath.

"It's supposed to be a safe town," said Fox. "That's what the sheriff said."

"I'd take his words with a grain of salt," said Tanya. "Did you see the bruise on his eye?"

"He was wearing shades."

"I spotted it when he turned. I'd like to know how he got it."

"Hey." Fox sat up and pointed. "Stop right here. That's the back gate of the Patel residence."

Tanya rolled the Jeep next to the small gate along the wall and turned the engine off.

Fox clicked his door open to jump out.

"Hang on," said Tanya. "Let's make sure no one's watching first."

"The coast is clear," said Fox in an impatient voice.

He was just about to step out when the screech of a metal door came from the side. He gently closed the door.

Tanya scooted down on her seat.

Someone was coming out of Patel's compound.

Chapter Thirteen

Tanya and Fox hunkered down, their eyes peeled just a few inches over the dashboard.

In the backseat, Max lay quietly, his head down but ears pricked, like he knew they were on stealth mode.

A young woman stepped through the gate.

Then another and another.

The three were dressed like fashionable influencers you'd see on social media. Their heavy makeup, trendy tops, expensive sneakers, and on-brand handbags screamed luxury. They were teenagers, at least a decade younger than Fox's sister.

"Models?" whispered Fox.

"Not skinny enough." Tanya frowned. "Unless the fashion industry has had a major change in conscience."

"Escorts?" said Fox in a cracked whisper.

Tanya didn't answer. It wasn't a question she wanted to say yes to.

The girls stopped as if they felt their presence. Their eyes darted back and forth, but they didn't seem overly frightened.

They stared at the Jeep for a brief moment, but from their vantage point, it looked empty.

After another check, they scurried down the road, clutching their enormous bags, giggling like they had just got away with something.

Tanya straightened up in her seat. "Why are they sneaking around like this?"

She opened her door quietly, and motioned for Max to jump out. Fox got out after them. They walked stealthily behind the girls, who were too busy chattering to perceive them.

Tanya wondered what these girls had been doing in a mansion where an old man lived alone. She could imagine many reasons, all of which made her stomach turn. But she knew better than to make hasty assumptions. In her business, guesses could get you killed.

She stopped in the middle of the road and raised her hand. "Excuse me, ladies?"

The girls jumped and spun around. They stared at her like she was an alien.

"Do you have a minute?" said Tanya.

She took a step forward, trying to look as non-threatening as she could, despite the German Shepherd and an off-duty officer behind her.

But before she could get any closer, the girls twirled around and sprinted down the road.

"Hey!" called out Tanya. "I just want to talk."

But they didn't stop. They were fitter than she had expected and were gaining speed.

"Get them, Max," said Tanya, as she dashed after them.

Max bounded their way.

The girls disappeared around a corner, screaming at each other to *run*. Tanya and Fox kept up their pace.

The alleyways in the neighborhood wound around the properties like a 3D puzzle, but the girls seemed to know the area well. By the time Tanya had turned three corners, she couldn't see them anymore. And she had lost sight of Max.

She stopped to take stock. Fox came over, panting hard.

"Where did they go to?"

Tanya turned around, hands on her hips.

"I can hear them. They can't be too far."

Somewhere in the maze, Tanya heard a bark.

Max.

He barked again, as if he was calling her over. Tanya and Fox turned into the pathway on their right, following his barks. They entered a small alleyway and stopped.

Max had cornered the three girls in a cul-de-sac. They were standing with their backs to a wall, clutching their bags.

"Call him off," screamed one girl as she spotted Tanya.

"Down, Max," called out Tanya.

Max backed off, but kept his face pointed at them. The girls cowered against the wall as Tanya and Fox advanced on them.

"Who are you?" asked one girl, a quiver in her voice.

"What do you want with us?" shouted another.

"Sorry about that," said Tanya, pulling Max back. "My pup used to work for the police, but he's really a sweetheart."

The girls' eyes widened, but they seemed to relax.

Tanya spread her arms, to show them she didn't mean any harm. "We just came to town and got lost in this maze. Thought you could give us directions to a friend's house."

The girls stared back, unsmiling.

Tanya noticed all three were wearing silver pins on their lapels. There were no letters or symbols on them, but each had a small red prism embedded in the middle.

Her mind raced back to the bracelet on the headless corpse's wrist.

What is that red stone?

Tanya dropped her shoulders and shoved her hands in her pockets to look as casual as she could, given the circumstances.

"So, do you gals know the area well?"

All three nodded.

Tanya smiled. "It's a beautiful neighborhood. You've got amazing views."

"It's nicer where we live," said the boldest girl.

"Really? Where's that?"

The girl pointed up the hill.

Fox looked up. "You live in that fancy castle?"

All three smiled proudly.

Tanya leaned over to the one who seemed the most talkative.

"We're supposed to visit Dr. Patel today. Do you know where his house is?"

Her eyes widened. "You know Dr. Patel?"

Tanya nodded. "We have an appointment with him in ten minutes."

"We just came from his place."

Tanya gave her a mock surprised look and turned to Fox. "You were right. That was the correct address."

"See, I told you," said Fox.

The girl shook her head. "No, you guys are in the back alley. You want to turn around and go to the front gate."

"Thanks," said Fox. "Good to know."

"So, what were you doing at Dr. Patel's?" said Tanya.

"We went to pick up our boxes. He told us they were ready."

"Boxes?" said Fox.

"They came in today." One girl pulled out a metallic box from her oversized handbag. "This cost me a grand."

"A grand?" said Tanya. "For a box?"

"No." The girl's voice was laced with impatience that said *don't you know?* "For the makeup kit."

What's this makeup made of? Gold dust?

"I thought you wanted to steal our boxes," said the third girl. "That's why we ran."

Suddenly, Max whirled around and growled. Tanya turned to see his heckles were up and his lips were drawn back into a snarl.

From somewhere in the maze came heavy footsteps, like army boots marching their way.

Tanya and Fox stepped forward.

Two muscled men in blue camouflage uniforms stomped into the alleyway.

Their black handguns were pointed straight at their heads.

Chapter Fourteen

"Hands up!"

The men hollered.

With one terrified glance at them, the girls fled back down the alleyway, screeching.

The men didn't even give them a second glance.

Tanya and Fox stood rooted to their spots, their hands in the air.

By Tanya's feet, Max growled like an angry lion.

The men's eyes flickered over to the German Shepherd. One man lowered his weapon and pointed it at Max.

"Behind me, bud. Now!" shouted Tanya as she stepped in front of her pup.

She turned her blazing eyes to the men.

"Who the hell are you and what the hell do you want?"

The guards gave a start as if they hadn't expected her to react so forcefully.

"Your vehicle's by our back entrance," growled one man. "What are you doing there? Trying to break into the property?"

Private security guards, thought Tanya, relief rushing through her. *These are the guys Sheriff Adams talked about.*

"We came to visit Dr. Patel," said Tanya, keeping her gaze and voice steady.

"We have an appointment," said Fox.

The two men exchanged a puzzled glance.

"Why didn't you come through the front gate?" said the first man. "We have the intercom there."

"These streets are a bloody maze." Tanya let out an exaggerated hiss. "If it was that easy to find, we wouldn't be running all over the place, asking for directions, would we, now?"

The men frowned. Neither had changed their aim, but their shoulders had relaxed and they no longer looked like they were ready to pull the trigger at a moment's notice.

"What do you want with Dr. Patel?" asked one guard, frowning.

"We have a confidential message for him. It's time sensitive."

"Tell us, and we'll take it to him," said the first man.

Tanya let out another annoyed hiss. "I don't have time for this." She turned to Fox. "We're wasting our time here."

She bent down and pulled on Max's collar. "Let's go, boy. We can tell the boss that Patel's men ambushed us, threatened us, and didn't give us the chance to do our job."

"What job?" said the second man.

Tanya let out a resigned sigh.

"There's been a change in the delivery of the makeup boxes. Supply chain issues. It's affecting everyone, and it's going to impact prices, but I need to speak to the doctor personally to sort out the next steps."

"How come Newton didn't come?" said the first man. "Isn't he in charge of this logistic stuff?"

HER LAST LIE

"Newton's sick. Influenza. He'll be off for a week or two," said Fox. "He phoned Dr. Patel this morning. Didn't he tell you?"

Tanya discreetly crossed her fingers, knowing they could call their boss and confirm her story within seconds, but she banked on the doctor being occupied with two local deputies as a good detraction for that.

"Let's go," said Tanya to Fox.

She glared at the men as she moved toward the alleyway entrance. "Dr. Patel isn't the only man in our business network, you do realize that?"

The guards lowered their weapons.

"Hang on," said one man. "How do we know you're not lying?"

Tanya shot him a disdainful look.

"Dr. Patel said he'd see us soon after his chat with the local sheriff's office. I believe Deputy Hatchet is seeing him now, isn't she?"

The men's eyebrows shot up.

"Look, either we talk to the doctor or we're going." She glared at them. "If you're that worried about security, why don't you frisk us? Then, let us in."

The men jerked their heads back like they hadn't thought of it. One of them came forward.

Max growled.

"Settle down, bud," said Tanya in a low voice. "Sit."

The first guard stayed in place and watched while the second guard frisked Fox first, then Tanya. His movements were fast and jerky.

Amateurs.

Tanya was thankful they had left their badges and guns in the car. The minute these goons sniffed out they were law enforcement

67

from out of town, and not authorized by Sheriff Adams, they would lose any opportunity to get inside the compound.

The guard turned to his mate and nodded. "All good."

The men holstered their weapons and gestured for Fox and Tanya to follow them.

The four walked abreast without speaking. Tanya and Fox were flanked by the guards and Max walked in between Fox and Tanya. His hackles were still up, but he had stopped growling.

They stepped through the small gate in the back of the Patel residence and into the main grounds. Tanya scanned the exits and surveyed the wall to see if it could be easily climbed from this side.

Always be ready for a speedy departure.

The men marched passed the staff quarters, toward the mansion in the middle of the compound. Tanya spotted Hatchet's cruiser parked next to a gleaming Cadillac on the driveway in front of the mansion.

The guards ushered them toward the back door, and into a large kitchen.

Tanya noticed figures in staff uniforms scurry off as they approached. She could feel their curious eyes on their backs, staring at them like they were exotic animals.

A plump man in a chef's hat looked up from his cutting board. His face turned purple as he spotted the intruders.

"This isn't a public walkway!" he spat at the guards.

The men didn't reply.

The chef shook his carving knife in the air. "This is the last time you walk through my kitchen. Next time you'll feel my blade, you hear?"

The guards hastened their pace, leading Tanya and Fox into a long corridor. They were heading toward the front of the house from where low, murmured voices came.

"I can't thank you enough, Dr. Patel," came a friendly female voice.

Deputy Kathy Hatchet.

Adams was right, thought Tanya. The deputies got along well with the doctor.

The guards stopped at a large entranceway. Through the open doorway Tanya could see an elaborately decorated room the size of a small apartment.

The two uniformed deputies were seated at the edge of a couch, their hands on their laps, their faces turned toward their host. They looked like eager students at the feet of their favorite teacher.

Across from them, seated on a grand armchair and surrounded by paisley-patterned cushions, was the man Sheriff Adams said was untouchable.

Chapter Fifteen

For one confusing second, Tanya wondered if they had entered a temple of an obscure sect.

Brightly colored silk saris draped the bay windows and embroidered pillows and cushions crowded the couches. The smell of burning incense was strong.

Dr. Patel was clad in baggy pants and a knee-length cotton shirt. Tanya judged him to be in his mid-sixties, but he wore his gray hair and beard long, which made him look much older.

Even from the doorway, she could see this man's smile didn't go all the way to his eyes. But it was the small button that flashed on his lapel that grabbed her attention. It looked a lot like the silver pin the three girls had been wearing.

The doctor and the deputies had been so focused on their conversation, they hadn't noticed them hovering by the entranceway.

While Tanya watched, Deputy Hatchet leaned forward with a thick envelope. The officer bowed deferentially to the doctor as she placed it on the coffee table.

"Thank you for everything, Doctor."

Hatchet spoke in a voice that sounded like the man could heal cancer by touch.

Tanya's brow furrowed. It was an odd scene. It certainly didn't look like a typical police interview.

One of the guards cleared his throat politely. The officers and the doctor turned toward the doorway. The deputies' faces fell as they spotted them.

"Newton's team, Doctor," said the guard, a slight tremble in his voice. "Seems like there's an issue with this month's delivery."

Without waiting for the doctor to reply, Tanya strode inside the room, with Fox and Max following her.

Deputy Hatchet opened her mouth as if to speak, then closed it. Her male counterpart got up hastily. "We should go," he said, straightening his gun belt. "Gotta get back to work."

This was supposed to be work, thought Tanya, wondering what they had been deep in discussion about all along.

Tanya and Fox stood by the coffee table, as the two deputies scrambled off.

As soon as the officers hurried out of the front entrance, Tanya pulled out her wallet and flashed it. There was an ID card issued by the Black Rock's police precinct mixed in with her credit and debit cards, but there was no need to take it out.

"We're not here with a message from Newton," she said, keeping her eyes on the man in the chair. "We're with the police."

The guards moved in.

The doctor waved them away, his lips curling in amusement. The men stopped, but didn't put their weapons away.

Dr. Patel turned to Tanya with the smile that didn't go to his eyes.

"I just spoke with the police," he said in a slightly accented English. "We had a very pleasant conversation."

His tone was melodic, designed to soothe, but that only made Tanya nauseous.

"We have a few more questions," she said, her voice steely.

"I am very happy to answer anything you want."

Something about him felt fake, but there was intelligence behind those beady black eyes. Unlike the guards, this wasn't a man who would be easily fooled. The way the local deputies had cowed in front of him confirmed the power he wielded in this town.

But before Tanya could say anything, Fox plunked his phone on the coffee table.

"Have you seen this woman?" he said, impatience in his voice.

"Sit, sit."

Dr. Patel gestured toward the couches and nodded, that plastic smile never leaving his face. "Why don't you take a seat, and we can have a very nice chitchat."

Fox leaned across the table, his face stony. "We didn't come here to have a chitchat. We're looking for a missing person."

He glared at the old man.

"I'm going to ask again. Have you seen her in or around your house?"

Dr. Patel's eyes flitted to the still picture of Eva. Fox had pulled up the video call his sister had made in front of this house and paused it. It would be hard for the doctor to deny she'd been near this compound.

With that smile still intact, the doctor shrugged and gave a dismissive wave.

"So many people come to see me every day. As much as I would like to, I can't remember them all, now can I?"

Tanya's eyes fell on the envelope on the table, the one Deputy Hatchet had left behind.

What's inside? Cash? Or something else?

"What do people come to see you for?" she said.

The doctor's smile widened. "I am retired now. My medical practice is no more. But if someone comes for advice, I try my best to help them. I have never forgotten my Hippocratic oath."

Tanya frowned. He was hiding something, just like everyone else seemed to be in this town.

"We saw three girls leave through your back gate carrying gold-laminated boxes. Can you tell us what they were doing here today?"

"Aahh." Dr. Patel waved his hands amiably. "Those bright young ladies are part of my new recruitment strategy."

Fox's eyebrows shot up. "Recruitment? For what?"

The doctor gave him a sympathetic look. "I can see you're not from town. Maybe you haven't heard. I run the largest retail-at-home organization in the region."

Tanya stared at him. *Retail at home? What does that mean?*

"What's in those gold boxes?" she said.

"Makeup kits."

As eccentric as that sounded, it corroborated with what those girls had said.

"I have many buyers and sellers in my network," said the doctor. "It is a wonderful fashion and beauty business that gives freedom and empowerment to everyone. Especially to women. That is what women want these days, is it not?"

Tanya blew a raspberry. The man was running a multilevel marketing scheme.

"With all due respect," said Fox, "you're not the first person who pops to mind when I think of a fashion and beauty program."

Dr. Patel let out a small laugh.

"You haven't been educated in this business, young man. If you will only let me tell you about it." He gestured toward the couch. "Come. Come. Shall we have coffee? Or tea? Chai, perhaps?"

Neither Tanya nor Fox moved.

"My clinical practice in Los Angeles did very well for me, you see." The doctor continued as he realized his guests weren't keen on banter. "All the beautiful people in the world came to see me. This project is just a natural progression of my vocation. Nothing strange or criminal about it, I assure you."

Tanya narrowed her eyes. "What did you specialize in at LA?"

Patel turned to her, his eyes traveling from her face, down her neck, and to her bust. Tanya felt her stomach turn. She suppressed the urge to slam her fist on the table.

My eyes are up here, pervert.

Dr. Patel smiled. "I was the best plastic surgeon in California."

Chapter Sixteen

F ox leaned back in surprise.

He pointed at his phone on the table.

"Did... did she...." He swallowed hard. "Did she come to see you for plastic surgery?"

Dr. Patel shook his head. "I am sorry, but I have never seen this pretty girl before. If I did surgery on her, I would have surely recognized her."

"What about this pyramid scam of yours?" said Fox. "Did you try to recruit her into it?"

"Scam?" The doctor put his hands over his heart and fluttered his lashes. "Oh, my goodness, no. Mine is a wonderful opportunity which allows women to do work they love from the comfort of their own home."

Tanya tried not to smirk.

You mean, peddling cheap products and recruiting even more gullible people to your sect?

"You can ask anyone." The doctor opened his arms wide. "They will tell you I create jobs in this town. I give opportunities and promotions to ambitious young women. And young men too. I spread the wealth through my business and my philanthropy."

He turned an innocent face to Tanya. "There's nothing illegal about that, is there?"

"The deputy who left this envelope," said Tanya, pointing at it with her chin, "is she part of your MLM organization as well?"

Dr. Patel beamed with pride. A gold tooth glinted under the light.

"Doesn't everybody want to look great, make a fabulous income, and take care of their families? That is what I help everyone do."

He wagged a finger at her.

"Do you know how much toxicity there is in the cheap products you buy at the drugstore? They cause cancer, stroke, and so many common chronic diseases. My kits reduce the impact of harsh chemicals that can make you sick for life. Not to mention, give you wrinkles too."

"You're evading the question, Doctor," said Tanya. "We're not here to discuss your business schemes."

"We're in the middle of an investigation of a missing woman who could be in danger," snarled Fox.

Dr. Patel turned to him and rearranged his face to show fervent concern. "But I am only trying to help you."

Tanya picked up Fox's phone and turned the screen toward the old man. While he watched with a puzzled look on his face, she zoomed in on Eva's hand.

"Does this bracelet mean anything to you?"

Patel's face froze for a split second. In that moment, Tanya glimpsed the cold and calculating nature behind his whimsical gestures and false smiles.

"I have never seen this girl. I have never seen this bracelet. I'm sorry I can't be of more help."

That's a lie.

He got up slowly, his arms shaking as he held on to the chair. A guard rushed to help him.

"My meditation practice begins in a few minutes. I really must wash up and prepare. Now would you kindly excuse me?"

Dr. Patel flashed his smile again.

"Thank you for coming to my home. It was such a pleasure to meet you both. I hope you will find all the answers you are seeking."

Tanya was about to reply, when Fox's phone buzzed in her hands. She clicked on the messenger icon automatically before realizing this wasn't her cell, but her colleague's.

A message flashed across the screen.

Tanya's spine chilled.

"I hope to see you again soon."

She looked up to see the doctor grinning at her, a peculiar glint in his eyes.

"Have a great day now. My men will show you out."

"We'll see our way out," snapped Tanya.

She nudged Fox to follow her and whistled to Max, who had been patiently sitting at her feet.

"Let's go."

Fox opened his mouth. "But, we haven't—"

Tanya gripped his arm and propelled him toward the main entrance. With Max in tow, she marched Fox down the front steps and onto the driveway. It was only when they were out of the front gates she offered his cell back to him.

Fox stared at her. "What's going on?"

"Either your sister is up to something you don't know, or someone has her phone and is pretending to be her."

He snatched the mobile and squinted to read the message that had just come in.

Stop looking 4 me. I'm fine. Leave Dr. P alone. U R making things worse.

Chapter Seventeen

"MLM, my foot."

Tanya rolled the Jeep back onto the road.

"Patel looks and sounds like a sick shyster who will pretend anything to get close to young women."

Fox was staring at his phone, barely hearing her.

"Why would Eva say something like this?" he said, shaking his head in bewilderment.

"It's time to get forensics to help us," said Tanya, wishing she could call up her team at the FBI HQ in Seattle. "Let's see if Sheriff Adams has contacts in the nearby counties."

Fox turned to her, his eyes red with stress. "Why doesn't she want me to find her?"

He had texted and called his sister repeatedly since that peculiar note, but Eva, if it was Eva on the other end, had remained stubbornly silent.

"How am I making things worse?" Fox's voice was strained. It was like he was barely keeping it together. "Why would she say something like that?"

Tanya kept her eyes on the road as they crawled through the narrow maze that sloped gently down the hill.

She suspected Fox and his sister hadn't been as close as he had imagined. One call, once a year, hardly constituted a relationship. Plus, Eva had refused to reveal anything about her life and had remained a living mystery for more than a decade.

Eva could be anywhere, doing anything.

But Tanya knew speaking the truth would be like a stab to Fox's already broken heart. He was being powered by guilt, guilt for not having rescued his sister from their neighborhood monster so many years ago.

"Once we find out where this message came from," she said, "we'll be in a better position to answer the harder question."

"Harder question?"

"Whether this is really her, or someone else."

"If anything has happened to her, I don't know what I'll do." Fox's voice cracked. "I couldn't live with myself if...." He rubbed his lined eyes. "Where on earth did she disappear to!"

Tanya gave him a side glance. She realized he was no longer a coworker on an investigation, but a distressed brother who would move heaven and earth to locate his sibling.

"We'll find her," she said, patting his knee. "I'm staying with you until we do."

He didn't answer, his face turned back on his cell, his fingers clicking as he sent yet another desperate message to his sister in vain.

Tanya took a corner and headed back down the hill, toward the precinct. She couldn't wait to interrogate the sheriff about his deputies. She wondered how much Adams knew about his own officers and their relations with the town's con man.

Her Jeep sped down the incline. Tanya tapped on the brakes, but the vehicle didn't reduce speed.

She glanced at her dashboard and frowned. A red warning light was flashing.

What's going on?

The Jeep started rolling faster.

Fox glanced up from his phone. "Hey, watch out, Speedy Gonzales."

Tanya gripped the steering wheel and pumped the brakes.

With an icy shiver, she realized that was a futile exercise. She leaned into her horn to warn pedestrians or vehicles that might cross her path.

"Slow down, for goodness' sake!" cried Fox.

Max barked, picking up on their panicky energy.

"Down, Max," snapped Tanya as she pressed on the brakes.

Fox turned an angry face toward her. "What are you playing at again?"

"The brakes," she said through gritted teeth. "Malfunctioned."

"*What?*"

Tanya didn't answer. She kept pumping the brakes, her eyes peeled on the road, praying no vehicle was coming up the hill.

They were heading straight to the busier part of town. If she didn't maneuver themselves away from the road, they wouldn't be the only casualties of a crash.

Tanya's heart raced.

A pedestrian was crossing the street five yards ahead.

"Watch out!" She yanked the wheel to avoid hitting him.

Fox dropped his phone and grabbed the door handle with both hands.

With her heart pounding like mad, Tanya switched the Jeep to manual mode. She shifted the gears down one by one, ignoring the protesting engine.

Fox clasped his hands against his ears.

"Stop the car!"

But they were rolling faster and faster.

A quiet voice in the back of Tanya's head was telling her this hadn't been an accident. Her Jeep was only a year old, and she had maintained it to spec. The brakes couldn't have broken down. But she didn't have time to think about that.

Not now.

With shaking hands, she pushed down the parking brake. With one eye on the dashboard's RPM meter and another on the road ahead, she pressed the brakes all the way to the floor.

That did nothing to stop them.

They were rocketing down the hill like an Olympic skier on a double black diamond run.

"Stop!" screamed Fox, his face white. His bare knuckles gripped his seat. In the backseat, Max barked nonstop.

"Look out for safe stops!" yelled Tanya.

Her eyes darted back and forth as she searched for a field, a soft surface, anything she could turn the Jeep into without killing themselves. Or anyone else.

Walls. Walls. Walls.

They were surrounded by a maze of whitewashed walls that would crush them on impact.

Suddenly, they came across an opening in the wall.

The Pacific Ocean appeared to her right. They were passing the viewing area with the picnic tables and the lookout.

Tanya turned the wheels a hard right.

"Heads down!"

Chapter Eighteen

"Noo!" screamed Fox.

They were minutes from dropping into the Pacific Ocean.

Max's frightened barks had turned into desperate whines. Tanya's brain swirled like a category five hurricane.

We have to get out.

How do I pull Max out? Will Fox jump out in time?

Her heart pounded like a jackhammer.

No. There's only one option.

She turned her wheels toward the lookout. No one was in the vicinity.

The tires rumbled from smooth asphalt to green grass, but the Jeep's momentum seemed unstoppable.

Tanya aimed the vehicle right in between the columns of the lookout platform.

The stakes that held the viewing deck on top were spaced apart just enough so they wouldn't snap and impale them. But that would be a moot point once they were crushed to death by the wall of wood at the end.

"Brace! Brace for impact!" she hollered over the engine's screeches.

Fox doubled over, holding his head, like they tell you to do during airplane safety instructions.

Tanya clutched her mother's sunflower pendant with her left hand and said a prayer under her breath.

Suddenly, it seemed like time had slowed down. She watched the distance between them and the platform recede, like she was in a terrifying dream in slow motion.

She yearned to say a few final words to Max, but her voice refused to work. She tucked in her chin and slid down in her seat, her hands still gripping the wheel, feeling the tension in every muscle of her body.

This is going to hurt like hell.

From somewhere behind them came the wail of a siren, but she kept her focus in front.

The platform loomed in front of them.

Fox screamed.

Max barked.

The Jeep rammed in between the planks and slammed into the back of the platform. Tanya's head whipped forward and back like a football.

The crash was deafening.

But they had finally stopped moving.

For a moment, the sound of creaking wood and the hiss of the busted engine was all she could hear. Tanya felt no pain. Fox and Max had gone completely silent.

Something was pressing against her face, suffocating her. She opened her eyes, and for a minute wondered if she had died. All she could see was darkness around her.

The airbags had deployed.

Tanya lifted her head slowly and leaned back. Her heart was beating so hard she was sure her rib cage would explode.

Someone was yelling from far away. The voice sounded strangely familiar.

She glanced to her right.

Stars swam in front of her blurry eyes, but she could make out Fox's outline. He was crouched in his seat, his face planted in his airbag, and his hands clutching his head.

"Fox!" She grabbed his shoulder. "Fox! Are you okay?"

He let out a moan but remained in his position, like he couldn't move.

He's not dead, was the only thought that crossed Tanya's mind. "Max! Max?"

She swiveled around in her seat and felt a sharp sting on her left arm. Ignoring it, she reached over the net to the back seat. As soon as her hand touched a warm furry body, she burst out crying.

"Max? Hey, bud? Are you okay?"

She felt a wet lick on her hand. With tears streaming down her face, she scrambled around in her seat.

Max was wedged in the back but didn't seem injured at first glance.

She leaned over the net and felt her pup for broken bones. He sat still with his tail tucked in between his legs, confusion and fear mixed in his big brown eyes.

"It's okay, bud," said Tanya in a shaky voice as she checked every inch of him. "It's all right. You're going to be okay."

Max thumped his tail once as if to say thank you.

Tanya slipped back into her seat in relief. For one horrifying second, she had been so sure she had lost him.

It was the net that had saved him from flying in between the front seats and through the windshield. And it was their seat belts that had saved her and her front seat passenger.

She grabbed Fox by the shoulder again.

"Hey, Fox? Stay awake! Stay with me!"

Fox lifted his head and stared at her, his face a ghostly white, his body trembling.

"Anything broken?" she said, as her eyes traveled down his body.

Fox let his head fall back. Tanya noticed the trickle of red that was running down the side of his forehead. He had cut himself.

"You're doing fine," said Tanya, giving his shoulder a squeeze. "Just don't move, okay?"

She leaned over to check the wound when a shadow appeared next to her door.

"Hey! You all right in there?"

The voice sounded like it was coming from a distance. Her ears were ringing. She had checked up on Max and Fox, but had no idea if she was broken or cut, herself.

Someone was pulling her mangled door open. Or trying to. She wanted to help them, but her arms felt weak.

She glanced up and realized the front of her Jeep was completely crumpled. For one maniacal moment, she wondered if her accidental insurance would cover malfunctioned brakes and a deliberate crash into a wooden structure.

"Hey, Stone!"

Tanya turned. Sheriff Adams had pulled the broken door open. She felt him clutch her arm.

"You okay?" he said.

Tanya nodded.

She stumbled out, her ears still ringing and her eyes still seeing stars.

The sheriff held on to her shoulders so she wouldn't fall.

He was still wearing those dark wraparound shades. The voice in the back of Tanya's head said, *What were you doing in this part of town?* But she didn't have the words or the energy to articulate that thought properly.

"Max. He's in the back. Get him out, now," she said in a slurred voice.

Why do I sound drunk?

Adams let go of her and popped open the back door. Max pushed his snout out and sniffed the air, like a frightened wild animal.

Tanya pointed at the front passenger seat. "Fox is bleeding. He needs serious medical attention."

"Medics are on their way," she heard Adams say in that far-off voice. "I was heading back to the station when I saw you roll down the hill like crazy. When you turned here, I knew something had gone horribly wrong."

His words floated in and out but Tanya got the gist of it.

More sirens wailed in the distance. Soon banging doors and loud hollers came from somewhere. But Tanya's head hurt too much to focus.

She clutched Adams's arm.

"Someone cut my brake lines. They planned to kill us."

She wanted to ask *was it you*, but that was when she fainted and collapsed into his arms.

Chapter Nineteen

"**S**tatus, please?"

FBI Director Susan Cross's voice was sharp.
As usual, she didn't allow for hollow pleasantries.

Tanya swallowed and clasped the phone to her ear.

"Nothing to report so far, ma'am," she said, hoping her voice sounded normal.

She had slipped into an empty ward room only moments ago. She limped around the hospital bed and turned her face away from the closed door. That way no one walking along the corridor outside could hear her.

Sheriff Adams and his crew had taken Tanya and Fox to the hospital at the next county. They had been there for three hours now. The medical staff had bandaged and medicated Fox, and an intern had checked up on Max after Tanya had first insisted, then threatened him to not ignore her pup.

The ringing in her ears had lowered in volume and she no longer slurred her words, but her head throbbed. The extra strength painkillers they had given her had yet to kick in.

"What are Black Rock's priority cases at the moment?" said Cross.

"I can't say," said Tanya, a hot flash of anger rushing through her. "I'll know more when I get back to the office on Monday morning."

I just escaped death. And you want a status report?

Tanya knew how irrational her irritation was. Susan Cross didn't know where she was or what she had been up to.

"Monday?" Cross's voice hardened. "Don't tell me you took the weekend off, Agent."

"No, ma'am, but I'm not in Black Rock at the moment."

"Where have you gone gallivanting to?"

Everyone in the bureau knew of the Seattle director's explosive personality. *Never get on her bad side*, had been her immediate supervisor's advice the day Tanya had accepted her undercover assignment.

Max looked up from the door where he was sitting, on guard.

Tanya's face softened as she looked at her dog. Max thumped his tail on the cold hospital floor. Right now, he was the only one keeping her sane.

"Crescent Bay," she said. "A hundred miles south of Black Rock."

"What in goodness' name are you doing over there? That's outside the territory assigned to you."

"I came here to help a friend."

"I sent you down for a job. Not to party."

Tanya closed her eyes and gritted her teeth.

Fox was bleeding and was getting sedated in the next room. Her dog had nearly got crushed. And her Jeep was totaled. She had no time or energy for politeness, even for the highest federal bureaucrat in the state.

She let out a breath before she answered.

"It was a matter of life or death. Deputy Shawn Fox is from the Black Rock precinct. His sister went missing a week ago and we believe she's in imminent danger in Crescent Bay."

"I'm not paying you to do private investigations, Agent Stone." Cross's voice sounded harder than steel. "Might I remind you it is the FBI that pays your salary?"

"Yes, ma'am," said Tanya, standing straighter, though every muscle in her body ached. "However, I believe this case—"

"I don't care what you believe. You're a contractor for Chief Jack Bold. You're not there to coddle the locals or do them private favors. Let them take care of their own issues. I need you on the ground in Black Rock, sniffing out organized crime."

Tanya swallowed a curse.

"Understood, but there seems to be an organized crime problem in this town as well. I thought I could hit two birds with one stone and see if there's a connection to the other incidents along the coast."

Silence.

The air in the small room felt suddenly heavy. Getting reamed out by the director was dreadful, but it was only second to her complete silence.

A sliver of sweat ran down Tanya's back.

I'm so fired today.

"What incidents are you seeing in Crescent Bay?"

Tanya almost let out a sigh of relief to hear Susan Cross's voice again.

"Deputy Fox's sister used to be a drug mule for the Hells Angels in LA. The local sheriff tells me there's no chapter in town, but I think a gang is setting up shop here. The sheriff clocked the town's first homicide in three decades. We discovered the headless body of a young woman floating in the sea this morning."

More silence.

The smarmy face of Dr. Patel came to mind, as Tanya waited for her boss to say something.

"Go on," said Cross.

"I don't have any evidence yet, but I feel there might be some form of trafficking going on here."

"Interesting."

A quiet male voice came from Cross's end, like someone had walked into her office.

Tom.

Tanya recognized it as Cross's assistant, the guard dog who worshiped his boss but treated everyone else like dirt. She waited while the director and her assistant conferred in hurried whispers about something seemingly urgent.

She flexed her arm and winced. The doctor had warned her about post-accidental symptoms. But the last thing she wanted to do was tell Director Cross about it.

Cross could pull her out in a minute, put her on mandatory sick leave, and replace her with someone else.

The director's voice came down the line again, crisp and clear. "I'd like a report on Crescent Bay when you're done, Agent."

Relief flooded through Tanya's body, as she realized she didn't have to lie or to fight to help Fox find his missing sister. She would have had to make up one heck of a story if she had to leave town in a hurry now.

After all that had happened, Tanya wanted nothing more than to hunt down the person who had murdered the headless woman and had tried to kill them. She was sure the incidents were connected.

"Will do," said Tanya, almost saluting, though the director couldn't see her.

"I want you back in Black Rock, latest Monday morning," said Cross. "I'll get a second agent to cover Crescent Bay if and when warranted."

She paused.

Tanya braced herself.

"Keep me informed of your movements, especially if you're traveling out of your jurisdiction, Stone. I have placed others strategically in the region and can't have you bumping into each other."

Tanya straightened up even more.

There are others like me? Who? Where are they? Do they know who I am?

But she knew better than to barrage the director with her questions.

"If you go AWOL on me," came Cross's voice, "you might not have a job to come back to in Seattle. Understood?"

Tanya swallowed hard. "Loud and clear."

Cross hung up without another word.

Tanya was about to put her mobile away, when Max barked in warning. She turned around to see the door handle turning slowly.

Someone's trying to get in.

Chapter Twenty

*H*ospital ward doors don't lock.

Tanya put a hand on her holster, glad she had plucked her Glock out of the glove compartment before her Jeep got towed away.

"Heel, Max," she whispered, keeping her eyes on the door.

He backed away but kept his snout pointed in front, so he'd be prepared to attack the intruder.

The door nudged open.

"Stone?" said a male voice.

Sheriff Adams poked his head in.

"I was looking for you."

Tanya quickly slipped her FBI-issued burner phone in her cargo pants pocket. "Private call."

Were you listening in?

Adams stepped inside the room and closed the door behind him.

"I need your help," he said.

If there was one benefit of getting a surprise call from the FBI director herself, it was that the fogginess had vanished from her aching head. Tanya was on full alert now.

She stared at Adams, wishing for the hundredth time she could see his eyes. She hated being paranoid, but staying suspicious until the other party proved their innocence had kept her alive.

"You were threatening us with imprisonment this morning," she said, her voice dry. "Now you want my help?"

"I was there when you crashed. That was no accident."

"How do you surmise that?"

"Someone cut your brake lines."

Adams looked at Max standing in between Tanya's legs. The look on his face said, *one step closer and I'll bite a chunk off you.*

The sheriff turned back to Tanya. "And I spoke to your boss."

For one disorienting moment, Tanya thought, *You spoke to the Director of the FBI?*

"Jack had glowing words about your work," said Adams. "He didn't know you were coming this way, though."

Tanya kept her face stoic.

Chief Jack Bold of Black Rock, of course.

"You heard Fox this morning," she said. "He didn't want anyone to know he was coming to Crescent Bay to look for his sister, for good reason."

Adams was silent for a few seconds, like he was gauging whether he could share with her what he was about to say.

"We think we know who the headless corpse is," he said, finally.

Tanya's eyes widened.

"The ME is still examining the body and hasn't handed in her official report yet, but Dr. Chen's preliminary and unofficial response is it's Julie Steele."

"Julie Steele? Was she from this town?"

"Our mayor's daughter." Adams peered at her across the hospital bed. "I'm sharing this in confidence. Without conclusive evidence, I can't have anyone talking."

Tanya could tell the man was worried, despite those dark glasses.

"The mayor is at the banquet hall this afternoon, chairing a fundraiser. Her husband is one of the most prominent lawyers in the region and they're always busy with charity events. I'm planning on asking a few discrete questions."

"If their daughter had vanished," said Tanya, "wouldn't they have reported her missing already?"

"She doesn't live with them. She was staying at Camilla Duvalier's house."

"A friend?"

"Her boss. Duvalier is a former actress from LA, retired here a few years ago. She's an active member of our community and a close friend of the mayor. She's always flying in and out of town, so she might not have even noticed Julie gone."

"How well do you know the mayor and her husband?"

The sheriff rubbed his forehead, like he was also nursing a bad headache.

"To be frank, Mayor Steele and her husband aren't my biggest fans."

Tanya shook her head. "Do you get along with anyone in this town?"

"The Steeles grew up here. We went to the same high school. They were from up the hill, and I was from the backwoods."

Adams straightened his shoulders.

"Don Steele ran for the sheriff's office two times in a row. They were brutal campaigns, but I always won fair and square."

"So they resent you?"

He shrugged.

"Let's say it created bad blood. Just inquiring about the disappearance of their only daughter is fraught with land mines."

"Do you have any idea who killed that girl?"

"Your guess is as good as mine, but I won't rest until I find who did this."

Tanya stared at him, trying her best to size him up.

"If I were you, I would talk to Patel again," she said. "Your deputies didn't ask any questions as far as I saw. They kowtowed in front of him like he was some god."

"What were you doing at the Patel residence?"

"We followed your people to his compound. His private guards accosted us, but we convinced them to let us in. That's when we saw them in the living room. They looked pretty cozy." Tanya paused. "I'm not impressed by this untouchable man."

Adams rubbed his head. "That makes two of us."

"Deputy Hatchet handed him an envelope," said Tanya, observing him carefully. "Is she involved in something she shouldn't be?"

"Kathy's an exemplary officer. She's my deputy sheriff. She's a smart cookie, too smart for the jobs I have for her."

Tanya shrugged. "Doesn't mean she isn't doing something behind your back."

Adams shook his head. "If you're talking about her MLM home business, I know about it. She runs a side hustle to keep herself occupied in her spare time. It's legit."

"Are you part of this network too, Sheriff?"

"No way." Adams shook his head violently. "Sometimes I feel these MLMs are run like cults."

"It doesn't bother you to have a deputy involved?"

"I can't speak for what she does in her private time as long as it's legal. Plus, Kathy was upfront about it with me."

Tanya raised a brow. *Maybe your right hand isn't as upfront as you think she is.*

"This morning wasn't her private time, Sheriff. She was in uniform and was sent to Dr. Patel on police business."

Adams rubbed his forehead again. "I'll have a talk with her."

Tanya leaned forward. "What I want to know is, do Julie Steele's murder and Fox's sister's disappearance have a connection?"

He looked up.

"That's why I came looking for you." He paused. "I'm heading back to Crescent Bay. Help me test a theory?"

Chapter Twenty-one

A dams pulled into the main driveway of the banquet hall.

"Felipe Fernando," said Tanya, as she spotted a man handing the keys of his yellow Ferrari to a valet.

The sheriff turned to her. "Seen his movies?"

Tanya shook her head.

"I only heard about him today. This fundraiser must be a pretty big deal to have a celebrity like him. That's what Fox said, anyway."

Tanya had checked in with her colleague just before leaving the hospital.

Fox had been dozing under his pain medication, but had woken up when she had walked into his room. She had barely explained to him where she was heading off to, when a nurse had shooed her out, scolding her for disturbing their patient.

After asking the nurses to watch over her friend, she had followed Adams to his car in the parking lot. With Max in the backseat, they had driven to the banquet hall in silence.

Tanya had many questions for the sheriff, but her head was hurting and her mind was buzzing.

The adrenaline rush was wearing off, forcing her to face the harsh reality of what had just happened. She couldn't believe they had escaped the crash with minor injuries. It had been a stroke of luck she hadn't hit an innocent pedestrian as they had barreled down the hill.

Did Patel's guards tamper with the brakes? Was it those girls? Or had someone else been watching them? How did the sheriff so conveniently turn up just as they crashed?

Tanya watched Adams from the side of her eyes as he surveyed the guests strolling around them. The main reason she came was to monitor him.

Crescent Bay's banquet hall was a modest building, but was now looking festive, decorated with bright lights and flower garlands.

An enormous banner announced the fundraiser as an annual charity event for a domestic violence prevention center. A wall poster had a smiling photo of the mayor with the town's tagline, *Best views on the West Coast.*

People in smart business outfits handed their car keys to the valets, greeted each other California style, and drifted toward the main entrance where servers carrying trays of champagne glasses waited.

Felipe Fernando extricated himself from a gaggle of fans and turned around. He lifted a hand in salute as he spotted the squad car idling by the entrance.

Sheriff Adams returned the salute.

Felipe grinned, blinding Tanya with his pearly white teeth.

"You know the man?" said Tanya.

Adams turned toward his window, his shades concealing his expression.

"We go way back."

With a nonchalant shrug, he opened his door. "Let's see if we can squeeze some information from the guests before the auction starts."

Tanya got out and opened the back door for Max to jump out. He barely had his front paws on the pavement when an ugly screech came from the doorway.

"No dogs allowed!"

Tanya whirled around.

A tall, white-haired woman in an elegant pink pantsuit was marching their way. The wonky way her lips curled told Tanya she was a regular user of Botox. The pearl choker gracing her neck looked like it would have cost as much as her Jeep.

But it was something else that drew Tanya's eyes. On her lapel was the same pin Patel and the three girls had worn. Tanya stared at the woman, her mind whirring.

Is this the symbol of the multi-level marketing pyramid?

A wave of expensive perfume wafted in the air as she stomped past Tanya, toward the sheriff.

Despite the Botox and the angry curl on her lips, she was stunning. She was the type of woman who exuded power and made everyone stop when she entered a room.

She strode up to the sheriff and grabbed his arm.

"John, you know the rules. There are folks here with allergies. I can't have anyone get sick in the middle of the auction. You should know better than to bring that mutt here."

"I understand," said the sheriff, putting his hands up as if to placate her. "He's a working dog, and I have a serious investigation underway—"

"I don't care if that's the president's pet. My rules are rules."

The woman turned to Tanya with a glare, her critical eyes traveling from her wrinkled shirt, to her cargo pants, and down to her dusty red boots. Tanya suddenly felt like she had just crawled out of a garbage dumpster.

"Don't you people have a uniform code or something?" spat the woman.

The sheriff opened his mouth to answer, but before he could, she let go of his arm and twirled around.

"Felipe Fernando!"

"Madame Camilla!" cried the actor as he spotted her too. He stepped toward her, his arms wide open for a hug.

Tanya turned to Adams.

"Madame Camilla?"

"Camilla Duvalier," said Adams in a low voice. "She lives at the castle on top of the hill. Got it built herself, about ten years ago."

"Does she think she's royalty or something?"

"People from Hollywood can be weird. They think they're the chosen ones. Then, when they get older and stop getting the attention and adoration they crave, they look for it someplace else."

"By building a *castle*?"

Adams shrugged. "Like I said. Hollywood folks are weird."

"Does she really have a say on who can come into the hall?"

Adams gave her an apologetic look. "Afraid so. She's very particular."

He looked down at Max, who was watching them, head cocked to the side, like he knew they were talking about him.

"Will he be okay in the car?"

With a resigned sigh, Tanya opened the back door of the vehicle and ushered her pup back inside. She lowered the windows enough so Max could get fresh air, but not low enough that he could jump out.

She closed the door and glared at the sheriff.

"He hates not being part of the action."

"Just keep your ears and eyes open," said Adams, wiping his forehead. "If you see or hear anything, let me know."

"I don't plan to sit back like a wallflower," snapped Tanya, pulling out her phone. "I promised Fox I'd ask around about his sister."

With a nod, Adams climbed the steps to the main entrance.

Tanya joined him, wondering if the person who had tried to kill them was here, mingling among these well-dressed folk, pretending nothing had happened. She kept her eyes peeled to see if anyone would be surprised to see her alive.

They walked behind Camilla and Felipe who were entering the hall now, arms linked, waving at the other guests like they were a royal couple.

A server came out with a tray of champagne glasses. Felipe picked up two and handed one to Camilla. They toasted each other before strolling inside.

Tanya observed them with curiosity. Camilla was close to her sixties while Felipe looked like he was in his mid-thirties, young enough to be her son.

"They're from Hollywood," said the sheriff, as if he was reading her mind. "They worked together on several movies."

"Madame Camilla was the dead girl's employer, right?" said Tanya.

"Camilla just got back to town from a business trip, so she probably doesn't even know Julie is missing. That is, if our victim is Julie Steele."

Tanya remembered their unexpected chat with the teens by Patel's compound. All three had said they lived in the castle.

"Did Julie Steele live in the castle on the hill?"

"That's correct."

Tanya turned to him. "How well do you get along with Camilla Duvalier?"

Adams shrugged nonchalantly, but Tanya could see that question bothered him. "She has her moments."

Does everyone in this town have a beef with the county sheriff? However did he get elected?

Tanya's frown deepened.

Is it him? Is he the culprit behind the dead girl and our crash?

Chapter Twenty-two

I nside the hall, guests congregated in small groups, chatting, and laughing.

Servers bustled around with canapé and drink trays.

A long table festooned with balloons stood against one wall. On it were wine and champagne bottles, jewelry in glass cases, expensive chocolate boxes, spa sets, and gold boxes like the ones the girls by Patel's house had in their purses.

Auction prizes.

"Sheriff Adams?" came an eager voice from behind the table. Adams walked toward an elderly woman to shake her hand.

Standing next to her and watching over the auction items was one of the girls who had sneaked out of the Patel residence.

Tanya opened the video call Fox had shared with her. Turning the sound off, she played the reel until she found a clear picture of Eva.

She took a step toward the girl.

"Hi there, I remember you. Small world, eh?"

The girl didn't smile back.

"Listen, have you seen this woman—"

The girl's eyes widened for one second. Then, she pivoted toward a guest who had been browsing the auction items. Tanya watched her studiously ignoring her, wondering why she was evading her.

I'll come back to her.

Tanya surveyed the room, looking for others to talk to. A group of four guests huddled in a small circle nearby, with champagne glasses in hand.

Tanya walked up to them.

"Excuse me. Have you seen this woman?"

They turned around with quizzical expressions.

"She's gone missing for a week," said Tanya. "She was last seen in this town."

One woman, wearing a bright purple fascinator hat, lifted her chin and narrowed her eyes. Her expression said *how dare you interrupt*. Another gave a dismissive wave without even a glance at the screen.

"Never seen her," said a man, swiveling away from Tanya, like he wanted nothing to do with her.

One by one, they turned around and closed in on their private circle.

For one furious second, Tanya yearned to flash her Black Rock precinct ID. Or better yet, her FBI badge. She let out a sigh, knowing the first wouldn't impress anyone and the second could get her fired from her actual job.

She was halfway down the room, trying not to feel discouraged by the cold shoulders she'd been getting, when she spotted Felipe in the corner.

He was standing in front of a young server who had a tray of canapés in her hands. Tanya recognized the girl. She was one of the three who had sneaked out of the Patel residence.

Even from where she was, she could see the girl was trembling. She realized the server was using her tray as a barrier.

As she watched, Felipe leaned over and grabbed the girl's breasts. The server lurched back in shock. Felipe chortled. He snatched the tray from the girl with one hand and groped her with the other.

A rush of fury shot through Tanya's spine.

She marched over, seized the tray from his hands and slammed it on a nearby table.

Felipe staggered back in surprise. The server scooted into the kitchen and disappeared.

"What the hell do you think you were doing?" snarled Tanya.

"Who the hell are you?" spat Felipe.

Tanya reeled back as the rich smell of whiskey hit her nostrils. The man had been drinking before he had arrived at the event. *Well before.*

"I saw what you did to that girl," she growled.

Felipe's face turned a slight pink. "I don't know what you're talking about."

He turned around to leave, but Tanya step forward, trapping him in between her and the buffet table.

"Let me go," hissed Felipe.

"I should book you in for harassment," growled Tanya.

"She asked for it."

"To be groped?"

"She came on to me." Felipe wiggled in place, but his eyes darted over her shoulder, like he was searching for a quick getaway. "She wanted my autograph. I thought I'd give her a bit more to remember me by."

He grinned.

Tanya gritted her teeth.

A vision of her grabbing him by the neck and slamming his face against the wall flashed across her mind. She could do it in a heartbeat, but she knew the consequences wouldn't help her.

For the hundredth time since she took on her undercover mission, she wished Susan Cross would have allowed her to keep her badge and let her do a proper police job in these small towns.

"Come on," whined Felipe. "I did nothing wrong. Lemme go. Maybe we can negotiate something."

"I don't negotiate with perverts."

Her eyes bored into his. A flicker of fear crossed his, as if he realized he had finally met someone he couldn't mess with.

Coward, thought Tanya. *Bullies always are.*

"What's going on here?"

Felipe turned around, relief crossing his face.

"Help me. She's harassing me." His voice was high, like a child complaining to a parent. "Do something. She was going to hit me!"

Tanya turned to see Sheriff Adams standing behind her.

Chapter Twenty-three

A dams's eyebrows shot up. "She threatened to *hit* you?"

"That's a lie," snarled Tanya. "I caught him groping a server. He had her trapped in this corner—"

"Felipe!"

They looked up to see Camilla striding over to them. Before Tanya or the sheriff could say anything, she grabbed Felipe by the arm and pulled him away.

"I need you to announce first prize," she said as they hastened toward the lectern with the microphones. Felipe didn't even look back.

Tanya turned to Adams.

"Aren't you going to do something?"

Even with his glasses on, Tanya noticed his face flush.

"I'll have a word with him when the event is over," said Adams.

"A word?" Tanya tried not to clench her jaws. "Stick him in the drunk tank for a few hours so he can contemplate how he treats people."

The sheriff let out a heavy sign.

"I have a headless victim on my hands. My entire team is focused on the murder investigation. I don't approve of this behavior any more than you do, but if I deal with him now, I can't focus on the case we're here for."

"So he gets away with it?"

"Look, I know Felipe well. I'll sit down with him and have a serious chat tonight."

"He doesn't need a chat. He needs to be charged with sexual misconduct."

"I'll ask him to apologize to the server. That might teach him a lesson."

With an exasperated hiss, Tanya turned away.

She locked eyes with the young server who was now lingering by the entrance to the kitchen. She had a tray of fresh drinks in her hands. Her nervous eyes peeked out like she was terrified to step back into the hall, but had to do her job, anyway.

Tanya felt for the girl.

She walked over to her. The server shot her a frightened look.

"I'm sorry I couldn't do anything about it," said Tanya, softening her voice.

"Oi!"

The angry yell came from inside the kitchen.

Tanya looked up to see the same chef who had been at Dr. Patel's stomp out. He was wielding his signature knife in his hands. He glared at the young server.

"We don't have all night. Get on with it."

The girl scurried off with her tray.

The chef turned to Tanya and shook his head.

"Help these days. Lazy as heck," he muttered as he headed back into the kitchen. "Can't find anyone reliable anymore."

Tanya wanted to pluck that hat off his head and ram it down his throat. Summoning all her willpower to stop herself from assaulting the chef, she stepped away.

She had a job to do.

"I don't give a damn about the dead girl!" The familiar female voice came from near the auction table.

Tanya whipped around.

Camilla had cornered Adams. She was poking a blood-red manicured finger on his chest, her furious face inches from his. The sheriff had his back against the wall and his hands up like he wanted to push her away but was trying to be polite about it.

Felipe was nowhere to be seen.

Tanya stepped closer to listen in. She pretended to browse the auction items but kept her ears pricked.

"You're ruining my night," Camilla was saying.

"Have some heart," said Sheriff Adams, "this could be anyone's daughter. Anyone's child."

"I'm trying to raise funds."

"I'm trying to catch a killer."

"Tell that girl to stop showing those pictures here. She's freaking everyone out."

Tanya kept her face down, but raised a brow.

She's complaining about me.

"I have a murder investigation in my hands," Adams was saying. "Given that a second woman is missing makes this even a bigger priority."

"Just remember that my business keeps this town employed," hissed Camilla. "If it wasn't for me, you wouldn't have a job."

Tanya looked up and gave them a discreet glance.

Adams's face had turned purple, but she could see he was struggling to hold his temper in.

A commotion by the entrance distracted Camilla. Dr. Patel had arrived. Guests twittered as they saw him. A dozen women surrounded him, pawing at him while he basked in their attention.

Tanya's stomach churned.

What did they see in this creepy old man?

She wasn't sure who she couldn't stand the most. Patel or Camilla.

A muffled cry came from behind her, but it had been so sudden Tanya wasn't sure she had heard it right.

"No!"

The cry again. It was a woman's voice.

Tanya spun around.

That had come from the kitchen.

Chapter Twenty-four

"**S**hut that damn door!"

The chef's roar was followed by a thud, like he had slammed his knife on something hard.

"Stop it!"

The frightened cry came again, this time louder.

Someone's in trouble.

Tanya rushed into the kitchen.

It was a typical industrial-sized space with stainless-steel fridges, a large range, and a counter that ran the length of the room. At the other end was the back door. There was a small room by the rear entrance that looked like an office.

Tanya scanned the space from one end to the other.

"What the hell are you doing in my kitchen?"

The chef was behind the main counter, his knife raised in the air, glowering at her like he wanted to boil her alive. She didn't reply.

Where did it come from?

As if in answer, a crash came from the office by the back exit.

"Stop it!" cried a woman's voice.

Tanya was about to rush toward it when Adams stepped into the kitchen, rubbing his forehead. His face was flushed, like he'd had enough of Camilla being on his case.

"Oi!" bellowed the chef, waving his knife in the air. "Who gave you people permission to come in here? Get the hell out of my kitchen, Adams, and take your people with you."

The sheriff gave Tanya a startled look that said, *What are you doing here?*

"Something's going on in the back," said Tanya as she marched toward the office, her hand on her holster under her jacket.

"You can't go in there!" the chef shouted from behind her. "Get out! All of you!"

The door to the office banged shut. Another cry came from inside, muffled this time.

Tanya stepped up to the door and kicked it open.

Felipe Fernando was yanking the shirt off a teenage girl.

Tanya recognized her. She had been part of the trio by the Patel residence.

The girl was fighting Felipe off. Even in his drunken state, Felipe seemed to have his strength about him. He was so busy trying to pin her against the chair, he hadn't noticed her.

"Felipe!" roared the sheriff from behind Tanya. "Get off her!"

Felipe didn't even turn to look.

Tanya stomped inside, clamped her hands around the actor's throat, and tore him off the girl. He struggled, trying to pry her hands off his neck.

Tanya tightened her grip. He flailed his arms and gurgled, choking.

"Release him, Stone," came Adams's warning voice from behind her.

If this had been in the battlefields of Ukraine, the man wouldn't have survived. Tanya would have made sure of it. Once a criminal commits a vile deed and gets away with it, they feel free to do it again. And again. Without retribution.

Felipe was wiggling like a sewer rat caught in a trap.

She slammed his head against the wall. She yanked his hands back and reached behind her belt, only to realize she didn't have her handcuffs on her anymore.

The sheriff stepped forward.

"I've got him," he said, pulling out a pair of cuffs from his belt.

Restraining herself from smashing Felipe's face again, Tanya reluctantly let Adams take over. The sheriff held Felipe's hands against his back as he read him his rights.

When he pushed him out of the room, the entire kitchen staff was staring their way.

Tanya turned toward the chef.

"You knew exactly what was going on in here," she said. "You should be taken in for accessory to assault."

The chef growled something incomprehensible.

Tanya turned back and glanced at the girl who was cowering in the office's corner, her chest heaving, barely holding her ripped shirt together.

"You okay, hun?"

The girl gave a quick nod, but Tanya knew this incident would scar her for life. Getting assaulted while others around her did nothing, even encouraged it, wasn't something she would forget soon.

Tanya softened her voice. "You need to come to the police station and give a statement, hun. Can I give you a ride?"

The girl shot her a frightened look and shook her head.

"It's really important that you do right away."

The girl didn't reply.

"You can stop him from doing this again, hun."

The girl turned away from her. "Leave me alone," she said in a hoarse whisper. "Go away."

With a resigned sigh, Tanya turned around and followed the sheriff out the back door, every bone in her body screaming in fury. This wasn't her jurisdiction, but she couldn't just watch and do nothing.

Outside, the sheriff was leading Felipe to his squad car, talking to him in a low voice. Tanya marched over, hoping whatever relationship these two men had wouldn't get Felipe off easy.

Seeing her come out, Max barked from inside Adams's car.

A screech of rubber on asphalt made Tanya whip around. The morning's events had made her jumpy.

It was Madden's unmarked cruiser racing across the parking lot. He screeched to a halt behind the sheriff's vehicle and lumbered out. He was so out of shape that even driving fast had made him wheezy.

He shuffled toward Adams, his face red with exertion.

"Came as soon as I got the call, sir," he said. "Good thing I was patrolling the block."

"Take him to the station," said the sheriff, pointing his chin at Felipe.

Adams turned to the actor. "I never expected I'd have to do this. I'm disappointed in you."

Tanya raised an eyebrow.

Disappointed?

It was like Adams was talking to a naughty kid, not an adult who had been caught trying to assault a young girl.

"I want you to know what you did was a very serious crime," said the sheriff, handing him over to the deputy.

Madden grabbed Felipe roughly by the arm.

The deputy didn't seem to have the same sentiments toward the actor as the sheriff. He propelled Felipe toward the back of his vehicle, opened the door, and shoved him inside. Felipe yelped as his head hit the car's door.

For one moment, Tanya wondered if Madden would have kicked the man in had they not been here to witness it.

Madden slammed the back door shut, stomped over to the front driver's seat, and drove off.

Tanya watched him speed through the parking lot, glad there was at least one officer in this precinct who knew the difference between right and wrong.

"Let's go."

Tanya turned around to see Adams opening his driver's side door.

"Did you talk to the mayor?" said Tanya, "About her missing daughter?"

"The mayor didn't come. She's at home with her husb—"

He didn't get to finish.

A blast of fire exploded, slamming Adams against his car.

Tanya dove to the ground, protecting her head with her hands.

Inside the car, Max barked like mad.

Shattered pieces of glass and wood flew across the parking lot. Something sharp rammed against Tanya's shoulders, stinging her.

The hall rang with panicked screams.

Tanya lifted her chin and glanced through the acrid smoky air.

A bomb had gone off inside the banquet hall.

Chapter Twenty-five

"It's a bloodbath in here."

Sheriff Adams wiped the sweat off his face.

"Madame Camilla?"

Tanya and Adams whirled around.

The faltering cry had come from Dr. Patel. He was lying on the floor by the entrance, a trickle of blood running down his face. A paramedic rushed up to him.

"Did she die?" cried the old man in a broken voice. "Did she....?"

Tanya stared at him.

That was an odd question to ask. Normally, a concerned friend would ask *is she okay?*

"This way!" called out a deputy, as he ushered out an elderly couple clinging to each other.

The first group of people who had spurned Tanya in the hall only a half hour ago stumbled toward the main door. Their pristine clothes were ripped, and their arms were tattooed by bloodied cuts and scrapes.

The woman with the bright purple fascinator floundered like she was lost. She stopped at the entrance and teetered on her toes, like she didn't know where she was. A deputy gently nudged her out.

A disoriented Camilla staggered behind them. Her pantsuit was torn, and her hairdo looked like it had been ravaged by a cyclone. She was shaking from head to toe, like a feverish spell had overcome her.

These were the lucky ones.

Those with serious injuries were being treated inside, at the scene. The medics would soon carry them in stretchers to the ambulances waiting outside.

At least, everyone was alive.

That's what Tanya thought at first.

She and Adams had rushed into the hall as soon as the explosion ended.

The building was still standing, its roof, walls, and structure intact. It was only when they got inside, they realized the extent of the destruction.

They had stepped around the broken glass and waded through the injured guests. Some had been staggering around in shock, and others had been crouching on the floor, screaming in fear or crying in pain.

Most of the light fixtures had blown out, but even in the semi-darkness, Tanya could see the blood splattered everywhere. On the tablecloths. On the furniture. On the carpet and the walls.

Mass chaos reigned while Tanya and Adams searched for those who needed help the most. They worked alone for several minutes, giving first aid, stopping the bleeding using the tablecloths for compression.

Soon, the air was filled with sirens, and emergency lights flashed in the parking lot. Tanya and Adams only stopped to breathe once a dozen first responders had rushed in to help.

Tanya raised her head now and looked around the banquet hall. It resembled a war zone.

She stared at the ashen faces of the guests who, only moments ago, had been greeting each other with smiles and laughter.

Her gut tightened.

Something told her whoever did this was still here.

Stepping around a medic who was bandaging a server's arm, Tanya walked to the back of the hall where the most damage had been done. Adams followed her, scanning the wrecked auction table, its contents now destroyed.

Tanya's leg hit the side of an upturned table. She leaned over to see if there was anything behind it, before moving it out of the way. Her hands stopped in mid-air as she spotted what was on the ground.

A bloodied foot.

Chapter Twenty-six

The severed foot was encased in a beige stiletto.

Its blood vessels were still visible. Tanya's stomach lurched as she stepped closer.

There was a body under the wreckage.

"Over here!" she hollered.

With her heart racing, Tanya pulled away the table and kneeled next to the teen who had been pinned underneath it.

She knew the girl. She had been tasked with welcoming guests at the auction table, the one who had avoided her earlier.

Her neck was angled to the side, like someone had snapped it back. Her legs were torn. Both her feet had been blown off, but Tanya couldn't spot the second foot.

"My goodness," breathed Adams as he kneeled across from her.

Tanya felt the girl's neck, searching for a pulse she knew no longer existed.

Two paramedics rushed in with a stretcher. Adams looked up at them and shook his head.

It was too late.

Tanya and Adams sat silently next to the victim till the medics returned with a body bag. There was nothing they could do for her. But a minute of silence for a young life that had been brutally cut short seemed like the right thing to do.

The screaming around them had stopped, overtaken by the occasional hollers of the deputies, and the inaudible murmurs of the paramedics as they tended to the injured.

The medics came back with a deputy who took his phone out to snap pictures for the forensics team. Tanya and Adams stepped away from the dead girl to give them space to work.

Adams pulled at the radio on his shoulder.

Tanya shifted through the rubble, while the sheriff barked instructions to the dispatch about getting forensics in ASAP.

Tanya glanced around the wreckage in the semi-darkness.

Wine bottles had been broken into smithereens, the red wine mixing in with the girl's blood. The spa baskets had burst open, spreading a fine powder like substance all over the debris.

If the perpetrator had wanted to hide a deadly device, they couldn't have picked a better spot. The jumble of auction items only made it harder to distinguish which glass and metal piece belonged to what object.

"Someone placed an IED in this corner," she said. "Whoever did this planned it well."

The sheriff shook his head, like he couldn't or didn't want to believe what she was saying. "The heat in this building runs on natural gas. This could have been an accident."

"Watch your step," said Tanya, pointing at a piece of broken metal by his boots. "That could be part of the explosive device."

She reached into her cargo pant pocket and pulled out a flashlight. She shone it across the floor, moving methodically from one end to the other.

She gave a start as she spotted the object hidden among the mess. "This was a pressure cooker bomb."

"*What?*" Adams turned to her. "How do you know?"

Tanya bent down and plucked something small and red from the floor. She lifted it up and held it to her light.

He frowned. "A plastic tomato?"

"A kitchen timer."

"That was probably part of the auction prizes."

Tanya shook her head. "Did you see the price list? Nothing on the auction table cost less than five hundred dollars, even the spa baskets. That begs the question. What's a common kitchen timer doing here?"

She surveyed the debris, more focused now as she knew what to look for. She bent down and picked up what looked like a steel plate contorted into a peculiar shape.

"What does this look like to you, Sheriff?"

"I don't know, but I think you're jumping to conclusions too quickly," replied Adams, his voice heavy.

Tanya stared at him for a moment. *Take off those darned shades,* she wanted to scream at him.

She placed the steel plate to the side and picked up a crooked nail from the floor.

"See these iron nails? This was a homemade IED."

"No one in my town would know how to make one."

"Anyone with access to YouTube could have done it."

Adams sighed and shook his head again, like he didn't want to believe her. "That would cover just about everyone in town. Makes little sense to me."

"That kitchen timer is the detonator," said Tanya. "If they were smart, they probably had more than one for backup."

From the corner of her eyes, she noticed something next to the nails, where the pressure cooker plate lay. Pushing the metal pieces aside, she pried the card out from underneath and flipped it over.

A shiver ran down her back.

She held it to the light and read it out loud.

"Last witness still alive."

Chapter Twenty-seven

"**B**reaking news..."

The terse voice of the TV news anchor rang through the hotel bar.

"An explosion ripped through Crescent Bay's banquet hall today, claiming one life and injuring many attendees at a local fundraiser dedicated to...."

Tanya took a sip of her beer but didn't taste it. Max was snoozing by the feet of her barstool, tired out from the day's events.

Tanya sent a silent note of thanks to Camilla for having been hard-nosed about her no-dog policy. If Max hadn't been locked inside Adams's car, he would have been the first to rush into the hall as people screamed for help.

"Heard you guys were at the scene today," said the bartender, pushing a tall beer toward Fox.

It was his third.

Tanya knew Fox was going to regret it later, especially after the strong medication he'd taken at the hospital. She was avoiding her usual vodka on ice for the same reasons, but she didn't have the heart to stop him. Fox had been through enough. The man deserved his drink.

It was past midnight now and they were seated at the bar of the Crescent Bay Hotel.

By the time Tanya had left the banquet hall, all casualties had been transported to the local hospital, and the dead girl to the morgue.

First responders from nearby counties, including firefighters and paramedics, had rushed in to assist Sheriff Adams's team. The hall had been cordoned off and a forensics team had sifted through the evidence.

That had meant Tanya couldn't stay, even after she had flashed her Black Rock contractor ID.

Sheriff Adams had refused to back her up or sign her in. But it was his rejection of her pressure cooker bomb theory that maddened her the most. The more she thought of it, the less she felt she could trust him.

She and Max had got a ride to the hospital in the back of an ambulance. Fox had been anxiously waiting for them, discharged but still groggy.

They had taken a taxi to their hotel in silence, Fox in shock at the news and Tanya's head buzzing with what she had just experienced.

She hated not knowing what was going on at the scene, and the news reporter on TV was telling her nothing new.

Tanya looked up at the bartender. "Did you find a spare rental yet?"

The bartender nodded. "My roommate says he'll lend you his truck for fifty dollars a day. As long as you bring it back with the gas tank full. Cool?"

"Is it in working condition?"

"Fifteen-year-old pickup, but it keeps on chugging." He made a face. "My buddy needs the money bad. He's late on his rent to me. I already told him you'd said yes."

"It's a deal if he can get it to the hotel parking lot before dawn tomorrow."

The bartender gave her a thumbs up and picked up the phone to call his friend. Tanya held her cold beer to her forehead, hoping it would deaden her migraine.

"You could have got yourself killed," said Fox, his words slurred.

"I've been in worse situations," said Tanya.

"You came here because I asked you to."

"I *want* to help you find your sister."

A tear rolled down Fox's cheek and fell into his beer.

Tanya put a hand on his arm. "We'll find her. I promise."

He looked at her, a pained expression on his face.

"Do you think she's involved in this... whatever's going on in this town?"

Tanya was silent for a minute.

"That text message you got is a red flag," she said. "Does she normally write like that?"

"It's exactly how she writes," said Fox, his voice grim. "Short and so cryptic, it drives Zoe mad sometimes."

He lifted his pale face.

"Do you think Eva's still alive?"

Tanya gave him a startled look. "Don't say that. Not until we have evidence. Do you hear me?"

Fox turned away and stared glumly at his beer.

"Two dead. And more would have died if the auction had started and the hall had been full. What's going on in this town?"

Tanya didn't have an answer to that question, but she had come across enough IEDs in the field to know that no one would have survived if a professional had carried this crime out.

Their suspect was an amateur. That much she knew.

Fox turned his reddened eyes to Tanya.

"What if Eva's the *last witness*?"

Chapter Twenty-eight

Tanya kept silent for a few seconds.

"The question then is," she said finally, "what exactly did Eva witness?"

"If she's not dead yet," said Fox, his eyes welling up, "she'll be soon."

Tanya grabbed him by the shoulder. He winced in pain.

"You've got to keep faith, man."

"Faith isn't going to help Eva."

"Listen to me. We're going to operate on the risk she's in danger, but we're not concluding anything further without facts." She shook him, ignoring his painful winces. "We can't panic now. We'd be chasing our tails like a bunch of monkeys if we do."

"I'm being realistic. I'm preparing myself for the inevitable."

Fox tried to shrug her hand off but careened to the side. Tanya pulled him back on his seat before he fell off the stool.

"I don't know what to do any more," he slurred, holding on to the bar.

"Call your wife and tell her you're fine. Lies always have a way of coming out. You don't want her to find out you were in Crescent Bay from a third party."

Fox blinked.

"You can't hide secrets like this from your family," said Tanya.

"No way. She'll get hysterical. She'd lose her mind if she knew what was going on here."

"If it was the other way around, wouldn't you want to know?"

Fox slammed his fist on the bar. "That's not gonna help her right now!"

Tanya raised an eyebrow at his unexpected outburst, and let go of his shoulder.

"Fine. But I don't want to hear any more of this defeatist talk. We're going to find your sister."

Fox shook his head. "Go back to Black Rock. I can't be responsible for your death too."

"I don't leave people behind. I'm here to finish the job I came to do."

Fox opened his mouth to protest, when his phone rang. He bumbled in his jacket pockets and brought it out, his face turning pale as he spotted the number on the screen.

Tanya leaned in to check, but he slipped off the stool and stumbled away before she could.

"Hey, babe," she heard him say as he walked toward the washrooms in the back.

Tanya turned back to her drink with a sigh.

Holding her beer glass to her head to lessen the pain, she peered down at Max. Watching her pup sleep was the best medicine she could ask for.

Unaware of the anguish his human companions were going through, Max was lost in a dream, his furry paws twitching like he was chasing squirrels in a far-off land.

When Fox returned from his phone call, Tanya had already downed her drink.

"I'm off to my room," said Fox, throwing a twenty-dollar bill on the bar and nodding at his colleague. "See you in the morning."

Without waiting for her to answer, he staggered toward the door. Tanya watched him leave, wondering if he was trying to give her the slip. She was about to follow him out, when her phone buzzed.

It was her public cell, the number she gave to her Black Rock colleagues and anyone else she needed to in her undercover role.

"Stone, here," said Tanya, feeling her head throb harder. All she wanted was to go up to her room and crash on her nice comfy bed.

"Tanya?" came a woman's shaky voice.

Tanya sat up on her stool.

"Zoe?"

"Are you alone?" said Zoe.

Tanya glanced around the pub. Fox had already disappeared.

Zoe let out a heavy sigh on the other end.

"Shawn's been lying to me."

Tanya's heart skipped a beat. She closed her eyes, wondering how to respond to that.

"He told me he was going to a martial arts program in Seattle with you." Zoe's voice was strangely reedy. "He told me you were teaching the class there. But he's not in Seattle, is he?"

Tanya swore under her breath. Neither was she. But the last thing she wanted was to start a row between Fox and his wife.

Zoe sighed. "I knew it."

Tanya cleared her throat. "Whatever he's up to," she said, racking her brain for what to say, "he means well. He cares for you—"

"If he cared for me, he would be with me this weekend."

Tanya narrowed her eyes. Her instincts told her something more was going on here than Fox lying about his whereabouts.

"What do you mean, Zoe?"

"How could he leave me in the middle of this, of all times?"

Tanya suddenly realized that Zoe was crying.

"Isn't he only gone for the weekend?" she said. "He'll be back on Mon—"

"Monday's too late," said Zoe with a sob.

"Too late? What for?"

Zoe took a shaky breath in.

"I'm dying, Tanya."

Chapter Twenty-nine

What's Deputy Madden doing here?

Tanya peered through the hotel parking lot.

She had just stepped out of the bar, when she noticed a familiar car idling next to a hotel shuttle. She recognized the large dent on the side of the unmarked Crown Victoria.

The lights outside the main hotel building were bright, bright enough to show anyone inside their vehicles. Deputy Madden was alone, in the driver's seat, his head down and his nose buried in his phone.

"Have a good night then!"

Tanya twisted around to see the bartender waving at her.

"My pal's gonna bring his truck early in the morning. It'll be out in the back. Car keys will be inside."

Tanya nodded her thanks, her mind elsewhere.

She had already passed him a wad of dollar bills, an advance payment for the truck rental. She would have a vehicle to get around, now that her Jeep was in the garage.

She closed the door behind her and let Max amble out ahead.

There was an entrance to the hotel from inside the bar, but she needed fresh air before she headed upstairs and confronted Fox.

If she had taken the inside route, she would have missed the deputy. Tanya watched Madden, hands on her hips. The deputy hadn't noticed her yet.

She glanced around the half-empty lot. It was the tail end of spring, so the hotel wasn't full. As far as she knew, she and Fox were the only guests who had anything to do with the current investigations.

Did Adams put us on a surveillance list?

If Madden had been tasked to watch over them, he made a lousy guard dog. But she had a more urgent matter to deal with than Adams and Madden right now.

"Come on, Max," she called to her pup as she turned toward the hotel's main entrance.

The doorman saluted as she walked by. "Good night, ma'am," he said, touching his hat. Tanya nodded and pushed through the glass doors with Max at her heels.

A spiral of shock had shot through her the second she learned about Zoe. She gritted her teeth as she thought of how Fox hadn't been honest with her.

She marched into the elevator with Max and punched the fifth-floor button with more force than necessary.

A small part of her knew she should forgive Fox. If there was anyone who kept her cards close to her chest, it had to be her. She understood why he did what he did.

Still, thought Tanya, as she stomped out of the elevator on the fifth floor.

You should have told me what was going on, Fox. How can I help you, if you can't trust me?

A mocking voice in the back of her head chuckled.

You're one to talk.

Tanya brushed the thought off and headed straight for Fox's door.

His room was next to hers at the end of the corridor, right by the fire exit. The plan had been to find adjoining rooms, so if anyone wondered why a "couple on holiday" weren't sharing a room, they could always say they just needed more space.

As if Max knew where they were headed, he trotted over to Fox's door, sniffed around the bottom, and wagged his tail. But Tanya didn't have time for niceties. She stepped up to the door and banged on it.

Silence.

She waited, wondering if he had gone off on his own to investigate. She wouldn't have put it past him to do that. But Max was still wagging his tail.

No, he's in his room.

She banged on the door again, louder this time.

Max barked and pawed at the door, as if to help her.

"Shh... bud."

The hotel had only allowed Max in on the condition that if anyone complained about him, she would have to find another place to stay. She couldn't afford to lose time. Not now.

She knocked on the door. "Fox? We need to talk. This is serious."

The chain rattled on the other end, and the doorknob turned. Tanya sighed in relief.

The door inched open and Fox's bleary eyes peered out. Tanya reeled back as the alcohol on his breath stung her nose.

She stared at him. Under the harsh hotel corridor lights, he looked like he had aged several years since he had left the bar.

His shirt was unbuttoned, his hair was a mess, and his face was blotchy. The bandage on the side of his head from the car crash was seeping with blood.

Chapter Thirty

F ox scowled. "What do you want?"

Tanya put a hand on the door so he couldn't shut it on her. "Can I come in?"

With a resigned sigh, he let go of the doorknob, turned around, and stumbled inside.

Max pushed through the narrow opening and scampered over to him, his tail a flurry of wags. Fox plopped on his bed and stroked the dog's back, pointedly ignoring Tanya.

Tanya closed the door behind her and looked over her colleague she was just beginning to know.

Fox looked like a shattered shell of his previous self. The anger that had been growing inside of her since Zoe's call rolled off her shoulders.

"I know about Zoe."

Fox didn't look up.

Tanya sat down on the second bed across from his. "She called me. She said she's starting chemotherapy tomorrow."

Fox stroked Max's neck. It was like that was all he could focus on at that moment. Max squatted in between his knees, licking his face, happy to get all this attention from him.

"I'm so sorry," said Tanya, feeling something catch in her throat. "Why didn't you tell me?"

When Fox lifted his head, his face was scrunched like he was about to cry.

"Zoe and Eva were best friends since kindergarten."

His voice sounded heavy, like he had taken the burden of the entire world on his shoulders.

"Zoe came from a broken family and was a single child, so she always thought of Eva as her sister. They were very close. It was Eva who introduced me to Zoe."

Tanya nodded but kept silent.

Fox rubbed his face. "I couldn't tell her Eva had disappeared. She'd break if she knew."

"Didn't she ask why Eva hadn't called on her birthday like usual?"

"I lied."

Tanya stared at him.

"I told her she called me while I was at work. I told her Eva was busy with a new job and didn't have a lot of time, so it was a quick chat. Zoe was disappointed, but she knows Eva likes her privacy."

Tanya sighed.

Lies on top of lies. And then, they stumble over one another.

"When did Zoe find out she wasn't well?" she said, softening her voice.

"Four weeks ago."

"Four...? That's so fast."

Fox ruffled Max's head. Max thumped his tail.

"There was no warning. She complained about a headache for a bit, but she was healthy. She was at her annual checkup when the doctor spotted the abnormal growth. It's in the back of her head. Stage four."

He sighed heavily.

"We just celebrated her thirtieth birthday. She's too young to...."

Something caught in his throat, and he swallowed hard. Tanya wanted to say something useful, but had no idea what the right words were for someone hurting this badly.

"There's nothing I want more than to be with Zoe this weekend." Fox's lips trembled. "But if something's happened to Eva.... What do I do?"

Tanya put a hand on his knee. "Go home. Your wife needs you right now."

"What about Eva? I'm wondering if I—"

"I'll take care of Eva. I'll find her and I'll find her alive."

Tanya knew it was madness to promise something she had no control over. But hope kept people going in the darkest of times, and if anyone needed hope right now, it was Fox and Zoe.

Fox stared at her, his eyes squinched, like he wasn't sure what she was saying.

"I was alone after they killed my mother and took my brother away," said Tanya.

She stroked Max's back, unable to make eye contact with Fox when sharing something so personal.

"Everyone was terrified of the Russian militia. No one would come with me to look for my brother. I wish I had a friend who stood by me then. I want to be that person for you. I couldn't live with myself if I didn't."

Tanya noticed the tears rolling down Fox's cheeks.

It was time to go.

She stood up. "Call your wife."

Fox wiped his cheeks with the back of his sleeve, and nodded.

Tanya turned to leave when she noticed what was on his bed. Littered among the jumble of clothes, personal items, and mobile phone was Fox's laptop. It was turned toward them, and on the screen was the smiling face of a pretty teenage girl.

Tanya's gut stirred. There was something haunting about her face.

Fox saw her look and pulled the laptop toward him.

"Who's that girl?" said Tanya.

"I think I found something," said Fox. "Don't know if it helps, but it's strange."

Tanya sat back down.

"Tell me."

"Dr. Patel voluntarily surrendered his medical license in four states."

Tanya's eyebrows shot up.

"Malpractice suits?"

"Complaints to medical boards," said Fox, "but none went all the way to court."

"Complaints regarding what?"

"Sexual assault and sexual advances to patients."

Fox rubbed his tired eyes.

"It's been done before by bad doctors. They say mea culpa, surrender their license, and shut down their practice. It's a trick to avoid jail time and legal fees. Patients don't pursue them because it's too expensive or they're ashamed by what happened. Probably both."

"So the physicians move to another state, open a new practice, and abuse more victims?" said Tanya.

Fox nodded. "Pretty much."

"What a sick game."

"There's no restriction on doing that at the federal level, at least when he was on the move, so he got away with it. He continued over and over again until he ended up here."

"And the man's supposed to be untouchable." Tanya shook her head and tsked.

She pointed at the laptop.

"Is that girl one of his victims?"

Fox turned his bleary eyes toward the screen.

"No, but it could be connected."

"How?"

"This teen went missing six years ago. A lobster fishing boat found her in the sea. Newspaper reports say it was a suspicious death, but because there was no evidence of foul play, the local sheriff closed the case."

"Sheriff Adams?"

"The articles don't give a name, just the title."

Tanya stared at the screen. The young woman with the pretty smile stared back at her.

So, she's dead.

"Who is she?"

"Deputy Madden's daughter."

Chapter Thirty-one

"What's he doing here?"

Fox peered through his hotel room window at the parking lot below.

It was harder to see inside the car from five floors up. But the exhaust escaping the pipes in the back of the dented Crown Victoria told Tanya that Deputy Madden hadn't left his vehicle.

"Watching us," she said. "Until you told me about his daughter, I was sure Adams sent him to keep an eye on us."

Fox turned to her. "Why would he do that? We haven't done anything wrong."

"Adams was the first one on the scene when our Jeep crashed. How did he get there so fast?"

Fox stared at her.

"Then, there's that bruise behind those shades," said Tanya. "He's hiding something."

"Maybe it was his wife or girlfriend. She punched him and he's too embarrassed to admit it."

Tanya shook her head. "He ran inside the hall with me after the explosion. He seemed horrified, but he really didn't like my pressure cooker bomb theory. Said I was jumping to conclusions."

"He said that?" Fox's eyes widened. "To *you*?"

"I know my IEDs. That wasn't an accidental gas explosion. It was a bomb."

"You think the sheriff's playing with us?"

Tanya had come across the world's best con men during her travels, and knew better than to trust anyone blindly. *Trust your instincts but act on evidence.* That was her mantra.

"I'm keeping my eyes and options open," she said. "At the moment, everyone in this town is a suspect."

Tanya pointed at his laptop on the bed.

"Madden could have been watching us to see if we can lead him to clues about his daughter's death. Maybe Adams has nothing to do with this."

Fox raised his chin. A flicker of hope came in his eyes.

"Maybe he can help us find Eva."

Tanya turned around and whistled at Max. "I think it's time to have a chat with the deputy."

Fox urgently buttoned up his shirt. "Wait for me."

Tanya pulled the door open.

"Leave this to me," she said, stepping outside of his room. "You have other priorities."

But Fox caught up to her at the elevator.

They strode in silence out of the main hotel entrance and toward the squad car parked out front. Tanya stepped up to the driver's side and peeked inside.

Madden was sipping on a straw, drinking what looked like an extra-large slushy. His other hand held a half-eaten burger. On his lap was his mobile phone to which his eyes seemed glued.

On the backseat lay a semi-automatic rifle, like it had been carelessly left behind and forgotten.

Tanya frowned.

Shouldn't he secure that?

She knocked on the window.

Madden jumped so hard, the slushy fell on his lap. With a yelp, he pushed the door open and tumbled out, wiping the mess of ice and soda from his wet trousers.

"Sorry about that," said Tanya. "Didn't mean to startle you."

Madden turned an annoyed face at her. "Do you always sneak up on people like that?"

"Do you always sneak around in hotel parking lots?"

He stared at her.

"I... er, I'm on duty tonight."

Fox pointed a finger at the officer's chest. "You were watching us, weren't you?"

The deputy put his hands up as if to defend himself. "Sheriff said to keep an eye out, because... because...."

"So, Adams sent you?" said Tanya, taking a step forward.

Madden took a step back in alarm. "All these bad things are happening, and it's ever since...."

Suddenly Fox swayed on his feet.

Tanya and Madden both turned to him.

"You all right, man?" said Madden, a concerned expression coming over his face.

Fox put a hand on Tanya's shoulder to steady himself. She shot him a disapproving look. The medication in his veins and the alcohol he'd just drunk were probably playing havoc in him.

You should be upstairs, in bed.

But Fox only gripped her shoulder tighter.

He turned toward the officer. "So bad things happened ever since we got here?"

Madden let his hands drop. "Look, guys, I'm just following orders. Sheriff said to keep an eye out for you."

"You mean an eye out *on* us," snapped Tanya.

With shaking hands, Fox pulled his phone out of his pocket and turned it toward the officer. Deputy Madden took one look at the young woman's photo and staggered back.

"Can you tell us what happened to your daughter?" said Fox.

Madden clutched at the roof of his car, bent over, and started wheezing like he was getting a heart attack.

"Hey, easy there," said Tanya. "Why don't you sit down?"

But Fox stumbled forward.

"I want to know if there's a connection between your daughter and my sister."

His voice wavered with fatigue, but his eyes blazed with determination.

Madden didn't look up.

"What happened to her?" said Fox. "Tell me!"

"She drowned," whispered Madden, clutching his chest. "She was only sixteen."

Tanya frowned. "How did that happen?"

"Lila had gone kayaking with a friend. She was an excellent swimmer, but.... Her friend came back. My girl never did."

"Who was this other girl?" said Tanya.

"Lila's best friend. They found her barely alive, clinging to a rock in the middle of the ocean."

"Was it an accident?" Tanya trailed off, not wanting to distress him any more than he already was.

"Her friend said it was a rogue wave," whispered Madden. "It hit them and turned the kayak upside down."

"Do you believe that?" said Fox.

Madden looked up.

His eyes had turned hard.

Tanya glimpsed a fury behind those eyes, a fury she never expected from a man like Deputy Madden.

Chapter Thirty-two

"The papers said it was an accident, but was it?" said Fox.

Deputy Madden was quiet for what felt like forever. He looked like he was fighting with himself to control his emotions.

Fox staggered toward the squad car and leaned against it as if he could barely stand on his own.

Madden sighed heavily.

"Lila was my baby girl." His face was etched in grief. "My only child. She was my everything."

"I'm sorry for what happened," said Tanya.

"It broke us. My wife couldn't take it. She blamed me for not protecting her."

"Where's your wife now?" said Fox.

"She took off." Madden's voice cracked. "She said she'd go mad if she stayed in this town after what happened. Someone told me she's in Florida and has a new family. I couldn't leave town, because if I did, it would mean forgetting Lila."

Tanya remained silent.

So many questions swirled in her head, but she could see Madden was still in pain, haunted by the loss of his daughter.

If she had thought Fox was broken from his sister's disappearance, Madden looked like a man who had spent a lifetime in prison—a prison of his own making.

As if sensing his hurt, Max trotted over to the officer and licked his hand. The deputy scratched Max's head absentmindedly.

"In one year," said Madden, addressing the pup, "I lost my daughter and my wife. It took everything in me to keep it together."

He looked up at Tanya, his eyes hard again.

"I know what everyone says about me."

"What do they say?" said Tanya.

"Sheriff told me to take a month of paid leave, but I need the work to keep my mind off things or I'd go mad. He keeps me on because he feels sorry for me. Gives me easy jobs. The other guys think I'm a burden. They only tolerate me because I retire in five years."

"The sheriff has good words for you," said Tanya, remembering how Adams had defended his employee in the interrogation room earlier that morning.

Madden turned away with a sigh. "That's what they all say. Everyone's polite to my face, but they all think I'm royally messed up."

Fox leaned toward the officer.

"Have any other girls gone missing in town?"

His voice was slurred, but he seemed like he was powering through his pain. Tanya noticed his hands were shaking.

He's going to crash soon.

Madden shrugged. "You really need to talk to the sheriff. I'm assigned to desk work and street patrol. I don't even get to look at case files anymore."

"Do you think what happened to your daughter has anything to do with the victim we found today?" said Fox.

Madden blinked like the question surprised him. "You mean that headless woman?"

"Who else do you think I'm referring to?"

Madden's face flushed. "Lila drowned. That's what happened. No one hurt her. If I had seen her like what I saw this morning, I would.... I don't know what I would have done... Probably wouldn't be here today."

He rubbed his eyes.

"You're trying to make connections where there are none. Look, I don't know what happened to your sister, and I don't know what happened to that woman we found today, but don't you put my daughter in the same...."

He looked up and glared at Fox.

"Leave Lila out of this."

"Who investigated Lila's death?" said Fox, undeterred. "Was it Sheriff Adams?"

"This was six years ago. It was the former sheriff."

Madden stared at Fox, then at Tanya, as if to say *are we done?*

"I understand this is hard for you," said Tanya. "Thank you for sharing your story."

The deputy took a deep breath in. He looked down at Max and ruffled his head.

"Lila had a pup too. Duffy was her name. A small black terrier. She passed away last year and broke my heart. She was my main connection to Lila for years after I lost my girl."

Madden's eyes had a faraway look, like he had wandered off into another world.

"That little fur bundle kept my daughter so happy."

"Lila had a good father in you," said Tanya. "I'm sure she appreciated everything you did for her."

Madden looked up, tears filling his eyes. It was like those were the words he had been yearning to hear all along. He wiped his face and nodded.

"I know what it's like to lose a loved one. I don't know what I can do, but I'll help you guys as much as I can."

Fox let out a sigh of relief.

"Why don't you start by telling us the girl who was with Lila when she drowned?"

Fox was slurring his words again, like he was drunk.

Madden peered at him. "You okay, man?"

Fox leaned against the cruiser, as if to stop from keeling over.

"Just answer the question."

Madden frowned. "It was Lila's coworker. They worked for Madame Camilla."

Tanya raised a brow. *Madame Camilla?*

"Can you share the girl's name?"

"Julie Steele," said Madden.

That was when Fox collapsed to the ground.

Day Two

Chapter Thirty-three

"We got duped, Stone."

Fox picked up the pile of coffee-stained paper and oily rags from the footwell of the rusty pickup truck. He threw them into the hotel's garbage dumpster.

"They probably stole this from the local junkyard."

It was five in the morning, but neither Tanya nor Fox had slept much.

After Fox had crashed with exhaustion in the parking lot, Madden had helped Tanya carry him back to the hotel. Fox had protested, saying he was fine, but had stopped after Tanya had threatened to tie him to his bed.

That hadn't been necessary as Fox had passed out as soon as his head hit the pillow. Tanya had pulled his shoes off and had thrown a blanket over him before leaving his room. From her combat days, she knew without sufficient rest, they could easily burn out, and that wouldn't help Eva.

The bartender had kept his word.

The red pickup truck was waiting for them in the back of the hotel by the time they had come down. The vehicle was greasy, grimy, and gross, and had probably not been serviced in years, but the car keys had been inside, and the tank was a quarter full.

In the back, Max seemed as skeptical as Fox about their new ride. He turned around in his seat, sniffing every nook and cranny. Then, he looked up at Tanya as if to say *you've got to be kidding me.*

Tanya reached over and nudged him down. There was no safety net in this vehicle, and the crash of the day before was glaringly fresh in her mind.

"Down, bud."

Fox got in and searched for the seat belt buckle that was stuck in between the seams of his seat. Tanya turned the key and cringed as the engine spluttered to life. She rolled out of the parking lot, wondering how far it would go before breaking down.

But now, they had an ally on their side.

Deputy Madden had promised to dig up old case files that morning—files from any case that had to do with missing women or girls.

They had agreed to meet him near the station before Sheriff Adams came in. Madden had a small window of time before the day shift started and would wonder what he was doing by the filing cabinets.

Their conversation the night before swirled through Tanya's head as she drove down Crescent Bay's main road.

She was still trying to piece the puzzle together and wished she could brainstorm with Fox. But she knew his imagination could run wild and he could panic again.

"It's strange Julie Steele was in the kayak with Madden's daughter the day they got overturned," said Fox, scrunching his forehead. "Then we find Julie with her head cut off in the ocean, six years later."

Tanya nodded. "Maybe someone tried to kill them both six years ago and came back to finish the job."

"We need to find out." He turned to her. "My gut tells me this is connected to Eva somehow."

Tanya shot her colleague a look.

Gosh, he looks terrible.

"I thought you were going to head home today."

Fox remained silent.

Tanya sighed. "Please tell me you called Zoe at least."

"She told me to stay and help Eva. She said it would make her feel better."

"Did you tell her—"

"No!"

Max lifted his head and gave a startled bark.

"She doesn't need to hear the grisly details of what we found." Fox's voice was rising. "I can't have her getting nightmares like I am. It will kill her!"

Tanya focused on the road, her ears trained on the cranky engine as it popped and sputtered like it would die at any moment.

"As far as Zoe knows, Eva has a nasty boyfriend in Crescent Bay and I came to help her move out," said Fox in a quiet voice. "If Zoe calls you again, back me up."

Tanya didn't reply. She hated lying to a woman who was already going through a lot.

But isn't this a white lie?

She hadn't forgotten her obligation to her boss in Seattle. Susan Cross hadn't minced her words when she gave her the deadline. She had to find Eva before Monday morning.

Tanya pushed Susan Cross to the back of her mind and turned onto the highway that hugged the coastline.

The early morning sky hung low, and the sea sounded even angrier than the day before. The dull gray around them said the storm clouds hadn't left town yet.

"What if he gets caught?" said Fox, all of a sudden.

"Who?" said Tanya.

"Madden. Adams can charge us with interfering with a police investigation. If he's got something to do with this, he'll be looking for an excuse to stop us from finding Eva."

"Let's hope Madden is smarter than he loo—"

Max barked, stopping Tanya in mid-sentence.

Her pup scrambled up and got on all fours.

"Hey, bud," said Tanya, peering at him through the cracked rearview mirror. "You've got to lie down when we're rolling."

But Max had his snout stubbornly stuck on the window that looked out to the sea. He whined and pawed on the seat, as if he wanted to tell her something.

Tanya narrowed her eyes. "What is it, Max?"

Fox sat up. "Who's that?"

She turned to see what he was pointing at.

A lone female figure was standing at the edge of the bluff. She had her back to them and was staring at something at the bottom of the cliff.

Chapter Thirty-four

Seagulls swooped over the woman at the edge of the cliff.

The blustery wind whipped her long blonde hair. She was a petite woman and could have even been an older teen.

Fox shook his head. "Don't these storm watchers have a life? Don't they ever go home?"

The silhouette by the cliff became clearer as they got closer. Tanya's heart skipped a beat.

"It's that girl Felipe attacked at the banquet hall," she said, taking her foot off the gas and tapping on the brakes.

Max whined again.

Fox peered through the window. "What's she doing out here this early?"

The girl was standing at the very end of the cliff with her face down. She was swaying, as if hypnotized by the waves below.

Beyond the precipice, Tanya could hear the ocean crash against the rocks. She pulled the vehicle to the side of the road and brought it to a complete stop.

She opened the door and jumped out. Max leaped through the front seats and out of the truck after her. He didn't wait for Tanya, but darted toward the cliff at full speed.

Her heart pounding, Tanya raced after him.

Hearing the dog bark, the girl spun around.

Her face was pale but expressionless.

Without a word, she turned back around, spread her arms wide, and bent her knees.

"No!" screamed Tanya. "Don't do it!"

Chapter Thirty-five

Max leaped on the girl and snatched her sleeve in his jaws.

For one horrific moment, Tanya was sure both the girl and her dog would disappear over the cliff.

But Max held on.

Tanya dashed over and yanked them back. All three came tumbling down, rolling away from the cliff. The girl let out a surprised cry and Max yelped, but Tanya kept her grip on both.

Fox came running over and grabbed the girl's arm.

"What do you think you're doing?" he said, shaking her.

Tanya sat back, panting hard.

"Good job, bud," she said, letting go of Max's collar.

She turned to the teen, who had tucked her chin into her chest like she didn't want the world to see her.

"What were you doing here?" said Fox, shaking the girl again.

"Easy there," said Tanya, putting a hand up to stop him. "Let her be."

She knew why he was reacting so harshly. Though this girl was a lot younger than his sister, all Fox could see was Eva in the place of the victims they had come across.

Fox stopped shaking her, but held on to her arm like he was scared she would run off and try to jump again.

"Good thing we came this way," said Tanya.

She touched the girl's shoulder and softened her voice.

"Honey, are you okay?"

The girl didn't answer, and seemed to withdraw even further. She scrunched herself into a ball and hugged her knees, like she was shrinking into herself.

Tanya leaned closer, trying to make out her expression, but her face was buried in her knees now.

"We're here to help you. Whatever you're scared of, we're here for you, okay?"

No response.

"We need to get her to her family," said Fox. He turned to the girl. "Where's your mum and dad?"

No reply.

Tanya appraised the teen and realized while she was small in stature, she must have been eighteen at the most. Technically an adult. Or almost an adult.

"What about a friend?" she said. "Can we get a hold of a friend of yours?"

Silence.

Fox plucked out his mobile and turned the screen toward the teen.

"Do you know her?" he said, bending down to get at the same level as her. "Have you seen her anywhere in this town or in someone's house?"

"Hey," said Tanya. "This isn't the time for this."

HER LAST LIE

But he pushed the mobile closer to the girl and shook it, as if that would do the trick. That only made the girl hug herself tighter.

"Leave her be," said Tanya. "She's gone through a lot."

Fox turned to her, his face dark and lined with worry.

"What about Eva? Where's she? What's going on here? We have to find her!"

Tanya pulled out her regular phone from her pocket and dialed the number she had got the night before.

"Madden, I need your help. It's urgent."

Chapter Thirty-six

When Deputy Madden arrived, Tanya, Fox, the girl, and Max were still huddled by the cliff.

The wind had picked up. Every minute had felt tortuously colder than the one before. Still, the girl had refused to budge.

Tanya had bundled her in her jacket, but the teen hadn't spoken or looked up at her rescuers. She had sat curled up in her spot in a haunting silence.

Madden's cruiser came to a screeching halt behind their pickup truck.

Tanya and Fox watched as the officer shuffled over to them, wheezing. His uniform was crumpled like he had slept in it, the stain from last night's drink spill even more glaring in the light of day.

"That was fast," said Tanya.

"I was on patrol all night." Madden put his hands up. "Not by your hotel. I swear."

"Looks like you're on a twenty-four-hour shift."

He shrugged. "All hands on deck at the moment." He pulled a USB stick from his pocket. "Got something for you."

Fox leaned over, snatched it, and pocketed it.

Madden bent down and peered at the victim.

"Now what do we have here? How are you doing, my dear?"

The girl didn't look up.

The deputy shook his head and tsked in sympathy.

"Do you know her family?" said Tanya.

Madden scrunched his forehead and scratched his head.

"She's not talking," said Tanya. "We've been trying to get her to give us her name, drink some water, but she might be in shock."

"Any ID?" said Madden.

"None in her pockets," said Tanya. "I checked."

"We need to get her somewhere safe," said Fox. "We can't just leave her here."

He turned his bloodshot eyes to Tanya. He looked like he was on the verge of a panic attack himself.

"We don't have time."

"I'll make sure she's fine," said Madden. "I'll get her checked over by a doctor."

Tanya turned to the officer. "Whatever you do, don't take her to Dr. Patel."

"Over my dead body," spat the deputy. "That will never happen, I can assure you of that."

Tanya raised an eyebrow.

The deputy's face darkened.

"Scum on earth. He's a psychopath."

Madden took a handkerchief from his pocket and wiped the sweat from his brow.

Tanya badly wanted to learn more, but she couldn't ask her questions in front of a young woman who had just contemplated ending her life.

"You can't take her to the precinct either," said Tanya, unsure she wanted to leave the girl with an officer who had his own issues. "She needs a safe place, not a police station."

"I'll take her to Dr. Chen, our medical examiner. They live at the big house at the end of the road. They're both doctors and they're good people. Her husband takes care of babies... He's a, er,...."

"Pediatrician?" said Tanya.

Madden nodded. "His wife does autopsies for the sheriff's office. I'd trust her with my life."

"The girl's family needs to be informed too," said Tanya, feeling like she was explaining his job to him. "They might be looking for her right now."

"Dr. Chen can talk to her family. She knows everyone in town."

The officer reached over and tapped the girl's shoulder. "Let's go, miss."

To Tanya's surprise, the girl slowly unraveled herself and got up on her shaky legs. She kept her face and eyes down, but she was moving.

"Come on," said Madden, nudging her forward. "We're gonna get you to a warm place, and get you a cup of hot chocolate, okie dokie?"

Tanya and Fox watched as the girl stumbled alongside the deputy toward the squad car.

"She knows him," said Fox as the girl slipped into the passenger seat. "Maybe she'll open up to him?"

Madden did a three-point turn on the road and drove off, his cruiser lights flashing and sirens blaring unnecessarily.

"I hope we're doing the right thing," said Tanya. "He may have his heart in the right place, but he's not the most competent officer I know."

"He lost his daughter," said Fox. "If anyone's in the position to treat that girl with the sensitivity she needs right now—"

A warning bark from Max made them whirl around.

"What's up, bud?" said Tanya, walking over to him.

Max was peering over the cliff, barking at a flock of seagulls squawking below. But it was something else that caught Tanya's attention.

She stared, unable to believe her eyes.

Fox stepped up to her and gasped out loud. "What in goodness' name is this?"

"That girl was going to kill herself here..." whispered Tanya, gazing at the sand art at the bottom of the cliff.

Someone had come in when the tide was low and written a note in large letters on the wet sand. The waves were sweeping the shore, and had already obliterated the top half of the words.

But the message was clear.

Last witness still alive.

Chapter Thirty-seven

S heriff Adams crossed his arms.

"I was so sure I caught the man behind this."

His eyes, still shielded by those dark shades, stared down the cliff at the markings below. The words on the sand were half gone, wiped by the waves that were growing stronger by the second.

Tanya turned to him in surprise.

"You have someone in custody already?"

Adams nodded, but pursed his lips, like he didn't want to share this information with an off-duty officer and a contractor.

Five minutes after Madden had disappeared around the corner, Adams's cruiser had shown up. He had parked his vehicle behind their truck and had strode up to them on the cliff.

Tanya and Fox had braced themselves, not knowing what to expect, but the sheriff had seemed curious and friendly, asking if they needed help.

Tanya's head whirled.

How did he know we were here? Did Madden alert him? Was Adams following us? Are they all in this together?

Tanya observed the sheriff but remained polite. Getting kicked out of town was not something she wanted, especially after what happened that morning.

"Maybe he had an accomplice," Adams muttered to himself as he peered over the bluff. "Someone he roped in to scare the townsfolk or deflect the accusations away from him."

"Can you tell us who you have in jail, Sheriff?" said Fox, his voice laced with impatience.

Adams stared silently at Fox as if he was scrutinizing him.

"Dupont," he said, finally.

"Who's that?" said Tanya.

"Chef Dupont," said Adams. "He has several pressure cookers in his kitchen. We found more nails in the drawers of his counter. Plus, he has enough butcher knives in his arsenal to do damage to a corpse."

"So you think it was a bomb then?" said Tanya. "Not an accidental gas explosion."

"The forensics team is still working on it, so I have no conclusive evidence yet. But it seems like you might be right." He made a face like he hated to admit to it. "Dupont is our most likely unsub right now."

Tanya knitted her brow.

She loathed the overbearing chef who seemed to think it was perfectly fine to permit a sexual assault in his back office. She was glad he was locked up, but something nagged her in the back of her brain.

"How do you know he was behind this?"

Adams turned toward her. "He was in the right place at the right time with the right tools."

"Circumstantial."

"He's denying it, that's for sure. I thought spending the night in jail might loosen him up, but he's not changing his tune. Says the cooker wasn't his, that he uses higher grade equipment, and that someone's trying to frame him."

Adams shook his head and sighed.

"The thing is he hasn't asked for a lawyer. He seems to think screaming at my officers is enough to prove his innocence. He's not helping his case at all."

"He doesn't fit the profile of someone who would plan such a meticulous act," said Tanya, speaking slowly like she was trying to figure it out herself. "What makes you so certain to make an arrest?"

"Because the entire town heard his death threats," said Adams.

"Death threats?" said Fox.

"Dupont had a fight with Camilla at the farmer's market last weekend." Adams blew a raspberry. "I shouldn't be sharing this, but since you're both in law enforcement and have skin in the game...."

"Tell us," said Tanya. "Maybe it will help us find Eva."

"Everyone knew Camilla keeps boy toys."

"Kids?" said Fox, with a grimace.

Adams shook his head.

"Men half her age, so they're adults. She makes sure of that. She cycles through them every year."

"What does that have to do with the bomb at the banquet hall?" said Tanya.

"The argument at the farmer's market was about her latest conquest. She got upset when she saw Dupont flirting with him. The boyfriend ran off, and Dupont told her he'd give up his new friend over her dead body."

"But nothing that's happened so far was an act of passion," said Tanya. "Especially the bomb. I'm willing to bet whoever committed either crime had planned ahead and planned them well."

"Dupont told Camilla he'd get her when she wasn't looking. The whole town was listening, and it was in broad daylight, so I have many witnesses."

"But Camilla hired Dupont for the banquet. Why would she—"

"These two have been going at each other's throats for a long time," said Adams. "They have a complex, love-hate relationship. He preys on her boys, but he has a Michelin star from a Marseilles restaurant from years ago. Having him cater her events brings out the crowds. Which in turn, means more funds for Camilla's charities."

Adams spread his arms out.

"Seems like he made good on his promise. He sabotaged her event and tried to kill her."

Chapter Thirty-eight

T anya's head whirled.

Adams' deduction didn't make sense to her. She felt like she was missing something important. A clue that was staring her in the face.

She glanced over the cliff.

The message was all but gone now. A faint outline was left on the sand, but that too would succumb to the sea.

"Dupont didn't write that," she said. "He was in custody. Whoever it was came here at low tide last night."

"Someone lured that girl here this morning," said Fox, thoughtfully. "She was supposed to see that message."

"This means Dupont has a partner in crime," said Adams.

"If the girl starts talking, we might have our answers," said Tanya.

"Maybe Dr. Chen can get her to talk," said Adams. "Madden briefed me over the radio while he was driving her over."

Tanya frowned.

So Madden told his boss about the girl. That's how Adams knew where to find us.

"Dupont's the type who'd throw a knife at you if he didn't like you," said Tanya, observing the sheriff while she spoke. "I can't see him leave secret messages or plot to kidnap and kill someone in cold blood."

Adams remained quiet, but she could see he was listening.

"Someone planted the bomb and framed the chef," she said. "The unsub has to be someone else."

The sheriff scratched his chin.

"What about this Dr. Patel?" said Tanya. "You said he might have a shady past. Maybe he's the mastermind behind all these events."

"He's a slippery fellow, but I have nothing to pin him down." Adams rubbed his forehead and sighed heavily. "My team's stretched to the limit. What I need is more resources."

"Time to call the big dogs, Sheriff," said Fox. "The feds have more funds than all of us combined."

Tanya's heart skipped a beat, but kept her face stoic. Neither man knew a federal agent with her K9 were standing among them right now.

She wondered how Susan Cross would react if the sheriff of this tiny county called for help. Cross's teams ignored requests from small offices, especially if they weren't within their purview. The FBI may be the big dogs, but they had their own mandate and budgets to worry about.

The sheriff furrowed his brow.

"Neither victim is underage, and there's nothing that says these incidents are in federal jurisdiction. They will never take my call."

Tanya turned to him, an idea crossing her mind.

"I worked with the FBI before."

Adams jerked his head back.

"As a contractor," said Tanya quickly. "If you want to get their attention, tell them you have a potential serial killer on the prowl. I realize you only have two bodies, but this message is a threat of potential future victims. That will be a good justification. I can help you craft your message to them."

Adams stared.

"I wish you worked for me. I might have a chat with Jack Bold about that."

Tanya kept her face straight.

I'm already juggling two jobs, Sheriff. Plus, I don't know if you're the unsub here.

Before she could reply, Adams's phone rang.

He put it to his ear. "Yes?"

Tanya and Fox watched as the sheriff's face flushed pink, then turned a dangerous red. He clutched his chest like Madden had the night before when they broached the topic of his dead daughter.

"You okay?" said Fox.

Adams lowered his phone.

"Felipe Fernando is dead," he whispered hoarsely. "They found him in his cell."

"How did that happen?" said Tanya.

"Choked on his own vomit."

Chapter Thirty-nine

"Zoe?"

Fox scraped his chair back and got up, his phone to his ear.

"What?"

Tanya jerked her head up, her heart ticking a beat faster.

Gosh, I hope she's okay.

She and Fox were back at the local precinct, but this time they had been invited in.

Adams had left them alone in his office while he went to get the details on Felipe's death from his deputies.

Whatever Chief Jack Bold from Black Rock had told the sheriff, it had impressed the man. Adams was treating them like colleagues now. They didn't need Deputy Madden's USB stick anymore.

But Tanya wasn't about to let her guard down.

She and Fox sat across from the sheriff's desk, reviewing old case files, the same files Madden had discreetly copied for them that morning.

Tanya watched as Fox leaned against the doorway to take the call from his wife.

At her feet, Max let out a loud sigh. He had been waiting patiently for the past hour, as they had tried to craft the best pitch for resources from the FBI.

"I promise you, babe," Fox was saying, his voice in earnest, "I'm coming home tomorrow."

He fell silent for a few minutes while Zoe spoke at the other end.

Tanya's antennas were up.

She wanted nothing more than to listen in, but she also knew that wouldn't be right. She stroked Max's ears, trying to figure out the best way to get her federal team over to help them find Eva, when she heard the words.

"Eva? You're kidding me?"

Tanya whirled around.

Fox was slumped against the door. "Are you sure it was her?"

Tanya pushed her chair back and got up. If Zoe had something to say about Eva, she wanted to know too.

Fox looked up as she walked over.

"Eva just called Zoe," he whispered, his eyes wide in shock.

"What did she say?" Tanya whispered back.

"Hang on, babe," said Fox to his wife. He switched the cell to speaker mode.

"Hey, Zoe?" he said. "Tanya's with me. Can you tell us what Eva said?"

Zoe laughed pleasantly.

Fox and Tanya exchanged alarmed glances.

"We talked like old friends," said Zoe. "She seemed so happy. It was so nice to chat with her after so long."

Fox raised his head and stared at Tanya.

Tanya shrugged.

Zoe seemed in a lot better mood than when they spoke the night before. There was a light giddiness to her voice.

Is it her medication?

"I needed that, especially right now," Zoe was saying. "With all I'm going through. It did me good to hear her voice."

"Did Eva sound scared?" said Fox.

"Goodness no." Zoe coughed before continuing. "I told her you were in town to help her with her boyfriend, but she told me you had it all wrong. She's found a man who's finally treating her well."

Fox's eyebrows shot up.

"Hey, Zoe," said Tanya, leaning in. "Are you certain it was Eva?"

"Of course. I recognized her voice. She hasn't changed a bit. What on earth makes you ask—"

"Did you see her face?"

"She didn't have her video on this time. I look like a right mess so I didn't turn mine on either."

"How long did you talk for?"

"Almost twenty minutes." Zoe coughed again. "Did you know she has an amazing new gig lined up?"

"New gig?" parroted Fox. "What kind of gig?"

"She told me you were overreacting as usual."

The lines on Fox's forehead deepened. "Overreacting about what?"

They could hear Zoe take a sip of water or something on the other end. It was clear she was having difficulty, despite her happiness at having talked to an old friend.

"You're always super protective about her," said Zoe.

"I agree," said Tanya, speaking quickly. "He even dragged me into this, in case the boyfriend got testy."

"That's what she said," came Zoe's voice, weaker now. "She said you two were like dogs hounding her. She told me to tell you to stop."

Fox stared at the phone like he couldn't believe his ears. He looked up at Tanya, confusion clouding his eyes.

Tanya leaned toward the speaker.

"Did you tell her you weren't well?"

Zoe went silent for a few seconds.

"She asked me why I was coughing, and I told her I had a touch of pneumonia. Everything is working out for her finally and she sounded so happy. I couldn't spoil that, could I? I just couldn't get myself to tell her."

Fox frowned. "Are you sure she sounded happy?"

"Shawn Fox." Zoe's voice hardened a notch. "Eva's not a kid anymore. She doesn't want us interfering with her new life right now. Respect her wishes, will you?"

"But... but...," stuttered Fox.

Zoe coughed a rough hacking cough. Fox winced, like it hurt him just as much to hear her.

"Did you get Eva's number?" said Tanya, before Zoe faded off.

"She's staying at a hotel, getting ready for an interview with a big accounting firm in Crescent Bay. It's her third interview, the last one where you negotiate salary and stuff."

"Did you see the number on the screen?"

"It was an unknown number."

Tanya raised a brow, as alarm bells went off in her head.

First, hotel names usually showed up on phone screens. Second, Crescent Bay didn't have a big consulting firm. The only large company was the one everyone talked about—the dubious MLM scheme.

Is Eva part of the pyramid scam?

"You sound like you're stalking her," said Zoe.

"We're not," said Fox.

"Stop harassing the poor girl and come home. Anyway, she has the job in the bag. I'm so proud of her."

Zoe coughed again.

"Besides, she'll tell us all about it when she visits us."

Chapter Forty

F ox almost dropped the phone.

"Eva's going to visit us?"

"Next weekend. She wants to introduce her new boyfriend to us."

Tanya heard a commotion and turned.

Loud voices were coming from across the precinct's bullpen.

It seemed like most of the local deputies had gathered at the doorway of a conference room. They were listening in, concerned expressions on their faces.

One covered his face with his hands and shook his head. Another stared at his feet. Whatever was going on in there had everyone on edge.

Suddenly, the officers parted, and Sheriff Adams stomped in between them. His scowl deepened the closer he got to his office.

Tanya's stomach tightened.

She had never been on a case where things seem to change at lightning speed, to the point she felt whiplash at every turn.

What now?

Seeing Adams make a beeline toward them, Fox switched the speaker mode on his mobile to private. Holding his phone against his ear, he slipped out of the sheriff's office and walked down the corridor, away from everyone.

Adams didn't seem to even notice Fox. He pushed past Tanya, marched inside, and threw his cap on his desk. Max sat up and growled.

"What's going on?" said Tanya.

"Felipe's death has been ruled a potential homicide."

Tanya stared at him.

"What about Chef Dupont? You said he was your guy."

"It wasn't him. He's still in custody."

"Is *he* still alive?"

Adams rubbed his face. "He is. I just hope it stays that way."

He dropped into his chair with a heavy sigh.

"I posted a junior officer by his cell."

Tanya stepped toward the desk. "How did Felipe get killed inside his jail cell?"

The sheriff shook his head. "I'm as stumped as anyone else."

"What exactly happened?"

"Kathy... Deputy Hatchet found him on the floor without a pulse during a routine check. At first glance, she thought he'd choked on his vomit. His blood alcohol level was five times the legal limit, so that wouldn't have been surprising."

"What makes you sure it's homicide?"

Adams's eyes turned dark. "There are ligature marks on his neck. Someone strangled him using his own bedsheets."

"Has the medical examiner checked—"

He put his hands up to stop her.

"Deputy Hatchet is in charge now. You can ask her all your questions."

Tanya put her hands on the desk and glared at him. "What's going on here, Sheriff?"

"I'm no longer sheriff. That's what's going on."

"Did you step down from your position?"

Adams stared at the files littered all over his desk. His shades made it difficult for her to see what he was thinking, but she could feel the air in the room get thicker.

"Conflict of interest," he said in a low voice. "I have no choice but to recuse myself. Hatchet is Acting Sheriff as of now."

Tanya pulled a chair and sat down.

"What exactly is your relationship with Felipe Fernando?"

To her surprise, Adams took his shades off for the first time since they had met. He rubbed his eyes.

Tanya stared at the large purple bruise on his right eye.

So, he had been hiding a black eye, all along.

Adams looked up at her with glazed eyes.

"Felipe is my half-brother."

Chapter Forty-one

Tanya leaned back in her chair and gripped the armrests.

Another whiplash.

"Were you two close?"

Adams slouched in his chair.

"Not as much as I thought. We were like night and day. He took after our father while I took after my mother."

He sighed.

"Our father used to be a.... They called him a ladies' man, but if I'm honest, he was a philandering, wife-beating jerk who didn't treat my mother or any of his partners right."

Adams looked even more broken than when he'd announced Felipe's death.

"He left my mother without a proper goodbye. Took off to LA on an acting gig. At least, that's what he told us. I never believed anything he said because he was a chronic liar. That's how he suckered all the women who dated him."

Adams fell silent for a second. Tanya sat quietly in her chair, one thought going through her mind.

Everyone carries a burden. Even this man who's built like an ox.

"Felipe's mother was a cleaner at one of his movie sets," continued Adams, like he needed to talk it out. "Our father took advantage of her, but left her when Felipe was only five. I'm surprised he stayed that long. Felipe's mother was so upset, she gave her last name to her son instead."

"Fernando," said Tanya.

Adams looked up, his face lined with sadness.

"Our father never cared. He died from a cocaine overdose in a crappy motel room in LA fifteen years ago. Live fast and die young, was his motto."

"When did you find out you had a half-brother?"

"Six years ago. Our father abandoning him haunted Felipe more than it did me. That was always in the back of his mind, so one day, he called around and found out he had family in Crescent Bay."

Adams wiped his eyes.

"My mother had already passed by then. She never recovered from my father leaving us like that, so it was just me."

"I guess meeting him meant a lot for you," said Tanya.

What she really wanted to know was who killed Felipe and why, but she knew better than to probe what seemed like a grieving man.

"We did DNA tests to make sure," said Adams. "It was good to find a blood relative, after being alone for so long. You know what I mean?"

Tanya nodded for his sake.

He didn't know that was one feeling she would never know in her life. She loved her found family back in New York with all her heart, but she no longer had blood relatives.

"He visited me on and off in between movies," continued Adams, his voice getting heavier. "He got along well with Camilla.

180

She used to work in Hollywood so they both hung around the same circles. She roped him in to headline her fundraisers. Everyone thought it was great to have a celebrity in town."

Adams looked up and met her eyes.

"Felipe was no angel. I haven't forgotten what happened yesterday at the hall. I know he's not the most upstanding citizen. He had a hot temper, and when he got upset, he got physical."

Tanya pointed at his black eye. "Did he give you that?"

Adams closed his eyes and opened them again.

"I invited him for dinner at a restaurant last weekend. I thought it would be a good way for us to get to know each other better."

He let out a sigh.

"The evening went sideways when I caught him groping a waitress. I put him on the spot and told him I never want to see that again. Let's just say, he didn't take it very well."

"He hit you?"

"He and our father didn't look alike, but their personalities were similar. I tried not to judge him. It's not like Felipe had a good male role model growing up."

He dropped his head in his hands.

"I'm sorry for your loss," said Tanya. "Do you know why anyone would want to kill him?"

Adams looked up, the strain of the recent events showing around his puffy eyes.

"He was an impatient, arrogant, and stubborn man who liked to have his way. But he is, I mean, he was my half-brother."

"Who had access to his cell?"

"My entire team."

"What about security footage?"

"That's the thing. Somehow, the camera that was trained on his door has malfunctioned."

Tanya raised an eyebrow. "Interesting."

"Convenient," said Adams, giving her a dejected look. "That's what everyone's saying."

Tanya leaned forward, finally realizing what he had been trying to get at.

"Are you being accused of murdering your own brother?"

Chapter Forty-two

A dams rubbed his tired face.

"Felipe always bragged about what he made for his movies. Last month he told the world he just updated his will."

"Who gets it all now?" said Tanya.

"Me." Adams gave her a defeated look. "He posted a funny meme. *Good thing my brother's a sheriff....*"

Tanya digested this news silently. Unless Felipe had been deep in debt, Adams had just become a rich man.

Did you do it?

She swallowed those words before they came out. There were better ways to find out if Adams had a hand in the murder. A direct question would only make him clamp up, regardless of whether he was guilty or not.

"I don't care about the millions," said the sheriff as if he knew what she was thinking. "I'd just like him back. He wasn't perfect, and he wasn't nice, but he was my only family left."

Tanya wondered what Felipe's death had to do with the headless corpse, the bomb that killed the girl, and Eva's disappearance.

A part of her wanted to find Fox, so they could get back on their hunt for his sister. But as she watched the sheriff's face churn from horror to anger to sorrow and back, she knew she couldn't just get up and leave.

Adams tapped absentmindedly on his desk. The rat-a-tat-tat of his fingers on the wood was like nails on a chalkboard to Tanya.

"They found a note in his cell."

Tanya jerked her head up. "What did it say?"

"Last witness still alive."

She stared at him, speechless, a sense of dread crawling through her spine.

How many more will die like this?

"Adams?"

The crisp female voice came from the doorway.

Tanya pivoted to see Acting Sheriff Kathy Hatchet at the threshold. She was standing at attention, posture perfect, chin up, and her face stern, like she was about to command a military parade.

Hatchet was ready for the sheriff's job and knew it.

Her eyes were on Adams.

"We have a ten-fifty-six," she barked.

Adams jumped to his feet.

"Location?"

"Three-five-one Hilltop Drive."

"Oh, man," whispered Adams hoarsely.

Hatchet hesitated like there was something else she wanted to say.

"I need all the warm bodies I can get. There are too many open cases."

Tanya pushed her chair back and stood up. "In my precinct, code ten-fifty-six refers to a suicide victim."

"Means the same in ours," said Hatchet in a dry voice.

Tanya felt her blood go cold. "Is it that girl we found by the cliff?"

"Madden handed her over to Dr. Chen this morning," said Hatchet. "She's at the clinic under medical observation."

Tanya frowned. "Who lives at three-five-one Hilltop Drive, then?"

Hatchet shot her an irritated glance and turned to Adams. "I'm on my way." The new sheriff spun on her heels and marched off without a word.

Adams plucked his jacket off the hook on the wall and pulled it on.

"It's the mayor's residence." He shook his head like he couldn't believe what was happening. "I was going to go over to talk to her just after the fundraiser, but—"

"I'd like to come with you," said Tanya. "This could be related to Fox's sister."

"It's no longer my call." He shrugged. "If we weren't so short staffed, I'd be heading home with my tail between my legs or stepping inside a cell in the back. As of now, I'm volunteering."

Tanya turned to her pup who had been listening to the drama, a curious expression on his face. "Come on, Max," she called out as she walked toward the door.

Fox barreled inside, bumping into her.

Tanya sprang back.

"I heard the sheriff just got ousted...." Fox trailed off as he spotted Adams standing behind her.

Without a word, Adams put on his cap and passed in between them, his head down and his shoulders slumped.

"Any more news on Eva?" said Tanya, sparing Fox the embarrassment.

He shook his head. "I was checking up on Zoe, making sure she'll be fine till tomorrow."

"Good. Come with me."

After whistling to Max, Tanya turned around and walked toward the precinct's entrance.

"What's going on?" said Fox, hurrying to catch up with her.

"Someone's taking out the residents of Crescent Bay, one by one."

"What?"

"They think it's suicide."

Fox grabbed her shoulder. *"Who?"*

"It's at the mayor's house."

She followed Adams out of the building and into the parking lot, with Fox walking silently beside her. She opened the truck's back door and helped Max get inside.

"Zoe is confident the call was from Eva," said Fox, sliding into the passenger seat. "It's hard to fake a conversation with an old friend. Maybe Eva's fine. Maybe I'm overreacting."

Tanya got in, a grim expression on her face. She knew he was only trying to reassure himself, but her mind whirled.

For all we know, someone could have been holding a gun to her head.

They drove silently, following Adams's cruiser through the winding labyrinth of streets that crisscrossed the hill. In the distance, they could hear the sirens of the squad cars that had got a head start.

Tanya's head swarmed with images of Eva lying on a bed, immobile, somewhere in the mayor's house. *Stop it,* she scolded herself silently. This wasn't the time to let her imagination run away from her.

Next to her, Fox fidgeted with his fingers, as if that would keep his mind occupied and away from the worst-case scenarios. Max remained quiet in the backseat, appearing to feel the tension inside the car.

Tanya slowed as she spotted the line of squad cars parked on top of the hill.

Fox peered through the windshield. "That's the Patel residence."

"Seems like the mayor lives next door."

"His gate is open."

Tanya stopped the truck across from Adams's cruiser and got out.

"Let's go, Max," she called out.

Max jumped out of the truck and darted after her.

Tanya raced inside the gates and up the driveway toward the mayor's house.

Please don't let it be Eva.

Chapter Forty-three

F ox jogged behind Tanya, panting.

Exhaustion was written all over his face. Tanya was sure the only thing that kept him from crashing was the hope of finding his sister.

A junior uniformed officer stood on guard at the front door of the mayor's house.

Max bounded inside, before Tanya could stop him.

"We're with Adams," she called out as she dashed in after her dog. She didn't wait for the officer to object or ask for identification, but he merely nodded. Fox followed in at her heels.

They stopped in the foyer and stared at the leather sofas, Persian rugs, and the grand piano in the corner. It was the kind of interior you'd find in a luxury home magazine.

Max was standing in the middle of the living room, his tail wagging, as if to ask *what took you so long?*

The living room was empty, but the pleasant aroma of gourmet cooking wafted to their noses.

A bottle of wine stood on a coffee table, beads of cold sweat still dripping down its sides. Surrounding it were three empty wineglasses with remnants of white wine at the bottom.

Tanya bent down to inspect them.

She pointed at one. "Lipstick marks."

"Where's everyone?" said Fox, turning around.

As if he understood, Max trotted over to the massive marble staircase. Muted tones and footsteps came from the second floor.

Tanya was about to run up the steps when a crash came from somewhere on the first floor. A loud curse followed soon after.

Max whirled around and barked.

Tanya stepped quietly over to the only other doorway from the living room and looked in, one hand on her holster. Two officers wearing forensics coveralls were staring at a broken decanter on the floor.

Tanya had seen them at the precinct earlier. One of them was holding his hands on his forehead. The second officer brought his phone out and snapped a photo of the breakage.

"You're in so much trouble, dude," he chuckled. "That probably cost three times your pay."

The first officer jerked up as Tanya stepped inside the dining room.

His face flushed. He turned to the credenza where a second glass decanter sat and moved it gingerly to the back, as if he was worried he'd break that too.

"Good timing." The second officer grinned at Tanya. "You saw what he did, didn't you? It wasn't me."

The two men returned to work, brushing surfaces for fingerprints and taking photos. Tanya wondered if Adams had already told everyone they were with the Black Rock police precinct.

"Seems like they were having guests over," said Fox, stepping inside the dining room and surveying the scene.

The long dining table, covered with a bright blue tablecloth, had been set for four. Surrounded by casserole dishes was a roasted duck on a silver platter. Someone had stuck a carving knife into the bird's breast. None of the chairs had been pulled back, and the plates and cutlery were untouched.

"They were just about to sit for a fancy lunch," said Tanya.

"Today's Sunday," said one officer, not looking up.

"What does that mean?"

"Mayor Steele has residents for lunch every Sunday. It's tradition."

The second officer jostled his partner with his elbow. "My ma says that's how she campaigns for the next election. But what do I know? I'm just a dumb cop."

His partner grinned. "You got that right. All you have in that empty head of yours is beer and chicks, man."

"Who was invited this weekend?" said Tanya.

"How would we know?" The first officer shrugged. "We're not on speaking terms with the mayor. You need to talk to the sheriff."

Which one?

Tanya knew Adams and the mayor's husband were rivals. But, Kathy Hatchet might be a different story. The image of Kathy kowtowing to Dr. Patel popped to mind. That woman knew how to play politics.

"Where's Adams and Hatchet?"

The first officer looked up. "You haven't been upstairs? You gotta see it for yourself, man. It's brutal, I tell you."

"Let's go," said Tanya, walking back into the living room and toward the staircase.

The voices got louder as she and Fox jogged up the stairs with Max. The noise was coming from the end of the second-floor hallway.

"The master bedroom," said Fox, pointing in its direction.

No one was guarding the doors on this floor. They walked along the long hallway, passing a series of bedrooms. Tanya peeked inside each one, but they were all empty.

Max trotted ahead of them and planted himself in front of the entrance to the master bedroom. Tanya and Fox stepped up to the open doorway.

Inside the room were three officers wearing vinyl shoe covers.

In one corner, Hatchet was talking urgently into her shoulder radio. Deputy Madden was taking photographs of something to the right that was hidden by the partially open door. Adams stared in the same direction, hands on his hips.

What's he looking at?

Tanya poked her head in. Her eyes widened at the sight.

Hanging from the open wooden rafters of the ceiling were a middle-aged man and a woman. Two chairs had been upturned by the king-sized poster bed.

The white ropes around their necks were tight, and their eyes bulged like they would pop out.

Tanya recognized the woman's face. It had been on the poster of the banquet hall.

The mayor had almond-colored skin, now a deathly pale, but Tanya could see the resemblance to the mutilated woman she had pulled out of the ocean the day before.

Julie Steele's parents.

Chapter Forty-four

Deputy Madden stepped up to the mayor's body.

He reached over to her hand, pulled on it, and let it go. The hand bounced back and hung limp by her side.

"Still warm and soft," announced the deputy. "But dead as doornails for sure."

"Madden! Didn't I tell you not to touch anything?" snapped Hatchet, whirling around, her hand on her radio. "Dr. Chen is on her way, and I want everything exactly as we found it."

All three officers were so preoccupied, they hadn't spotted the newcomers by the threshold.

Tanya put a hand on Max's collar to hold him back in case he decided to join the others. She and Fox remained at the doorway, knowing how easy it would be to contaminate a crime scene.

"Why on earth would they kill themselves?" said Adams, shaking his head. "They were doing so well. This doesn't make any sense."

Hatchet turned to him.

"Wasn't Mayor Steele supposed to be at the banquet hall yesterday? I saw her name on the speech itinerary."

"That's why I went to the fundraiser," said Adams. "I wanted to talk to them about Julie, but they never showed up. According to Camilla, the mayor changed her mind at the last minute."

"Any idea why?"

"Got sidetracked by an urgent call. City business, or so I was told." Adams shrugged. "I was about to drive over here to talk to them when...." He threw his arms in the air. "The whole world blew up, and I had other priorities."

Tanya's mind buzzed.

First impressions never tell the complete story.

"The dining table was set," she called out from the doorway, "and the food was already out."

All three officers whirled around in surprise.

"What are you doing here?" barked Hatchet.

"That means they were just about to sit down for lunch," said Tanya, ignoring her question. "No one creates an elaborate meal, then goes upstairs to end their lives."

"Maybe it was like the Last Supper," said Adams. "It was their way of ending things on a high note."

"Wouldn't they have finished their fancy luncheon, then?" said Fox.

No one answered.

"There were supposed to be four people," said Tanya. "Who are the other two?"

Hatchet glared at her, but didn't answer.

"I've worked for law enforcement in many places," said Tanya, gesturing at the couple swaying from the rafters. "I've never seen anything like this. I doubt this was suicide."

"We'll let the medical examiner decide that, shall we?" said Hatchet, her voice turning hard.

Adams turned to her. "I would investigate this as a potential double homicide myself."

Hatchet's scowl deepened.

Madden didn't seem to notice the power play between his two bosses. He had been taking photos while everyone was talking. He stopped in mid action, as if struck by a thought.

"What if they killed their daughter, and then killed themselves? That would make one hell of a story, wouldn't it?"

Adams grimaced. "Let's show some respect for the victims, shall we?"

"Could also be murder-suicide, sir. One of them offed the other and hung themselves. It's not like that hasn't happened before."

Tanya's eyes scanned the room. "If this was a legitimate case of suicide, there's usually a note. If we can find it, we might glean—"

A strange whimper made her stop. She took a small step inside and scanned the room.

In the far corner of the bedroom, peeking through the partially closed door of the closet, was the face of a wizened man. He was crouched low to the ground and was shaking hard. On one hand, he was clutching a phone.

Tanya clenched her jaws.

"What are *you* doing here?"

"He called it in," said Hatchet, her tone defensive, as if Tanya had accused him of murder. "He found them and did the right thing."

"What's he doing in the closet?" said Fox.

"Leave the man be. He's in shock."

"Were you a guest today?" said Tanya, her eyes on Dr. Patel.

"I... I... I came for lunch," stammered Patel. "I always come for lunch on Sundays."

"Who was the fourth person invited today?"

Despite his shakes, Patel shot her an angry look from under his bushy eyebrows.

He turned to Adams. "Help me, Sheriff. Someone's trying to kill us all, one by one. Help me!"

Adams stepped up to the old man in the corner and squatted next to him as if to calm him down. Patel reached out to him with a trembling hand.

"It's going to be me next. They're going to get me."

By the doorway, Tanya and Fox exchanged a curious glance.

"Who's out to get you, Dr. Patel?" called out Tanya.

The old man snapped his head to her and narrowed his eyes. For a fleeting moment, she spotted the fury that crossed his face. The instant switch from fear to anger told Tanya he knew more than he was letting on.

Just as quickly, Patel turned back to Adams, his eyes pleading.

"Give me protection. I need your team at my house. Please help me, Sheriff. *Please.*"

He clamped his hand on Adams' arm and held on, like a toddler would with their parent.

"I'm afraid we're severely under-resourced," said Adams, gently prying the man's fingers from his arm. "You already have a good security team. I think you're well taken care of."

"No!" screeched Patel. "They'll kill me next—"

"Found it!"

Tanya whirled around.

Madden was next to the bedstand behind the two bodies, waving something excitedly in the air.

"The suicide note!"

Chapter Forty-five

M adden beamed triumphantly.

Tanya grimaced. The man was too dense to not realize how inappropriate his behavior was, given the circumstances.

"Where are your gloves, Deputy?" hollered Hatchet.

"Sorry, sorry," said Madden, fumbling at his belt.

With a frustrated hiss, Hatchet stomped over and grabbed the note from him. Using her gloved hands, she unraveled the paper.

"What does it say?" said Adams, walking over.

"I think I know," whispered Tanya to Fox.

Hatchet squinted at the note in her hand. "Looks like a kid scribbled this." She frowned. "I can't make head or tail...."

Adams stepped over and peered over her shoulders. He read it out aloud.

"We're paying the price for being the parents we shouldn't have been."

He looked up, a puzzled expression on his face.

"What the heck does that mean?" said Madden.

Fox shook his head. "I was so sure it would say the same thing as the other notes."

"Me, too," said Adams.

"*Parents they shouldn't have been?*" said Hatchet, staring thoughtfully at the two bodies. "They treated Julie like a princess. Everyone thought she was spoiled, to tell the truth."

"Was Julie their only child?" said Tanya.

Hatchet nodded.

"Maybe they were so distraught, they couldn't take it anymore," said Fox. "Finding your daughter killed and maimed would drive any parent insane."

Hatchet glared at him. "That information was confidential!"

Fox put his hands up in defense.

"Dr. Chen hasn't had time to confirm the identity of the first victim yet," yelled Hatchet. "No one knows who we suspect her to be. No one, except for those of us at the precinct."

She shot an irate look at Adams. The message was clear. She resented him for pulling Fox and Tanya into the investigation.

But Adams's eyes were on the two hung bodies.

"I think we can be pretty sure of the first victim's identity now. It has to be Julie Steele."

"Did anyone have a grudge against—" Tanya didn't get to finish.

"Out of my way!"

She and Fox whirled around. They glanced down at the petite woman with neatly trimmed gray hair glowering at them. She was wearing white overalls and booties and was carrying a metallic briefcase.

She was about five foot tall. She barely came to Tanya's chest, but the scowl on her face made her look like a bulldog who'd shred you to bits, given the chance.

She swung her briefcase at them. "Move!"

Max growled.

"Dr. Chen," cried out Hatchet, relief flooding her voice. "Thank goodness, you're here."

Tanya and Fox quickly stepped aside.

Dr. Chen marched in like a military general taking over her domain. Two young interns, also in white overalls and booties scurried behind her, lugging black cases.

The medical examiner turned around. "Everyone out!"

Madden didn't wait to be told twice. Hunching down like he was avoiding an oncoming missile, the deputy scurried along the wall and slipped out of the room. Adams picked up Dr. Patel by the arm and pushed him outside.

Patel was still whimpering as he passed Tanya. She stared at him, wondering how long he would keep up this charade. She was sure Adams saw right through it, but it was Hatchet she was worried about.

Tanya and Fox followed the officers down the marble steps and into the dining hall on the first floor.

The two junior officers were nowhere to be seen. Outside the open front door, Tanya could see the deputy on guard, arms crossed behind his back.

"I'm next. I know it!" came an anguished wail.

She turned to Patel, who was now seated at the end of the dining table.

"They're going to get me," he cried, rocking from side to side.

Hatchet fished out a blanket from a nearby cabinet and draped it over the man's shoulder.

"There, now," she said in a soothing voice. "Take it easy, Dr. Patel. I'll get the medics to look over you soon."

Madden turned to her. "How do we know he didn't do it?"

Patel's head shot up. His eyes turned icy cold.

"I'm a reputable man. You insult my honor."

"That's enough, Deputy," snapped Hatchet, an angry flush creeping up her neck. "I'll ask the questions from now on."

Tanya watched Patel's transformations with interest. The man's emotions seesawed in seconds.

"I apologize for this, Dr. Patel," said Hatchet, a hand on his shoulder. "Why don't we get you home, and you can tell me what you saw."

Fox turned to Tanya and whispered, "He couldn't have hung two adults from the ceiling by himself."

"He could have had help," Tanya whispered back. "We still don't know who guest number four is."

"The couple would have put up a fight though."

"Not if they'd been drugged."

Fox's eyebrows shot up. "Drugged?"

Tanya nodded.

"If I were in charge, I'd get those wineglasses in the living room tested and checked for fingerprints."

Chapter Forty-six

A buzz came from one of Tanya's cargo pant pockets.

She plucked both her mobiles out to check. It was her FBI burner phone.

Restricted Number

The only people who contacted her on her burner were Susan Cross and her team. Most of the time, it was Cross's assistant who enjoyed calling field agents and barking instructions as if they were his own.

She pocketed it discreetly and nudged Fox.

"Keep an eye on them."

"Where are you going?" he said, but Tanya had turned around and was walking toward the front door. Max saw her leave and trotted after her.

Tanya hurried out of the mayor's house and toward her truck. Half a dozen police cruisers and an ambulance were parked along the roadside, their occupants milling around the vehicles, waiting for instructions from Hatchet or Adams.

They turned around expectantly as Tanya came out, but she deliberately kept her face turned away. She didn't have time to answer their curious questions.

She opened the truck's door. Max jumped in and settled himself in the passenger seat. He looked at her, his tongue hanging out, an eager look in his eye.

"Sorry, bud," said Tanya as she fished out her burner phone. "Hang in there for now. I'll find you some action soon."

She scrolled down.

No messages.

She clicked on the number for Cross's office.

"Where were you?" barked Cross's assistant.

"At a crime scene. I called as soon as I could find a quiet spot."

"What took you so long?"

Tanya swallowed a curse.

He really needed to learn office manners. This was exactly why everyone in the bureau had dubbed him Toxic Tom behind his back. She didn't even remember if Tom was his real name, but the moniker fit him to a T.

"Well, I'm here now," she said, trying hard not to snap.

"The director wants to talk to you."

Tanya grinned to herself as the irritation in his voice came down the line. Tom hated it when senior executives spoke directly with front-line staff. It took away the power he wielded.

There was a click on the line and Cross's voice came on. She was terse as usual.

"I need you out of Black Rock by midnight tonight."

Tanya frowned. "May I ask why?"

"I have handed Crescent Bay to another agent. They'll be on ground next week."

"We're close to solving the case here. I just need—"

"Absolutely not," snapped Cross.

"Permission to speak freely, ma'am?" said Tanya.

Cross was silent for a moment.

Tanya gripped the phone. Speaking with the top boss was always a gamble. Every time she did, she felt like it would be the last phone call she would ever make to anyone in the bureau.

"Permission granted."

"I'll be glad to collaborate with the new agent," said Tanya. "We could partner up. It might speed up the case."

Cross let out a frustrated hiss.

"First, I need you in Black Rock on Monday. Second, you should know better than to ask. You're both undercover. I can't have any of you knowing each other's identities. That could lead to disastrous consequences."

Tanya's mind swirled like a whirlwind as she tried to guess who that other agent would be.

"This is not up to debate," Cross was saying. "The decision has been made. I need you to touch base with Tom at midnight tonight to confirm your location. I trust it will be Black Rock."

Tanya felt her chest constrict briefly. Sometimes, working for a federal department was suffocating.

There was no need for her to call Toxic Tom like a schoolkid with a curfew. As far as she knew, all field agents' phones were being tracked via GPS, and their locations were easily identified. This was just another bureaucratic check.

"You're not a lone ranger, Agent. You're part of a complicated system with many cogs and wheels. Respect it."

"Yes, ma'am," said Tanya.

A click told her Susan Cross had hung up.

Tanya turned to Max, who thumped his tail.

"Bud, you're the only one in the whole world who understands me." She leaned in and nuzzled her dog. "You're better than anything therapy can buy."

He licked her face. She squinched her eyes as he slobbered on her face.

"I only have a few hours to find Eva now," she said to her pup, who licked her nose in reply.

With a resigned sigh, she opened her truck door and jumped out.

"Back to work, bud. Let's see if I can find you a job—"

That was when a gunshot came from inside the mayor's house.

Chapter Forty-seven

M ax whirled around in his seat, barking.

The crew outside rushed through the gates to the mayor's home.

"Stay," said Tanya to Max. "I'm not having you in the line of fire."

He whined loudly.

"Sorry, bud."

She shut the truck's door before he could leap out, and darted down the driveway, trying to ignore Max's annoyed barks from the car.

The officers had gathered by the main entrance, backs hunched, weapons drawn, their heads swiveling around to catch the shooter.

"All clear!" came Hatchet's voice from inside.

Tanya pushed through the crowd and dashed in. She came to a halt by the dining room's entranceway.

It was Patel.

His hair was askew, and he was prancing around the dining table like a man gone mad.

"They're gonna kill me next! I'm telling you. Why don't you believe me? Do something!"

Hatchet was trying to calm him down in vain.

Madden lurked in a corner of the dining room, like he wanted to distance himself from the raving man. Fox stood by the doorway, staring at the chaotic scene like he couldn't believe what was happening. And Adams waited by the table, a firearm in his hands.

Tanya scanned the room.

No one seemed injured. Or dead.

"What happened? Did Adams shoot someone?"

Fox turned to her. "Patel pulled out Hatchet's gun from her belt. Adams grabbed it before he killed somebody."

"But I heard a gunshot."

Fox pointed at the credenza with his chin. The second crystal glass bottle had been smashed into smithereens.

"He murdered a decanter."

Who was Patel aiming at?

"Calm down, Dr. Patel," Hatchet was saying. "We're trying our best to help you. But you've got to settle down."

"I didn't do it!" screamed Patel, pulling on his hair. "I'm as good as dead! And you think *I'm* the criminal!"

Hatchet shook her head. "I haven't accused you of anything—"

"I have."

Tanya turned to the deputy in the corner. Madden straightened up. His face was hard, like he would throttle the doctor if he could get away with it.

"I asked before and I'll ask again. Where were you were when the mayor and her husband died?"

Patel shot the deputy a furious look. "How could you? You... you... stupid cop!"

"That's enough, Madden," snapped Hatchet. "I won't tolerate unwarranted allegations. We don't even know if these deaths are suspicious. We have no evidence."

Because you're not looking for it, thought Tanya.

The midnight chat they'd had with Madden at the hotel parking lot flashed to her mind.

Did Patel have anything to do with the death of Madden's daughter?

Madden certainly seemed to think the doctor was guilty.

Patel stopped flailing. Throwing his blanket off his shoulders, he spun around, moving surprisingly fast for his age. Before anyone could do anything, he leaned across the table and plucked the carving knife from the duck's breast.

"Put that down!" roared Adams.

With an earsplitting screech, Patel raised the knife and rushed at Madden. Madden reeled back, his hands up in defense.

Tanya jumped on the doctor and pulled him back by the shoulders. Adams tried to snatch the knife away but Patel kicked and flailed, slashing the air in front of him.

Tanya struggled to hold him back, feeling like she was wrestling a tornado.

"Duck!" cried Fox as the blade came dangerously close to her head.

She and Adams lunged. Tanya heard the swoosh of the blade as it cut through the air, inches above her head.

Adams reached up to grab the knife.

But it was too late.

It sliced through his arm.

Adams fell back with a yelp.

Tanya yanked Patel back. Fox leaped in and grabbed his wrist. The doctor twisted his hand out and stabbed Fox's face.

"Watch out!" yelled Tanya.

The knife slashed Fox's cheek and fell to the ground. Blood spluttered from his face as he staggered in shock.

Tanya yanked the doctor's arms behind him, slammed him to the floor, and rammed her knee on his back.

"Someone get me cuffs!" she hollered.

Hatchet stepped in and nudged her off him. Tanya stepped away as the acting sheriff took over.

Where was she all this time?

Panting hard, Tanya wiped the sweat off her forehead.

How did it take three of us to wrestle this crazy old man?

"Man down!" shouted Adams, clutching his bleeding arm. "We need a medic!"

Tanya whirled around to see Fox sprawled on the floor.

Next to him lay the carving knife, stained with his blood.

Chapter Forty-eight

"Patel is strong for his age," said Adams.

"Stop moving," snapped Dr. Chen. "You want to bleed some more or what?"

Adams shrank in his chair like a schoolboy being scolded by the headmistress. Dr. Chen opened her cabinet and pulled out a handful of medicine bottles for the cut on his arm.

Tanya still couldn't believe how easily she had sneaked into the clinic.

A flash of her wallet with her Black Rock precinct's contractor ID had been enough for the receptionist to buzz her in. She had peeked through the open door to the examination room, surprised to find the demoted sheriff in the patient's chair.

Dr. Chen had swiveled around on her stool.

"You came to hold his hand?"

Tanya had jerked her head back. "Hold his...?"

She suddenly realized the doctor had handed her the perfect excuse.

"Is he going to be all right?"

Adams had stared at Tanya in confusion, but hadn't objected when she had stepped inside the room and took the spare chair.

He looked like a wounded soldier who had returned from the field. His forehead was bandaged, and his eyes were bloodshot. Tanya glanced around her, thankful Hatchet wasn't here.

Soon after Fox had fainted, Hatchet had taken over.

Her instructions had been clear.

She would interrogate Dr. Patel, while Adams would return to the office to write up the report. Hatchet had chased Madden away, reminding him he was only a patrol cop, and wasn't welcome at any crime scene.

The deputy had left without protesting, but his furious face as he stomped toward the exit hadn't escaped Tanya.

A team of paramedics had tended to Fox.

He had blacked out from pain and exhaustion, the knife wound culminating in his weakened state. The medics had cleaned and dressed his wound and had given him painkillers with an ultimatum.

Either come to the hospital or stay in bed to get his much needed rest.

Tanya had driven a badly bruised Fox back to his hotel room. He had passed out as soon as he had got into bed. Leaving Max behind so Fox had company when he woke up, she stepped out of his room.

Max had a bowl of water and the DogTV channel to keep him occupied. Tanya felt bad for leaving them both behind, but bodies were piling up and she had even less time to find Eva now.

She got in her rusty truck and headed out of the hotel parking lot.

Her mind whirred as she went through her options.

Adams was a lame duck. Hatchet was a bumbler. Though Hatchet blustered around like she was in charge, it was Dr. Chen who held the cards.

The physician ran the city's makeshift morgue and the town's clinic. That was where all the bodies and the girl who had attempted suicide had been taken.

If she wanted to solve this deadly puzzle and find Fox's sister, she would have to make friends with that bulldog of a woman.

With another glare at Adams as if challenging him not to move, Dr. Chen swabbed his wound with a translucent liquid.

Adams winced in pain.

Tanya grimaced at the sizzling sound, like a piece of steak had been thrown on a hot barbecue. Her nose stung from the smell of strong antiseptics.

"This is a good hurt," said the doctor in a stern voice. "If it hurts now, it will heal faster."

She glanced at Tanya. "Don't come to my clinic if you're looking for a mollycoddling."

Tanya put her hands up. "No, ma'am."

"The only people I like are dead people," continued Dr. Chen, pressing a cotton wool against Adams's arm. "They don't talk back. And they know how to behave."

Adams shot Tanya an exasperated glance.

Tanya was glad he hadn't worn his shades since Felipe's death, which meant she could finally see his expressions freely.

She suddenly realized why he had shown up at the clinic. His knife wound was a good excuse. With Hatchet micromanaging the investigation, he had come to the only place where he could glean information.

Just like she had.

"It's all psychological," Dr. Chen was saying. "You know how a mother can lift a car if her child is stuck underneath? That's what happened. That means, whatever instigated this knife attack had brought Dr. Patel to the brink."

"Could he have killed the mayor, her husband, and her daughter?" said Tanya.

The doctor looked up at the ceiling, like she was contemplating the question.

"You need force to cut a human head off, but Julie Steele was clearly attacked with a power chainsaw."

Tanya grimaced.

Dr. Chen looked at her.

"But there are no shortcuts to strangling a human and hoisting the body up. It requires power and energy. The Steeles wouldn't have given up without a fight, even if they had been drugged...."

Tanya and Adams waited for her to finish, but she threw the extra gauze into the trash can and put her medicine bottle away, her hands moving fast like she needed to move to think things through.

Tanya leaned in. "What if he had help—"

"We're done here." Dr. Chen slapped Adams's thigh, making him jump.

She lifted his arm, as if she was admiring her handiwork. "Now that's the correct way to clean and bandage a knife wound. They don't train EMA staff the way they used to. They're more like glorified ambulance drivers these days."

She wagged a finger at him.

"Don't touch it. Don't scratch it. Do you understand me?"

"I do," said Adams meekly.

Tanya cleared her throat. "Dr. Chen, I'd like to see the girl who was brought in this morning."

The doctor spun around and narrowed her eyes.

"She's under sedation."

"I stopped her from jumping. I was there with her. She might talk to—"

"I don't care if she was your goddaughter. Nobody's going to disturb her until I say she's ready."

"We're searching for a missing person who could be in grave danger. She might know something to help us with our search."

Dr. Chen stared at her. "A missing person, you say?"

Tanya nodded.

"I think you have more important matters than a missing person."

Before Tanya could ask what she meant, Dr. Chen spun around and stepped out of the room. Tanya and Adams exchanged a curious glance.

"Are you coming or not?"

The doctor's high-pitched voice had come from down the corridor. Tanya scurried out with Adams.

They followed Dr. Chen through a winding hallway toward a thick steel door at the end. The sign on top of the entrance said, *Staff only beyond this point. Phones off.*

It was the morgue.

Chapter Forty-nine

A blast of cool air hit Tanya as she slipped past the heavy steel doors.

It was like she had entered a massive sub-zero fridge.

A young woman in scrubs was hunched over a row of scalpels. She looked up in surprise.

"Masks and gloves for our guests please, Alice," said Dr. Chen before stepping up to the sink to wash her hands.

Tanya put her mask on and surveyed the room. A row of steel gurneys was laid out in front of them. Five dead bodies.

She almost gagged at the pungent odor of flesh and blood. Thankfully, the harsh cleaning chemicals slightly overpowered the human smells.

The two gurneys closest to Tanya were only covered to the cadavers' necks.

Mayor and Mr. Steele.

The ambulance had transported their bodies here while she had taken care of Fox. Though Tanya had never met the power couple, a pang of sorrow crossed her to see them both lying side by side.

Next to them were two more gurneys, which she presumed was Felipe Fernando and the girl who had died in the banquet hall explosion.

The fifth gurney had been set in the far end, separated from the others. On it, she could see the distinct outline of a corpse without a head under the plastic sheet.

A shiver went through her.

Julie Steele.

Placed around her were a handful of stainless-steel containers. The one on the weighing machine looked like it held Julie's bloodied heart.

Tanya looked away and swallowed hard.

Though her combat experience had given her a strong stomach, the cold and clinical world of autopsies repelled her.

Adams stood by the door, his hands drooped to his sides, his eyes flitting from one gurney to the next, an anxious look in his eyes.

He's looking for his half-brother.

Dr. Chen stopped lathering her arms and turned to her assistant.

"Number three. Uncover the body, please."

The intern stepped up to the third gurney and flipped back the plastic sheet.

Adams didn't move from his spot, but his face turned pale, making the purple bruise by his eye even more pronounced. He clutched the wall.

"You want a chair?" said Dr. Chen.

Adams remained quiet, his eyes on Felipe's deathly face.

Dr. Chen squinted at him, like she was examining an interesting test subject.

"You weren't that close to him really, were you?"

"He... I.... " Adams looked away. "I guess it doesn't matter any more."

Tanya felt a tug in her heart. He had lost the only family he had and his job in one fell swoop. His life would never be the same again.

He's taking it better than I would have.

The former sheriff was an enigma, but he was clearly struggling with his emotions. He'd have to be a talented actor to pull this off.

Maybe you didn't kill your half-brother, thought Tanya as she observed him.

Dr. Chen pulled a towel from a rack and wiped her arms with vigor.

"It's getting crowded in here. We haven't had this many bodies before. You have a very interesting killer in town, Sheriff."

Tanya wondered when the news of Adams' demotion would get around town.

Adams straightened up, like he had just woken up from a bad dream.

"Have you found anything to help us catch the perp?"

Dr. Chen shrugged.

"The victims are from different demographics and psychographics, so I wouldn't normally expect it to be a serial killer. But I suspect, and that is the operative word here, I *suspect* this to be one person's mad handiwork. A psychopath on a rampage."

"Do you have any evidence?" said Adams. "Any clues we can use to hunt them down?"

"I'm a lone medical examiner with two interns." The doctor pursed her lips. "If you're expecting *CSI* results, I suggest you quit watching television. Authenticity isn't what sells on TV. Even on those inane and vapid, so-called reality shows."

"The mayor and her husband bought a track of ocean-front property recently," said Adams, his brow knotted. "They were planning to build a world-class yacht club."

He gazed at the two cadavers, their lips now a tinge of blue and their skin a deathly white pallor.

"They were an ambitious couple. The whole town knew of their big plans. They were the last people to do something like this. Why would anyone frame their deaths as suicides? That's not very smart of the killer."

Dr. Chen turned to him.

"Almost everyone who ends up in my morgue has died a thousand deaths before they took their last breath."

Tanya raised an eyebrow. *A physician and a philosopher.*

"Their lives may look rosy to outsiders, but they're hurting inside," said Dr. Chen. "Then, one day, they succumb to their inner demons and make unforgivably poor decisions."

Tanya frowned. "Are you saying the mayor and her husband—"

"I'm saying if anyone found out what was really going on with their private lives, all they needed to do was play up those demons. And voila. You could drive them to suicide. Or, kill them and make it look like suicide, and no one would be the wiser."

Adams gave her a thoughtful look. "If the killer wanted their deaths to look like suicides, wouldn't they have also exposed their inner demons?"

"The suicide note," said Tanya. "It said something about feeling guilty for not being good parents. The killer could have left it."

Dr. Chen whirled around to the intern.

"Alice?"

"Yes, Dr. Chen?"

"Get that phone out."

Alice scrambled over to a sideboard by the back entrance of the room. A stack of indiscriminate items, secured in zipped plastic bags, were neatly piled on the table. She sorted through them, picked one up, and brought it over to her boss.

Dr. Chen nodded.

"Show the sheriff what you found."

Chapter Fifty

"Whose phone is this?" said Tanya.

"It was in Mayor Steele's pocket," said Alice.

Pulling on a fresh pair of gloves, the intern extracted the phone from its bag and placed it on the closest table. She bent over it and punched a series of numbers on the screen.

"You hacked the password?" said Tanya, appraising her.

"It was easy." Alice looked up and smiled. "The password was *Crescent Bay.*"

Dr. Chen turned to Adams. "See the extra services I give your office? You really should pay me more."

Alice picked up the phone and turned it toward everyone.

"Text messages. They all came in a flurry over the past twenty-four hours."

She scrolled through them one by one and read them out loud.

"I know who you really are. Shame."

"I'll tell the whole world the sick things going on in this town. Pay up or else."

"You're not going to get away with it. Pay me."

"This whole town's going to burn."

Tanya looked up in alarm. "This whole town's going to burn?"

Dr. Chen gave her a wry look. "I told you. You've got bigger problems on your hands than just one missing person."

Tanya turned to Alice.

"Did you find out who sent these texts?"

"They bounced off a series of numbers." Alice shook her head. "They were international, so it's hard to say who was on the other end."

"This means we're looking for someone with serious tech cred, right?" said Adams.

"It's actually not that difficult to spoof phone numbers these days," said Alice. "Download an app and punch a few numbers. That's about it. Totally do-able but totally illegal."

"All I know is spoofing will get you a ten grand penalty per violation." Adams scratched his head. "So, how can we identify the perp?"

"You could call the cellular provider, but they don't always succeed in tracing these calls," said Alice. "The FBI in Seattle has a cool IT forensics lab which probably could do the job, but they're not open to the public."

She paused.

"If the sender really wanted to stay hidden, they could have used a onetime burner phone and thrown it away afterward. That would make it hard to find him. Or her."

Tanya smiled inside.

Alice would make a good recruit for the bureau.

Dr. Chen beamed. "She's a clever girl, isn't she?"

"I don't get the tech stuff," said Adams, pointing at the phone, "but I sure know blackmail when I see it. The mayor didn't pay up as demanded, and so they killed her and her husband."

He looked at the doctor.

"This threat to burn the town is a ruse. They sent it to rile the mayor."

"You've had five deaths in the space of twenty-four hours," said Dr. Chen, moving over to the mayor's corpse. "I'd say your county is burning, Sheriff."

She gestured at Adams and Tanya to come closer.

"Put those special glasses on and look at this."

Alice handed them what looked like goggles. After putting hers on, Tanya shuffled behind the medical duo and peeked over their heads.

The intern was holding a black gadget much like a speed gun state patrol officers use on highways. She fiddled with its controls and turned a switch.

Alice began scanning the mayor's throat, the blue light from the device casting an eerie illumination on the dead woman's skin.

"Alternate light source," said Dr. Chen, not looking up. "Got it last week. Didn't expect to use it so soon."

"What does it do?" said Tanya, adjusting her goggles to see better.

Dr. Chen pointed at a red bruising on the mayor's neck that Tanya hadn't noticed earlier.

"See these marks?"

Adams and Tanya nodded.

"These are definitely ligature marks. I would surmise it was someone with fairly large hands. A male, I suspect."

Adams tightened the straps on his glasses and leaned closer to the mayor's body, his goggles almost touching her pallid skin.

"Did she fight back?"

"I would infer they had both been drugged before they were strangled and hung. But we will be checking for DNA evidence under their nails."

"The wine," said Tanya, remembering the half-drunk glasses on the living room coffee table.

"Precisely." Dr. Chen gestured at Alice. "That's what she'll be testing next. The results, I believe, should be interesting."

"So, we can be sure this was homicide, not suicide," said Adams, straightening up.

"Hanging by suicide often bloats the face and neck above the rope," said Dr. Chen, "because the person is obviously still alive and kicking. No pun intended."

She paused.

"But when an already deceased body, thus with no blood circulation, is hung, there is no bloating effect."

She pointed at the mayor's throat.

"During a strangulation, the hyoid bone can be fractured. This doesn't happen all the time, so it's not conclusive, but it could indicate murder."

Dr. Chen turned to Alice.

"Scalpel, please."

The doctor took the knife and placed it on the mayor's smooth skin.

Tanya's stomach churned. She fought back something that was about to come up to her throat.

She turned and rested her eyes on the sideboard where the bagged evidence sat, to settle her gut for a moment.

Her eyes scanned the back wall.

Behind that table was the exit door.

With a quick look to make sure Dr. Chen and the others were occupied, Tanya stepped away from them and walked toward the table.

She scrutinized the evidence for a few minutes but found nothing of interest.

She glanced at the group hovering over the dead body. Their attention was on something inside the mayor's open throat.

Tanya removed her goggles and let out her breath.

Adams has a stronger stomach than me.

She placed the glasses gently on the table and stepped toward the back door, crossing her fingers that no alarm would go off.

She slipped out to the corridor, closed the door behind her, and took a deep breath of fresh air in.

She took stock. To her right was the examination room and reception area. On her left were a series of closed doors.

Tanya turned left and treaded down the corridor. With her heart beating slightly faster, she pushed the first door open.

It was a sparsely furnished room with a hospital cot and a metal table. It smelled faintly of medicine but was empty.

Tanya stepped over to the next door and peeked inside.

An elderly patient was sound asleep, hooked up to an oxygen machine. Computer screens surrounded his cot. It was quiet inside, except for the sound of the respirator and a machine beeping at regular intervals.

She closed the door quietly and scanned the corridor.

No one had noticed her gone yet.

Tanya stepped toward the third door and pushed it open.

Bingo.

Chapter Fifty-one

*T**he girl by the cliff.*

Tanya opened the door another inch.

The teen was huddled under a coverlet, sitting half-upright on her bed.

Her head lay on a pillow, and her eyes were closed. She wasn't hooked up to any machines, so she likely didn't have serious injuries, but the handful of pill bottles by the bedside table showed she wasn't well.

Tanya slipped inside and closed the door behind her.

The silver pin.

Tanya stepped closer to get a better look at what had been attached to the patient's lapel.

The girl's eyes sprang open.

Tanya put a hand to her lips.

The girl sat up with a gasp.

"Hey, it's okay," whispered Tanya. "I just came to see how you're doing."

The girl stared at her wordlessly, seemingly uncomprehending.

"Do you remember me?"

The teen scrunched her eyes like she was trying to recollect her face.

"I saw you at the banquet hall yesterday. Remember?" whispered Tanya. "And I, er, I saw you by the cliff this morning. I gave you my jacket when it got a little cold up there."

The girl's eyes widened.

"I just wanted to make sure they were taking care of you."

The girl leaned forward. Tanya braced herself for a scream. But she merely stared, like she was scrutinizing her.

Taking that as a positive sign, Tanya shuffled closer and squatted on the floor by the bed, hoping Dr. Chen and the others would be occupied with the mayor's body for a while.

"How are you feeling, hun?"

Silence.

Tanya remained in her position, trying not to alarm the girl with big movements. After a few minutes, she felt a cramp in her leg and shifted.

"You saved me."

Tanya gave a start.

Didn't Dr. Chen say she hadn't spoken since she arrived?

"Sorry, what did you say, hun?"

But the girl had fallen quiet again. Tanya wished she had brought Max with her. He had a calming effect on most people.

"I hate Felipe," whispered the girl.

Tanya sat up.

So, she can talk.

"Me, too."

"He always does that," said the girl.

Tanya nodded silently.

Felipe won't be harassing anyone, anymore.

"I'm sorry," she said, instead. "What happened to you wasn't right. It happened to me too, a long time ago."

The teen's eyes widened.

Tanya offered a small smile. "My name is Tanya. What's yours?"

"Valerie."

"It's nice to meet you, Valerie. I'm happy to see you're doing okay."

Valerie's eyes filled with tears.

Tanya leaned in. "Did they get in touch with your family, hun?"

Valerie shrugged. "They told Camilla, but she's busy as usual."

"You're related to Madame Camilla?"

Valerie shook her head. "She's my boss. I don't have a real family."

Tanya had so many questions, but she knew she had to tread gently. If this was the first time Valerie had opened up to anyone, she was lucky she was speaking at all.

The cogs in her brain whirred. She badly wanted to ask why Valerie had tried to end her life, but she knew that could trigger many horrors. What Valerie needed was not Max, but a professional psychiatrist.

To her surprise, Valerie's lips curved into a small smile.

"Thanks for coming to see me."

Tanya smiled back.

"Hey, hun?" She paused. "Would it be okay if I showed you a picture of someone special?"

Valerie nodded.

Tanya reached into her jacket pocket and pulled out her regular phone which had Eva's videos and photographs. She scrolled to a still picture of Fox's sister in front of the Patel residence and turned the screen toward the girl.

"Have you seen her?"

Valerie clutched her coverlet to her chest.

So she recognizes Eva.

"Do you know her well, honey?"

Valerie looked at her, her eyes wide.

Is that a yes?

"Can you tell me when you saw her last?"

Valerie looked away, like she didn't want to answer.

Tanya pointed at the pin on her shirt. "Is she part of your club too?"

Silence. But a nervous tick on the girl's face told Tanya she was on to something.

"I need your help, Valerie. She's gone missing and I'm looking for her."

Valerie started trembling, like a drug addict undergoing withdrawal.

Tanya quickly slipped her phone back in her pocket, wondering if it was Eva's face or if it was something else in the picture that terrified her.

"It's okay. You don't have to look at the photo. No more questions. I promise."

"Why are you looking for her?"

Valerie spoke so softly, Tanya wasn't sure she heard the question right.

"Her brother thinks she's in danger. Maybe even dead. He's very worried."

Valerie lifted her chin and looked Tanya in the eyes. Pretty blue eyes, thought Tanya. They looked sincere and innocent.

"She's alive," whispered Valerie.

Tanya's eyebrows shot up.

"Does she live in Camilla's castle with you?"

Valerie let out a heavy sigh and leaned back against her pillow.

Please don't stop talking to me.

"Would you like some water, hun?" said Tanya.

Valerie opened her eyes and nodded.

Tanya got on her knees to reach for the jug on the bedside table. She had just finished pouring a cup of water when Valerie reached out for it from under her coverlet.

That was when Tanya saw it.

On Valerie's wrist was a diamond bracelet with a ruby pendant.

Chapter Fifty-two

Tanya froze.

Her heart thumping hard, she held the water jug in mid-air. She stared at the jewelry twinkling on the girl's wrist.

"Honey, where did you get that bracelet?"

With a startle, as if she just realized what she had on, Valerie thrust her hand under the coverlet.

Tanya put the jug down and turned toward her.

"It's gorgeous. Can I see it?"

Valerie turned her face away from her.

How come I didn't see it on her when she was on the cliff?

"Did somebody give it to you?" said Tanya. "Was it someone special?"

"I hate it," hissed Valerie.

Those words sounded like snake venom.

"I think it's stunning," said Tanya. "Where did you get it from, hun?"

"I never wanted it."

"Why do you say that?"

"You can have it."

Valerie pulled her hand out from under the coverlet, ripped the bracelet from her wrist, and threw it at her with force.

Tanya stumbled back in surprise and lost her footing. She grabbed on to the bedstand to stop the fall, when she heard a scrunch under her right boot. She pulled her foot up and gasped in dismay.

Valerie turned around in bed, and slipped under the covers, sobbing.

Tanya stared at the broken bracelet on the floor.

The ruby pendant wasn't really what she had thought it was. It was a tiny glass cannister which her boot had smashed into pieces.

The diamonds had remained intact, but they were covered in what looked like splatters of blood.

"How dare you intrude!"

Tanya whirled around.

It was Dr. Chen.

She stood at the doorway, looking like a pit-bull terrier ready to tear her limbs off.

Chapter Fifty-three

T anya pulled herself to her full height, her head still spinning.

"What's going on here, Dr. Chen?"

The physician bared her teeth.

"You cannot disturb my patients like this. This is unacceptable."

Tanya looked over at Valerie. She had pushed herself so far under the coverlet that only a few strands of her hair showed. But she was sure the girl could hear every word.

She turned back to the doctor. "Until I'm certain she's safe, I'm not moving."

"How dare you accuse me of anything untoward?" snarled Dr. Chen. "You're the one sneaking into my private rooms."

"She's the only survivor so far," said Tanya. "That means her life is at risk."

The doctor shot her a startled look. "What do you mean by that?"

"Maybe you can tell me?"

Dr. Chen opened her mouth to speak, then closed it. She shook her head.

"I have no idea what you're talking about. If you think I'll let anyone harm her, you're wrong."

"Do you know who the killer is?" said Tanya.

"I'm beginning to think it's you." Dr. Chen shot her a furious look. "*You* sneaked into my clinic!"

Tanya sighed. "Your premises aren't as secure as you think. I only had to flash my Black Rock contractor ID for your receptionist to let me in."

The doctor frowned. "Black Rock? I thought you were with Sheriff Adams's team."

"She is."

A shadow loomed by the doorway. It was Adams.

"She's helping me with my murder investigations," he said. "It's a temporary assignment."

Dr. Chen turned from Tanya to Adams and back, her brow furrowed in confusion.

"Stone is correct," said Adams. "This young woman is in danger. We still don't know who the perpetrator for all these crimes is, but I have a feeling she does. That means they'll target her. That also means you and your team are in the line of fire."

The doctor stepped inside the room and grabbed the footrail of Valerie's bed, like she needed something to hold on to. Her confident posture had evaporated.

"I usually get to see the aftermath of a crime. It's clinical. That's how I like them. I've never been in the middle of... one."

Her face scrunched into what looked like genuine anguish. She turned her troubled face to Adams.

"Are you telling me the killer will come here, looking for her?"

Adams didn't answer.

"What am I going to do?" said Dr. Chen. "Someone has to watch over Val. And my team."

Tanya frowned. The doctor was a highly intelligent woman who could easily manipulate words and people.

Can I trust her?

Adams pulled his mobile out and put it to his ear.

"Get James to Dr. Chen's clinic right away. I need emergency backup." He paused and frowned. "I don't care what Hatchet says, get him over here now."

Dr. Chen stepped around the bed and stared at the lump under the covers.

"What's happened to this town? It was so peaceful. Has been for years, and now..."

Adams slipped his phone into his jacket pocket and pointed his chin at the cot.

"She okay?"

"Terrified and traumatized," said Tanya in a low voice. "But she's seen Eva. She told me she's alive."

Dr. Chen's eyes widened. "She *talked* to you?"

Tanya nodded.

The doctor plucked a stethoscope from a nearby table and walked to the head of the bed.

"Val? It's me, sweetie."

Valerie didn't move.

Dr. Chen perched at the edge of the bed and placed the stethoscope in her ears.

"Wake up, Val. It's me."

A moan came from the lump in the bed. Valerie peeked from under the covers.

Dr. Chen leaned toward her. "How are you feeling, sweetie?"

To Tanya's surprise, Valerie pulled a hand out of the covers and reached toward the doctor. Dr. Chen grasped the girl's hand.

"Don't you worry. We won't let anything bad happen to you. The police are here. You'll be safe, okay?"

Valerie clutched her hand and nodded.

It seemed like Dr. Chen had a maternal side Tanya didn't realize existed.

"Now lie back and relax," she was saying. "I'll check your vitals, then you have to eat. Once we get some good tomato soup inside of you, you'll feel better in no time."

Valerie lay back on her pillow and closed her eyes. She held on to the doctor's hand while Dr. Chen checked her heartbeat.

Tanya's mind spun as she watched them. A single name kept swirling in her head. She was getting close to finding Eva. She felt it in her bones.

When Dr. Chen pulled her stethoscope out of her ears, Tanya leaned over and tapped her shoulder.

"Did Camilla come to the clinic, this morning?"

Chapter Fifty-four

D r. Chen leaned over Valerie and felt around her throat.

"She's her official guardian," she said, not looking up. "Val works for her."

"Did Camilla come alone?" said Tanya.

"If you're asking me if she sailed in with her usual entourage, the answer is no. She knows I would never allow that. Val was sleeping, but I let her in for just a minute."

Tanya glanced at Valerie. The teen had her eyes closed, but something told her she was listening intently.

"What does she do at Camilla's?"

"The girls are members of the MLM program. Those with the most sales get to stay at the castle. She built a separate house in her compound for them. They live in luxury. It's one of the perks."

Tanya pointed at the pin on the girl's lapel. "Like that silver pin?"

Dr. Chen nodded. "All members get that pin when they join."

Tanya's eyes traveled to the doctor's white coat. It was hard to see if she was wearing anything on her jacket underneath.

"Are you a member too, Dr. Chen?"

"Goodness me. No. I don't approve of these pyramid schemes, but to each his or her own."

"What about your intern? Alice?"

"How would I know?"

"I've met three young women her age who are part of this club," said Tanya. "I get the feeling they're recruiting in her demographics. "

"What my employees do in their private time is none of my business. All I'm concerned about is how they perform at their job."

Tanya felt eyes watching her. She turned to see Adams was observing her keenly from the doorway.

Are he and the doctor in this together? Are they both playing with me?

"Did Camilla leave anything in the room?" she said.

"I don't hover over my guests," said Dr. Chen. "I left her alone with Val and told her not to say anything that would disturb the girl if she woke up."

Tanya observed the doctor carefully as she spoke, but her instincts told her Dr. Chen wasn't lying.

A knock made them turn. A fresh-faced deputy by the door touched his cap.

"Sir? You called?"

Adams gestured at Valerie who was lying quietly on her pillow, pretending to be asleep.

"Stand guard, James. No one can come in or out."

The deputy clicked his heels. "Yes, sir."

Tanya turned back to the doctor.

"Do you know what this bracelet signifies?"

Dr. Chen glanced around the room, a quizzical expression on her face. "What bracelet?"

Tanya pointed at the floor by the bedside table. Adams stepped inside and stared at the broken piece of jewelry.

"Wait. That looks exactly like—"

"The one Julie had on her wrist when I pulled her out of the sea," said Tanya.

Adams frowned. "Madden bagged it and took it to the precinct."

"Eva was wearing a similar bracelet in the video she took in front of the Patel residence."

Tanya looked over at the cot, but Valerie still had her eyes shut.

"She had this on her wrist. When I asked her about it, she didn't want to talk about it. She pulled it out and threw it at me. It fell to the floor, and I stepped on it by mistake."

"I've never seen this before," said Dr. Chen, squinting at it. "I would have noticed it when I was examining her."

"That's because Camilla gave it to her."

"A gift to make her feel better?"

"Or something else," said Tanya, watching Valerie for changes to her face, but the girl remained completely still.

Adams crouched low to examine the bracelet.

"Did you cut yourself?"

Tanya shook her head. "That little red pendant, which I thought was a ruby, is actually a vial made of glass."

"What's all this?" said Adams, pointing at the red splatter.

"If I have to guess," said Tanya. "That's human blood."

Adams gasped.

"And it's not mine."

Dr. Chen stared at her, seemingly speechless for a moment.

"I have worked all around the world and back. In all my years, I've never seen anything so bizarre as this."

Chapter Fifty-five

"Room five-ten, please."

Tanya kept driving as she waited for the hotel's front desk staff to put the call through.

This was the third time she had called Fox, but he hadn't picked up.

Where are you, Fox? Did the medication put you out?

Tanya could imagine Max sitting on the floor, staring at the phone on the bedside table, listening to it ring over and over again.

Poor Max.

She glanced at the road ahead.

Adams' cruiser was turning into a smaller road, several yards in front of her. They were heading to Camilla's castle, as Tanya was certain that's where Eva was.

She sped up to catch up to him, cringing at the grinding of the truck's gears. For what felt like the hundredth time that day, she wished she had her Jeep back.

The ringing cut off, and the receptionist's chirpy voice came through the phone's speakers.

"Hi there! It sounds like our guest isn't in at the moment. Would you like to call again, ma'am?"

Tanya glanced briefly at her phone on the truck's dashboard. Fox couldn't have passed out completely and for that long. Her imagination whirled.

What if he's in serious medical trouble? Max wouldn't be able to help. What if Fox is...?

She shook her head to clear it. Ruminating on potential worst-case scenarios wasn't going to help.

"Did you see a man walk out of the hotel with a dog, by any chance?"

"I'm sorry, ma'am," said the receptionist, her cheerful voice tuned a notch down. "Did you say a dog?"

"A large German Shepherd."

There was silence on the other end, as if the staff member wasn't sure what she had heard. Then came low murmurings as she conferred with her colleagues.

"Sorry, ma'am. Nobody saw a dog, or a man with a dog in the lobby."

Tanya took a deep breath in.

"Have you been at the desk all day?"

"Yes, but a bus load of tourists checked in an hour ago, so we were busy."

"Could you go to his room and see if he's okay?"

"I don't think we're allowed to do that, ma'am."

"Look, I'm not some stranger. I'm one of your guests."

"We're not permitted to go inside an occupied room unless it's for cleaning or an emergency."

"I'm telling you this is an emergency."

Tanya could hear paper rustling. More murmurings came on the other end of the line. She looked up to see Adams had already disappeared down the road.

Her stomach tightened. She couldn't help but feel something was wrong.

After a quick look at the rearview mirror, she pumped the brakes, and spun her wheels sharply to the right. She pulled the truck on to the shoulder. The vehicle behind her honked loudly, and the driver flipped the middle finger as he revved past her.

Ignoring the man, Tanya pulled her phone on her lap. She ended her call with the hotel and dialed Adams.

"Go to Camilla's," she barked before he could even say hello. "I'm heading to the hotel."

"What's going on?" came Adams's voice.

"Fox isn't answering the phone. He might be sicker than I thought."

"Ten-four," said Adams.

"I'll join you as soon as I check up on him."

"Roger that."

Tanya hung up and pulled the truck back onto the road. She pushed on the gas pedal and crossed over to the left lane.

It took her five minutes to get to the hotel. She raced down the driveway toward the main entrance, pushing the truck to its limits. The doorman jumped back as the vehicle screeched to a stop, inches from his feet.

He stared as Tanya jumped out.

"Valet parking, miss?"

Tanya didn't respond. She pushed through the main doors and dashed inside.

The lobby was unusually busy. The receptionist had been right. It seemed like the entire bus load of guests were milling in the lounge. She bustled past the crowd and dashed toward the bank of elevators in the back.

Tanya punched the up button and tapped her foot impatiently. *Come on. Come on.*

She glanced up at the bar of lights on top. The elevators were stopping at every single floor.

With a hiss of frustration, she whirled around and yanked the door to the fire exit. Tanya raced up the five floors, her heart pumping hard.

She burst through the fire doors on the fifth floor and raced down the corridor, almost bowling over a cleaner folding towels on her trolley.

Tanya raised her hand to bang on Fox's door when she realized it was ajar. With her heart in her mouth, she pushed it open and peeked inside.

"Max?"

Tanya's eyes widened.

A hurricane had passed through the room. Pillows were lying on the floor and the bedside lamp had been overturned. Fox's bed was unmade, but he wasn't in it.

A chill went through her. She stepped inside, her mouth dry. "Fox?"

That was when she spotted the naked feet sticking out from behind the bed.

Chapter Fifty-six

"Fox!"

Tanya rushed in.

Fox was sprawled on the floor next to the bed, like he had fallen over. His face was squashed on the carpet and his legs were splayed apart.

She fell to her knees and put her hand on his neck. His skin was hot like he was fighting a fever. His heart was beating fast.

He's alive!

Tanya swiveled her head.

"Max? Where are you? Max!"

Fox moaned.

She grabbed him by the shoulder. He groaned in pain. She gently turned him around and saw a trickle of blood rolling down his forehead.

What happened?

Fox fluttered his eyes open and gazed at her with glazed eyes. His left eye was swollen, and the right side of his mouth had been cut.

Tanya pulled out her phone and dialed emergency services.

"Ambulance, ASAP. Room five-ten. Crescent Bay Hotel."
She hung up and stared at Fox. "What happened?"
Fox opened his mouth to speak but winced in pain.
"Did someone come in?" said Tanya. "Tell me."
"I ... heard a noise..." whispered Fox through his swollen lips.
"It... it woke me up. I got up... to see... then someone hit me."
He closed his eyes like it took too much energy to speak.
She helped him sit up and lean against the bed. She pulled a
pillowcase off and used it to put pressure on his wound.
"Superficial," she said in relief. "They punched you near the eye
but they didn't do too much damage. You'd be fine if you were in
better shape."
Fox nodded weakly and raised his arm as if to protect his face.
"I tried to stop him... but I... blacked out."
"Him? Did you see who it was?"
He gave her a baleful look.
"I... think it was a man.... I was half asleep... All I know... I saw
this shadow. Then... a punch. Next thing... I was on the floor..."
Tanya was trying hard not to shake all the answers out of him.
"Where's Max?"
Fox placed his head in his hands like it hurt too much. Tanya let
go of his shoulder and jumped to her feet.
"Max?"
She stepped inside the bathroom and checked the shower.
Where is he?
She scoured the room, checking every nook and closet. Fox
watched her as he lay on the floor, taking raspy breaths.
A cold tingling sensation crawled up Tanya's body.
"Where are you, bud?" she said, her voice cracking.
She spun around the room, her heart pumping hard.
Max was gone.

Chapter Fifty-seven

Tanya's mind raged like a violent windstorm.

Max wasn't just a good K9. He was her baby. Her baby boy. Her everything.

She let out a roar and slammed the wall.

A knock on the door made her swivel around. The chambermaid was peeking inside, her eyes widening at the mess in the room.

"Are you all right, ma'am?" she said.

"Did you see a dog?" said Tanya, exasperation laced in her voice. "A large German Shepherd? Did anyone walk out with him?"

The chambermaid shook her head.

"I was on the floor all morning. Never saw a dog in the hallway." She glanced quickly over her shoulder. "But if they left through the fire exit, I might have missed it."

"Did you hear barking? Howling? Anything?"

"I thought I heard a dog bark about an hour ago. But I was sure someone had their TV on—"

She stopped as her eyes fell on Fox by the bed. She put a hand over her mouth.

"Oh, my lord. Is he sick? Should I get my manager?"

Tanya nodded curtly. "And call security ASAP. Tell them someone broke into this room and assaulted a guest."

The woman's face turned pale.

"*Assault?*"

"Stone?" came a male voice from the corridor.

Adams appeared behind the chambermaid, towering over her. Tanya frowned.

How did he get here so quickly? Wasn't he supposed to be on his way to Camilla's castle to find Eva?

Adams stared at Fox. "What's going on here?"

"Blow to the head," said Tanya. "I'd guess they used the bedside lamp."

"Who's the perp?"

"He didn't see."

"How did this happen?"

"He woke up to find someone in the room. He wasn't in the best of shape, so he felt it harder than usual, but he'll survive."

Nudging the chambermaid aside, Adams stepped inside the room, and pulled on his shoulder radio.

"I need a first responder team immediately," he barked. "Crescent Bay Hotel. Room five-ten. Get Hatchet to send a couple of deputies to secure a crime scene."

He crouched low in front of Fox. "Hey, you okay?"

Fox opened his eyes and gave him a feeble nod.

The sound of a siren came from the distance. Adams sprang up and turned to the window.

"That was quick."

"I dialed emergency when I got in," said Tanya as her eyes desperately searched the room. "What I want to know is where's Max."

Adams turned to her with a raised eyebrow.

"What do you mean, where's Max?"

"I left him with Fox, but he was gone when I came in." Her voice faltered. "He's trained to stay with an injured victim."

The chambermaid peeked into the room again, her phone in her hand.

"Security is here, ma'am."

The sound of someone wheezing came from the corridor, and soon a large man in a navy uniform appeared at the threshold.

His eyes widened at the sight of Fox. He gave a start when he spotted Adams.

"Hello, Sheriff."

He paused, as if unsure whether to come in.

Outside, the sirens were getting louder.

"I swear I saw nothing," said the guard as if he just realized the magnitude of the problem. "If I did, I'd have called your people. I just heard right now about the break-in and assault, but I—"

Adams put a hand up.

"I'm sure you did your job, Paul. I just need one thing from you."

"Anything, Sheriff."

"Can you bring up this morning's surveillance footage for this floor?"

Relief crossed the guard's face. "I'm on it."

With an awkward salute, he spun on his heels, and disappeared from view.

The sound of running footsteps came from the hallway, and soon, two paramedics appeared by the doorway with a stretcher and a first-aid kit in their hands.

They pushed passed the chambermaid who had taken a permanent position by the door, as if unable to turn her eyes away from the scene.

Tanya stepped away to give the medics space. Adams removed his cap and scratched his head.

"This is getting more complicated by the second."

Tanya didn't reply. Her eyes had caught something. She stepped up to Max's water container in front of the television set.

"What is it?" said Adams from behind her.

In the background, Tanya could hear the medics as they checked up on Fox. Fox kept saying he was fine in a shaky voice that said anything but.

Tanya squatted and pushed the stainless-steel bowl to the side with the back of her hand.

Adams leaned over to look.

"Max's breakfast?"

Tanya stared at the half-eaten sausage that had been hidden under the bowl's rim.

"I don't let him touch this processed crap." She looked up, her face lined with concern. "He only gets raw organic food once a day, and he had his meal this morning."

Adams turned to the chambermaid.

"Did room service come here today?"

The maid stepped inside the room, looking glad she was needed.

"Room service doesn't start till noon, sir. Breakfast is served in the dining hall. They only have morning room service from April to October, and I'm happy about that. Less work for me in the winter and spring months."

"But someone brought this in here," said Tanya.

"Would Max eat it if a stranger gave it to him?" said Adams, squatting to get a better look.

Tanya sighed. "He's well trained, but he's a dog first. If he knew I wasn't looking and the food was tempting enough, he'd chow it down."

Adams pulled on a pair of gloves and picked up the sausage. It was sliced in the middle. He tore the weenie in two and scrutinized it.

Tanya stared at the white residue that coated the sausage.

Adams turned a worried face at her. "Somebody drugged your pup and kidnapped him."

Chapter Fifty-eight

T anya winced.

She had already suspected Max had been dog-napped, but to hear the words out loud felt like a punch in the gut.

A faint clang made her and Adams turn around.

The chambermaid had dropped something in the trash bin. An embarrassed expression came over her as she realized they were looking her way. She wiped her hands on her apron.

"Just tidying up. I, er, have lots to do today." She glanced around Fox's room, her eyes narrowed, as if to say, *How on earth am I going to finish on time?*

Tanya got up. "What did you just throw in the trash can?"

"Oh, just some pin."

Tanya walked over and peered at the silver pin lying at the bottom of the bin.

"Where did you find it?"

"On the floor, by the can. Someone missed their aim. It happens all the time."

Tanya reached in, plucked the pin out, and held it up.

Was the perpetrator wearing this?

How convenient it is for us to find it.

"A badge for that MLM club," said Adams, staring at it.

Tanya glanced at him.

"Did someone plant this? If so, who did it?"

Adams scratched his head, like he couldn't make head or tail of it either.

"Sir?"

The hotel security guard was hovering by the doorway. He was looking at Adams, an expression of dread on his face.

"I er…" He wiped his forehead and swallowed. "I don't know how it happened, sir."

Adams stood up. "What are you talking about, Paul?"

"It's only me on duty in the mornings. I've been asking management for a partner for a while now, but they've told me that's overkill."

Tanya stepped toward him. A flicker of fear crossed the guard's face as she loomed over him.

"What are you trying to tell us?"

The guard shuffled his feet.

"I only left the s… security booth for half an hour."

He was sweating now.

"I was doing my rounds outside in the morning, like usual. And it seems like…." He gulped. "Someone came in and turned off the security cameras."

Adams and Tanya stared at him.

"Do you have anything from today?" said Adams.

"They erased everything on this floor."

Chapter Fifty-nine

"What made you come to the hotel?" said Tanya.

"Your voice," said Adams.

They were walking to their vehicles parked in the front of the Crescent Bay Hotel. Fox trailed out of the entrance behind them, limping visibly.

He had threatened to sue the paramedics if they had forced him into the ambulance. Tanya had wanted to tell him to stop fighting the people who were trying to help him, but she knew exactly how he felt.

Just like she was prepared to move mountains to locate Max, he would go through hell to find his sister.

"What do you mean, my voice?" said Tanya, squinting at Adams.

"You sounded strained, like you knew something bad had happened. Glad I came to see what was going on."

Tanya stopped.

"Chef Dupont is a convenient scapegoat. Felipe, the mayor, and her husband were all killed while he was in jail."

Adams's face darkened. "That's what bothers me too."

"I don't believe our unsub is a psychopathic serial killer like Dr. Chen thinks, either," said Tanya. "Everything that happened so far required organized effort."

"Organized?"

"I suspect the MLM organization is a front."

"A front for what?"

"A gang."

"I told you, there are no gangs in my county."

"They don't exactly advertise."

Adams didn't reply, but his face flushed.

"What about this Patel dude?" said Fox. "He's a creepy, modern-day Rasputin."

Adam's furrowed his brow. "I can't think of what his motivation would be to go on a killing spree like this."

"He could be in cahoots with someone else," said Tanya. "Camilla. She's another powerbroker who might be involved."

"She wields influence, that's for sure," said Adams. "Getting an invitation to her castle is a big deal for folks around here."

"She's the one who stopped Max from entering the hall," said Tanya. "She might have been worried he'd sniff out the explosives."

"You think she planted the bomb and framed her chef?" said Adams.

"Nobody would have questioned her if they had seen her messing around the kitchen or by the auction table," said Tanya. "The staff would have thought she was checking up on things."

"The explosion bruised her like everyone else." Adams frowned. "For an actress who cares about the way she looks, that's a big deal."

"But if the goal was to kill that girl and silence her," said Tanya, "she accomplished her objective."

"What happens now Hatchet's in charge?" said Fox.

"As Acting Sheriff," said Adams, "I would hope she documents evidence from the crime scenes, reads Dr. Chen's autopsy reports, and calls the forensics lab at the next county for help. But I believe she's already made up her mind."

He gave them a pointed look.

"I may be on administrative leave until Felipe's murder is solved, but I plan to get to the bottom of this."

"She's not going to be happy about that," said Fox.

Adams looked at him, then Tanya, a strange expression coming on his face.

"My team tells me Hatchet left the office in a hurry an hour ago, and no one's heard from her since."

Fox placed a hand on Tanya's shoulder to steady himself.

"Hatchet's gone AWOL?"

"Seems like it."

Tanya raised her brows.

Did she take Max?

"Hang on," said Fox. "You said Hatchet is a member of the MLM cabal, but I didn't see a silver pin on her shirt."

"Our uniforms have strict specifications."

"What about you?" said Fox. "Are you a member of this MLM club?"

Adams gave a start.

"Me? Not my thing."

"Really?"

With an angry shake of his head, Adams opened his car door, got in, and slammed the door shut.

Chapter Sixty

"The creepy castle," said Fox.

The grandiose building loomed on the hilltop.

Adams took a sharp curve on the road and pulled in front of an elaborate wrought-iron gate. Tanya kept close to his rear bumper.

Two security guards stood at attention in front of the sentry cabins. Tanya put the truck on park and waited as Adams gestured to one of the uniformed men.

Her gut told her they would find Max when they found Eva.

Please be okay, bud. Please be okay wherever you are.

Her heart felt hollow without him by her side. Her fingers dug into the steering wheel as she tried to stop from crying.

"That's serious firepower." Fox pointed discreetly at the assault rifle the guards were carrying.

Tanya blinked her tears away and scanned the fortress.

Are we walking into a trap?

A fortified wall, an electrified wire on top, and a couple of private security guards were understandable for a famous retired Hollywood actor. But Russian Kalashnikovs?

She peered through the gate into the massive grounds inside. "What's Camilla hiding in there?"

"Whatever it is, it has to be important," said Fox, staring at Adams and the guard who had got into an argument. "Look, even the sheriff has to negotiate to get in."

"News of his demotion must be getting around town," said Tanya. "If he has to fight to enter the premises, that means he may not be part of this club after all."

"What if Hatchet's behind these killings?" Fox turned his bloodshot eyes on her. "She's an MLM member, just like Camilla, Patel, and those girls. Felipe and the mayor were probably part of the racket as well. Maybe Eva was forced to join the club too."

Tanya didn't reply, but her heart ached.

Max's disappearance had been the last straw. She was holding on by sheer willpower.

They had been thrown into a roller coaster ride the minute they had entered Crescent Bay. So many ghastly things had happened so fast, she no longer knew when they would get hit with the next twist.

She was sure of one thing. Nothing in this town was what it seemed.

"I think I know what's going on," Fox was saying. "It's the result of infighting in the MLM club."

Tanya frowned. "What do you mean?"

"Someone probably didn't get their million-dollar bonus. Or they got the wrong order one month and lost a lot of money. Or someone else got promoted in the club before they were. Think of any stupid reason. People have killed for less."

In the car up front, Adams was getting animated. The guard was shaking his head, but the former sheriff didn't seem like he was letting up either.

"I hope he doesn't have to produce a warrant," said Tanya, tapping her fingers on the steering wheel.

"If they turn him back," said Fox, "I swear I'm climbing this wall and getting inside come hell or high water. So, shoot me."

Tanya turned to him. "What if those silver pins stand for something else?"

Fox gave her a puzzled look.

"The diamond bracelets with the blood vials don't point to a business deal gone bad," said Tanya. "Not a political rivalry, a family feud, an anarchist group, or even plain old vigilante justice. Something else is driving these killings."

"Like what?"

"Those three girls live in this castle with Camilla, right?" Tanya pointed at the building. "They were cocky when we met them, but they were hiding something. Something that frightened them. Valerie started to shake when I asked what she did here."

She paused, as she tried to sort out the puzzle in her head.

"Adams said Camilla built the castle after she retired from acting. He said something about Hollywood types being desperate to maintain their fame and status...."

She trailed off, frowning.

"But what does that have to do with these killings?"

Fox rubbed his face.

"Oh, Eva. What did you get involved in?"

"You said Eva was a drug mule for a Hells Angels chapter?" said Tanya.

Fox nodded, forlornly.

"Did she do any other work for them?"

"What are you implying?"

"Sex work."

Fox whipped around. "So, a girl is abused as a kid, and she automatically becomes a prostitute?"

"That's not what I—"

"Not Eva!" shouted Fox, making a guard glance over at their truck momentarily. "She may have dealt in drugs, but she didn't sell her body. She has more self-respect than that."

"They could have forced her."

"She would have told me. She would have asked for help. No. Not my sister."

"I'm only trying to connect the dots to find her."

"She did a lot of things she shouldn't have, but selling her body, that's just...." Fox shook his head. "That would kill her. And me."

He turned his tear-filled eyes to her.

"She's my baby sister. How can you even think of such a thing?"

Tanya looked away, guilt rising inside of her. Maybe she had asked too directly, but she still stood by her suspicions.

Fox was deluding himself if he thought his sibling, who had hung out with an organized crime ring for years, hadn't been used and abused.

"If the hotel employees are in Camilla's pockets," she said, changing to a safer topic, "she could have easily asked them to destroy the footage. Same goes for the footage in the precinct when Felipe was killed."

"You think the local cops are getting a payola?" said Fox.

"Hatchet's part of the MLM club. Camilla could easily manipulate or bribe her into doing her bidding."

"What does she want with Eva? And why take Max?"

"They took Max because we're getting warm." An acute feeling of pain sliced through Tanya's heart. For a second, she couldn't breathe.

Please be okay, bud. Please be okay.

She gripped the steering wheel tightly and gnashed her teeth.

I swear I'll put a bullet through the head of anyone who had anything to do with Max's disappearance.

"It was a warning to us," she whispered.

"If they think kidnapping your fur baby is going to stop you, they don't know you."

Tanya glanced at her colleague. Cut up, beaten, bruised, and bandaged, Fox looked like a shell of himself, but there was a fire in his eyes.

"You're a good brother, Fox," said Tanya. "Your sister would be proud to know how far you've gone for her."

His eyes filled with tears.

"I don't care if Eva is dead or alive. I just want to find her."

"We need to go in believing she's alive. She's probably been waiting for you for a long time."

A loud clang made her look up.

The castle's iron gates in front of them were swinging open.

Chapter Sixty-one

A dams rocketed through the gate before it was even fully open.

It was like he was worried the guards might change their minds.

Tanya jumped on the gas pedal. The old truck engine screeched. The guards frowned as they bucked by them. One man put his hand up.

"Halt!"

Tanya stuck her head out of the window.

"We're with the sheriff!"

She slammed on the accelerator and lurched through the opening without waiting for them to answer.

"Are you crazy?" cried Fox, throwing himself into the footwell as if he expected bullets to fly.

But the guards didn't fire.

And Tanya didn't reply, her mind on Max.

Is he on these grounds? Why would anyone bring him here? Where is he?

She sped up and caught up to Adams. They raced through the driveway that led to the massive mansion on top of the hill.

Surrounding the path was a green park with a large pond in the middle. A fountain spouted water high in the air. Tall fir trees lined the wall that enclosed the grounds.

There were no adjacent houses or staff quarters here, like they had seen at the Patel residence or inside the mayor's compound. The castle was enormous enough to house a dozen families or more.

The setting sun cast eerie shadows on the estate. A warning chill filled Tanya's gut as they approached the building. She couldn't help but feel they were walking into the lion's den.

"Keep a sharp eye out," she said as she scanned the area, alert for signs of ambush. "We're being watched."

"Who?" Fox raised his head and swiveled around. "Where?"

"I'd bet you there's a whole range of security cameras trained on us, and a bunch of armed guards on the grounds."

"I just want to find Eva and get her the hell away from this place."

"Watch Adams too," said Tanya. "He may act like he's on our side, but we don't know what his true motivations are."

"We would have never got inside without him, though," said Fox as they pulled up next to the former sheriff's cruiser.

Adams was inside his car, busy with something.

Tanya peeked through the windshield. The castle was dark. Heavy curtains were drawn across the windows on all floors, making it difficult to see what was inside. While the building looked empty, something told her there were people within it.

She jumped out of the truck and stepped over to the cruiser. Adams got out of his vehicle, his sidearm in his hands.

"What's with all the security?" said Tanya, eying his gun.

"Camilla used to be a popular actor," said Adams, holstering his weapon. "The paparazzi swarm her when she goes to LA."

"This isn't LA."

Before Adams could answer, Fox strode up to them.

"Eva. She's our priority."

Adams nodded. "I'll do my best to locate her."

He glanced over their shoulders.

"I told the guys at the gate I had an urgent private matter to discuss with Camilla. It's a pretext and will only work until Hatchet makes sure everybody knows I'm on administrative leave."

"Didn't they call to check with Camilla?" said Tanya.

"The guard hut has an intercom linked to her phone, but she never picked up. My lucky day."

Adams's eyes flickered down to Tanya's belt.

"You got your Glock on you?"

Tanya nodded.

"Stay here and keep an eye on your phones," said Adams as he turned toward the main entrance.

"Hey." Fox stepped up to him. "We're coming with you."

"If we all walk in, they'll see it as a threat. Security will throw us out in a second."

He rubbed his forehead like he was tired and just wanted this to end.

"Stand guard here. If you see Hatchet, stall her. I need to have a quiet chat with Camilla."

Fox scowled. "How do we know you're not with them?"

Adams placed a hand on Fox's shoulder.

"Somebody killed my half-brother. I want to find out who did it just as badly as you want to find your sister."

He let his hand fall. Then, without another word, he marched up the driveway toward the front entrance.

Tanya glanced around to check if anyone was watching, but an eerie silence had fallen on the perfectly manicured castle grounds.

She still couldn't shake off that feeling there were others milling around, people who were watching them, people she couldn't see.

An idea was forming in the back of her head.

But first, Max.

Fox turned to her, his face flushed in anger.

"How could you let him boss us around like that? Why didn't you put him in a chokehold or something?"

"Keep your voice down."

"If I wasn't so beat up and medicated, I'd—"

"Hey," said Tanya, lowering her voice. "We need to let him think we're with him."

"What do you mean?"

She pulled on his elbow. "This way."

Chapter Sixty-two

Tanya slipped into the shadows of the castle.

Fox scrambled to follow her. Crouching low, they scuttled behind the buttresses that reinforced the stone walls of the building.

"I don't have a good feeling about this," whispered Fox.

"Keep your head down," whispered Tanya.

She pointed at the row of decorative columns that had been placed around the grounds.

"See those black dots on top of the pillars? Those are cameras. If we stay under here, they won't be able to see where we've gone."

Keeping their heads just below the windows, they crept along the facade of the castle, stopping every few seconds to check the windows. But they were too high to reach or were latched tight.

They had just got to the end of the front wall when Fox tapped Tanya's shoulder.

"Do you hear that?" he whispered.

She stopped to listen. A low hum was coming from a distance. It peaked and fell, more organic than machine-like. Goose bumps sprang up on her arms.

What's that?

"Is that coming from *underground*?" said Fox, staring at the cobblestones beneath his feet.

Tanya nudged him. "Keep moving."

They turned the corner toward the rear of the building and stopped.

Tanya gaped.

Fox gawked.

Fifty odd sedans and oversized SUVs were parked in rows at the back of the castle. Tanya took stock of the Mercedes, Cadillacs, Audis, Bentleys, one Ferrari, and three long black limos.

Normally, she would have expected to see chauffeurs, valets, and staff milling around the vehicles, but there was not a soul in sight.

A large sign said *Staff Parking Only.*

"These aren't staff cars," whispered Fox from behind her.

Tanya nodded. "Looks like a party is going on inside."

"There's lots of guest parking in front. Why didn't they park there?"

Tanya scanned the luxury vehicles. "Whatever they're doing here, they're going to great lengths to keep it quiet."

A feeling of dread came over her.

Where's Max?

Gesturing for Fox to follow, she crept along the facade, keeping her profile low. She was halfway down the back wall when she spotted them.

She stopped and peered in between the buttresses. The two Crown Victorias were parked at the very end, by the tree line, where they would be least visible to anyone coming around the back.

One vehicle was unmarked but had a large dent on the driver's side door. The other car had the sheriff's decals on its panels.

"Deputy Madden is here," whispered Tanya, raising her head to see if she could spot him inside. But the cruiser was empty. "Who does the other squad car belong to?"

"Wait a minute," said Fox. "We've seen that before."

He pulled out his phone, scrolled through his recent photos and videos, and turned the mobile toward her.

"Here's the video I took when we first went to Patel's house. I wanted to make sure we could trace our steps back through the maze."

Tanya squinted at the screen. "What am I looking at?"

Fox zoomed in on the still video to enhance the license plate of the squad car they had been following. Then, he pointed at the second cruiser in the castle's parking lot.

"Same plate number."

"So, Hatchet's here." Tanya stared at the empty cruisers. "Either Adams is with her, and has been playing us, or he's about to get into serious trouble."

Fox shook his head. "I told you Hatchet was the mastermind behind all this."

"She's got her claws on Madden too," said Tanya, remembering the midnight conversation they had at the hotel parking lot about his dead daughter.

Fox made a face. "That's why she was so quick to shove Adams out and take control of the investigation."

Tanya nodded. "Let's go find her. I bet you she knows where Eva and Max are."

HER LAST LIE

After another scan to make sure no one had seen them, she pointed at a small door halfway down the back wall.

"That's our entry point."

Without waiting for Fox, she scurried over and tried the handle.

Locked.

She pulled her Swiss Army knife out and plucked out the tweezers and the toothpick.

"What are you doing?" Fox whispered, breathing down her neck.

Tanya bent the tweezers and checked the pointy end of the toothpick.

"Where did you learn that?" said Fox.

"Keep watch," said Tanya gruffly as she focused on her task. "And turn on your phone camera."

"What for?"

"So we can show justification for the break-in." Tanya jiggled the lock using the tweezers as a tension wrench. "It will help us plea for a reduced charge."

"Reduced charge? Are you serious?"

"Do you want to find Eva or not?"

Fox fell silent. Tanya kept working on the lock. By the time she heard the *click,* sweat was pouring down her back.

She drew her weapon and motioned for Fox to stand back.

She nudged the door open and listened.

Nothing.

It was a spooky silence, the kind you'd hear when there's a room full of people around the corner, waiting quietly.

Tanya pushed the door open fully and peeked inside. A large foyer greeted her eyes. She scanned the area, her heart racing.

It was quiet.

Too quiet.

TIKIRI HERATH

"Where *is* everyone?" whispered Fox, panning his phone around the space. "What are all those—"

The sound of a girl's frightened cry rang through the air.

Chapter Sixty-three

Tanya and Fox raced into the foyer, their weapons drawn.

They halted as they reached the open entrances on the other end.

Where did that cry come from?

Tanya swiveled from side to side, scoping out the four corridors which branched off and entered the bowels of the castle.

The strange, muffled hum was back. It was clearer here. Haunting but faint, it sounded like it came from the belly of the building.

What is that?

"Which way?" said Fox, whirling from one corridor to the next.

His face was drawn but his eyes flashed in fury. Sweat had gathered on his forehead and there was a dangerous twitch on his neck. He was minutes away from another breakdown.

"That can't be Eva," said Tanya, shaking her head. "It was a kid. A girl."

The cry came again. It stopped abruptly this time, like someone had covered the girl's mouth.

"Over there!" cried Tanya.

They spun to their left and dashed into the first corridor, their weapons aimed forward.

There was a closed door to their immediate right. The commotion was coming from inside.

Tanya stepped up to it and kicked it hard. The door flew open with a crash. Fox shoved her aside and burst inside.

"Eva!"

Tanya leaped inside after him to see a young girl on a bed, struggling to get out of Patel's clutches. She didn't look over thirteen years old.

"Hey! Stop that!" shouted Fox.

But the doctor's claws dug into the girl's shoulders. One of his hands was clamping her mouth shut. He turned to Fox and barred his teeth.

"Get out of my room!" snarled Patel.

"Get off her, you pedo scum!" shouted Fox, aiming his weapon at his head. "I will shoot you!"

Tanya jumped toward the bed, raised her arm, and pistol-whipped Patel on the crown. He crashed to the floor with an angry screech. She grabbed him by the scruff of his neck and slammed him on the wall.

"This will teach you," she growled.

"Let me go!" he squealed. "Police brutality!"

Tanya raised her knee and slammed it on his lower back, pinning him against the wall.

"Brutality, eh?" she snarled.

While holding him in place with her knee, she turned around and whipped the top sheet off the bed. She ripped a long piece from the side.

"What do you call what you were doing just now, sicko?"

She pulled his arms behind him and tied his wrists together with the cloth.

"Let me go! You'll never get away with this. I know people in high place—"

"Shut up," snapped Tanya. "We'll be taking you to the local precinct for the sexual assault of a minor."

"You have no proof!"

"Oh, really?" Tanya stepped away from him, appraising her makeshift handcuffs. "Our phones captured everything."

"I never touched her! She said she wanted a massage. I did nothing wrong!"

Tanya gritted her teeth. She would have given anything to smash his face on the wall till it bled, but she knew that would only give him justification to wriggle out of serious charges.

She turned to look at the girl when she spotted the packet of condoms on the bedside table.

A ripple of disgust crawled through her skin. Tanya had felt Patel's creepy vibes the minute she had met him, and now she had proof.

She turned to the pedophile.

"Your MLM racket is a front for creating a pool of vulnerable young girls for your sick pleasure, isn't it?"

"Lemme go! You can't arrest me—"

"Camilla recruited the girls and sent them to you, didn't she? All under the guise of a pyramid scheme to sell makeup."

Patel fell silent and didn't look up.

Tanya's eyes bored into the back of his head like laser beams.

"We know of the malpractice complaints you've had in four states. All for sexual interference of minors. That's not going to help you."

He turned around halfway, his face pale, like he couldn't believe she had found out.

"You're a psychopathic freak who preys on children," spat Tanya.

"It's all right," came Fox's voice from behind her.

Tanya turned around to see the girl had buried her head in Fox's jacket and was covering her ears. She was shaking uncontrollably.

"You're safe now," said Fox, giving an awkward pat on her head. "You'll be fine. No one's going to hurt you, anymore."

Fox looked up at Tanya, his face even more haggard.

"We can't trust Hatchet or—"

Loud footsteps came from down the corridor.

Tanya spun around.

Is that Patel's security team?

"One peep from you and I'll rip a bullet through your head," she hissed as she shoved Patel to the ground.

With her Glock aimed forward, she crept to the half-open doorway. She peeked out to see a male silhouette marching toward them.

She jumped out and shouted.

"Hands up! Or I'll shoot."

Adams threw his arms in the air.

Chapter Sixty-four

Tanya glared at Adams.

"What are you doing down here?"

"I have the same question for you," he said, his voice calm.

"You were supposed to be talking to Camilla."

"I heard someone cry for help," said Adams, his hands still in the air.

"And Camilla?" said Tanya, her steely eyes on him.

He shook his head. "She has a front office where she usually meets people, but no one's in today."

Tanya raised a brow. "There are fifty cars parked in the back. I'd say there's a party in the castle, and we haven't been invited."

Adams's eyebrows shot up.

"Care to explain what's going on?" said Tanya.

He gave her a frustrated look.

"How would I know? I haven't been able to get past the front foyer." He glanced over her shoulder. "What the heck's going on in there?"

"We caught your pal, Patel, red-handed, trying to assault a child," said Tanya through clenched jaws.

"He's not my friend." Adams grimaced in disgust. "Would you lower your weapon, please?"

"Not until you tell me what's going on here."

"Look, I have the same questions you have. And now I'm forced to return to the precinct."

"Why, did Hatchet find you?"

Adams looked at her, startled.

"She's here? Why didn't you call to warn me? You had one job."

Tanya didn't reply.

"I only saw Linda." Adams gave a frustrated hiss. "Camilla's business partner. She told me to get a search warrant before I could take one more step inside. I was just about to head out, when I heard the cry, so I ran down."

The sound of a door opening came from the end of the corridor. Adams spun around.

A female figure stepped into the hallway at the other end. She was in a stunning purple ballgown with a bell-shaped skirt that spread around her like a balloon.

Camilla?

Tanya whipped her weapon at her.

Can't be her. Camilla's thinner and taller.

Whoever she was, she was unafraid. It was as if the gun in Tanya's hand meant nothing.

The woman moved toward them, her heels clicking on the stone floor. Dangling from her right hand was a large bunch of keys. Tanya stared as the eerie apparition got closer and closer, feeling like she had been thrown inside a Dickensian horror novel.

Adams jerked his head back. "Linda!"

The woman approached them, gliding through the corridor like a Victorian ghost.

"What on earth is going on here?" she barked at Adams.

Her voice was raspy and cut like sandpaper.

Tanya recognized her.

She was the guest wearing the purple fascinator at the fundraiser, the one who had snubbed her when she had shown her Eva's photo.

"What are you still doing here?" she snarled at Adams. "Didn't I tell you to leave? You cannot and will not enter our premises without a warrant."

"I was just about to head back out, Linda," said Adams, his voice weary and his hands still in the air. "I thought I heard a cry for help and came to investigate."

Linda turned and glared at Tanya, completely oblivious to the weapon trained on her.

"You're off bounds," she snarled. "This is private property."

She turned back to Adams.

"Tell your people to back off and stay off our grounds. You're giving us an excellent excuse to sue your department. Do you want us to bankrupt your county?"

Adams gave her a helpless look. "She's got a gun, if you haven't noticed."

Tanya stepped forward, maintaining her aim on the woman.

"We just found a man assaulting a young girl in one of your rooms down here. I think it's *you* who will have to answer to the authorities."

Linda blinked.

"It was Patel," said Tanya, her voice hardening. "But I think you already knew."

Linda gave a dismissive wave.

"He was probably giving her meditation lessons like he always does with new recruits."

"If that was meditation," Tanya spat, "I'm the queen of India."

"Dr. Patel is an honorable man. He'd never do anything like that."

"Do anything like take advantage of the young girls you and Camilla send him, you mean?" said Tanya. "We know your MLM club is a front for a trafficking ring."

Linda opened her mouth and shut it. Her neck was flushing pink.

Bingo.

"You must be out of your mind," snarled Linda. "The girl's lying if she told you that."

"We caught him red-handed, and we have it on video."

Tanya mentally crossed her fingers.

Fox had held the phone but had crashed through the door so helter-skelter that she wasn't exactly sure he got any good footage. But they should have had audio, if the phone hadn't turned off or died in the critical moment.

But Linda didn't know that.

Tanya glowered back at the woman. She could never understand how anyone could commit such unspeakable crimes and fight to justify them.

The sound of sobbing made her turn.

Fox had pushed the door open and was ushering the girl outside. She had her face buried in his jacket like she was too ashamed to face them.

Tanya lowered her weapon, but kept it close, ready to aim and fire at a moment's notice. Adams brought his hands down and stared at the girl. His face scrunched like he was genuinely upset.

His eyes flickered around the corridor. "Where's the suspect?"

Tanya pointed at the opened door. "Tied with a bedsheet on the floor. You'll find condoms in there too. He was prepared."

Adams pulled on his shoulder radio.

"We have a code three. I repeat code three. I need a team at Camilla's residence. Get a paramedic and deputies immediately."

He turned to Linda, whose face was slowly turning purple.

"I don't need a warrant for that, Linda," said Adams, his eyes narrowing. "If I'd known what kind of racket you were running here, I would—"

"How dare you?" Linda stomped her foot. She pointed her keys at Adams, jangling them angrily in his face. "You have no care for our reputation!"

"I care for justice."

Tanya raised a brow.

Linda stepped up to Adams and slammed her keys in his face. He turned and blocked her with her hand, just in time to save his eyes.

"I can't have a bunch of stupid cops running round here. Not today!"

Linda's furious screech echoed through the corridor.

Chapter Sixty-five

Tanya stepped up to Linda.

"What's going on at the castle today?"

Linda glared, but her lips shut into a thin grim line.

"We know you're hosting an event," said Tanya, her eyes traveling down the woman's fancy ballgown. "We saw the cars outside."

Linda swirled around with an angry swish of her skirt and stomped back down the corridor. The sound of her heels clicking on the floor and the keys jingling in her hand echoed through the hollow space.

Suddenly, the faint hum started again.

Tanya glanced up at the ceiling and at the walls.

Adams seemed just as confused, swiveling around to identify the source of the sound. "What the heck is that?"

Tanya's stomach tightened.

There was something odd about this place. There was something more here than girls being handed over to pedophiles. But what? She didn't know, but she felt danger in her gut.

"Camilla will sue you all!"

Linda's screech came from the other end of the corridor, drowning out the hum. They watched her yank the door open and disappear.

Adams turned to Tanya, his eyes becoming hard.

"Never point your weapon at me again."

"I didn't know if you were part of this... whatever this is."

"I'm at the end of my tether trying to figure out why folks are falling like flies in my county. For heaven's sake, let me do my darned job."

Tanya stared at him. A deep anguish was etched on his face. His tone said he meant every word.

"I don't know who to trust anymore."

Adams let his shoulders drop. "You and me both."

"Did you see Eva?" came Fox's voice from behind them.

Adams turned to him.

"I didn't get past Linda and her screams for a search warrant."

"Do you know Madden and Hatchet are on the premises?" said Tanya.

Adams eyes widened. "Madden too?"

"Do you have any idea what they're doing here?"

Adams didn't reply, but his face told her he was surprised at the news.

"Their squad cars are parked in the back," said Tanya.

Adams straightened up and squared his shoulders.

"Show me."

Tanya gestured toward the back foyer. Adams pushed past her and marched down the corridor. With a quick nod to Fox, Tanya hurried after the former sheriff.

Adams stepped out of the back entrance and scanned the parking lot.

Tanya stepped out, next to him. "Do you recognize any of these vehicles?"

Adams stood with his mouth open like he was at a loss for words.

"Half the town is here," he said, finally.

Tanya pointed at the squad cars parked by the tree line at the end of the lot.

"Including your colleagues, it seems."

Adams jumped down the steps and stomped toward them.

Tanya followed him out in the open, knowing there was no reason to stay hidden from the cameras anymore. The entire castle should know they were here. Camilla was probably on the phone to her high-priced lawyers right now.

Adams walked up to the dented Crown Victoria and peeked inside. Littered on the passenger seat were crumpled food wrappers and an empty paper bag.

"It's Madden's, all right," he said. "And this is Hatchet's for sure."

He opened the driver's side door to the second car. He ducked his head and put a knee on the passenger seat to survey the inside of the vehicle.

"What is she doing here?" Tanya heard him mutter as he checked the back seats.

He turned around and flipped open the cubbyhole. A dozen shiny buttons clattered to the footwell.

"More silver pins," said Tanya, peeking over his shoulder.

Adams picked one up and held it to the light. "She was probably recruiting."

"Recruiting for—"

Tanya stopped as a curious sound came from behind the tree line.

"Did you hear that?" she said in a hoarse whisper.

Adams pulled his head out of the car to listen. The sound of crickets came from the small woods behind the lot.

But Tanya's heart thudded.

She was sure she'd heard a whine. She stepped behind the cars and surveyed the wooded area in the back of the castle.

Did I imagine that?

The whine came again.

A chill went up her spine. She sucked in shallow breaths.

"I hear it," said Adams. "It's coming from that end."

Without waiting for her, he darted into the woods. Tanya dashed after him, her heart thumping hard. They crashed in between the trees and stopped as they came to the wall in the back.

The whine came again.

"Max?" cried Tanya, whirling around, her heart in her mouth. "Where are you, bud? Max!"

"Over there."

Tanya spun around, her eyes tearing, hardly registering that her entire body was shaking.

Adams grabbed her by the arm.

"He's alive," he said, pulling her toward a large fir tree.

The whining was coming from inside a cage at the base of the tree. It was just large enough to hold a German Shepherd.

"Max!" cried Tanya, falling to her knees.

Wrapped around Max's snout was a black leather muzzle.

Chapter Sixty-six

With tears streaming down her face, Tanya fumbled at the lock.

Inside the cage, Max blinked and gazed at her with his big brown eyes. They looked glazed.

"He was drugged," said Adams, peering over her shoulder.

"I'm getting you out, bud," said Tanya in a trembling voice. "You're going to be okay, bud."

But her hands were shaking so hard, she was having trouble with the bolt. Adams squatted next to her.

"Let me try."

Tanya pushed him away and raised her weapon. She banged the gun barrel on the padlock, breaking it in half. She twisted the broken pieces off the latch, yanked the door open, and reached for her pup.

Max gave her a confused look.

She pried him out gently, one leg at a time, letting him stretch his muscles after being squeezed inside the cage for so long.

Tanya felt him all over, checking for bruises, broken bones, or, heaven forbid, bullet wounds. But other than being muzzled and jammed in that space, he was in one piece.

She buried her head in his neck and hugged him tight.

"You might want to get the gag off him," she heard Adams say.

Tanya ripped the muzzle off of his snout and threw it over her shoulders. Adams pounced on it. He picked it up after putting on a glove.

"This is evidence," he said with a stern look at her.

But Tanya wasn't listening.

Max put his front paws on her shoulders and whined. She pulled him close and wrapped her arms around his body. She nuzzled her cheek against his fur, holding him tightly. Max licked her nose, his tail wagging a million miles a second.

Tanya didn't know how long she snuggled with her dog, her heart bursting with love and tears pouring out in relief.

Oh, Max. I missed you so much, bud.

The sound of sirens came from somewhere behind them.

"My team's here," said Adams.

"You go," said Tanya, barely able to speak. "I'll join you."

Adams headed back out of the woods, but stopped, and turned.

"I'm glad you saved that girl."

Tanya wiped her eyes and nodded.

"We're on the last stretch," he said. "I can feel us closing in on the unsub soon."

Tanya didn't answer, but Adams was already stomping back out through the trees. The sirens were coming from the back parking lot now.

Tanya turned toward Max who was limping around, trying his legs gingerly, like he was learning to walk for the first time.

"First, we're going to get you some water. Then, we're going to find out who nabbed you. And then, I'm going to shoot the thug."

Max wagged his tail as if he agreed with her plan.

"Wish you could talk, bud."

By the time Max was comfortable walking and they got back to the parking lot, Adams was huddled with a handful of his deputies.

Patel was inside one of the squad cars looking miserable, like the worst of offenses had been committed to him. Not the other way around.

Tanya shot him a disgusted look as she passed him.

You sick pervert.

She knew he would wrangle his high-priced team of defense lawyers shortly.

There were times when Tanya felt the justice system didn't play fair for the victims, but bowed to the demands of criminals. She hoped this wouldn't be one of those times.

But the more she thought of it, the more she was sure there was an even bigger man behind the curtain.

Camilla.

Camilla had to be the head of this trafficking ring. She had the resources, the influence, and the power in this town. Patel was just one of her side goons.

Tanya could see Camilla ordering someone to kidnap Max. It could have been the guards up front, Hatchet, or any one of her paid minions.

Whoever it is, she thought, *they're going to feel my fist on their face.*

Adams spotted them and walked over. He bent down to pet Max, who reacted like he'd just met a long-lost friend.

"You already look a lot better," said Adams fussing over the dog. "You're a good boy, aren't you?"

He glanced up at Tanya. "As soon as we get the warrant, we'll rip this place apart." He narrowed his eyes. "If Fox's sister is inside, we'll find her. That's a promise."

"Thanks, Sheriff."

Tanya realized she was seeing him in a new light. She gave him a wan smile.

"I've stepped on your toes more than once. Sorry I stuck my gun in your face."

"You better be. I could have you arrested for threatening an officer of the law." He smiled a tired smile.

"Truce?" said Tanya.

"We're on the same side," he said, offering his hand. His handshake was brief but firm.

Adams spun on his heels and returned to his team, who was busy on their phones and radios. Tanya scanned the parking lot.

The young girl they had rescued was seated in the back seat of a squad car. Through the open door, Tanya could see she had a blanket around her shoulders and a bottle of water in her hand.

A female deputy was sitting beside her, talking to her quietly. The teen was holding on to the officer like she was scared they would leave her behind. Even from where she was, Tanya could see the tears running down her face.

Tanya wondered how she had ended up at the castle. She wondered if she had been kept here, like the other girls. And she wondered if Eva was here, or if they had come in vain.

If Eva is here, what's she doing in this place?

Tanya had so many questions. And she knew who had all the answers.

Camilla.

It was time to confront that woman.

Chapter Sixty-seven

F ox gave a start as he spotted Tanya and Max.

He stepped away from the cruiser he had been leaning against. He crouched low and spread his arms wide.

"Max! Come here, big boy!"

Max bounded toward him, his tail wagging hard, like he hadn't seen him for years.

"So good to see you, buddy," said Fox, rubbing the pup all over his back.

"I'm sorry I didn't stop the goons from taking you." Fox turned his head to avoid getting doggy slobber on his face. "So happy to see you, boy."

Tanya walked up to them.

"Did the girl talk?"

Fox looked up. "Not to me."

He pointed with his chin to the female officer sitting next to the teen. "But when Deputy Yarrow started asking questions, she started talking."

"What did she say?"

"Camilla and Linda lure the girls with Felipe's help. Felipe's job is, or was, to bring them to parties at the castle. That's when the two ladies recruit them into their MLM club. They give them expensive gifts, trips, and the chance to become instant influencers on social media."

Tanya raised her brows. "An attractive proposition to a teen."

"But what they experienced wasn't exactly what they were promised."

"Let me guess. They get entangled in a pyramid scheme within a pyramid scheme?"

"The girls are rotated through the club members. Both men and women. Apparently, it was Patel's turn tonight."

"That's sick."

"You were right. This is a trafficking racket." Fox sighed heavily. "I never thought in a million years that Eva... I should have asked her more questions. I should have come to find her sooner."

Tanya put a hand on his shoulder.

"Where is she?" Tears rolled down Fox's face. "Is she getting rotated tonight, too?"

Tanya turned and glanced at the forbidding facade of the castle. It seemed impenetrable.

"We need to get inside."

Fox wiped his cheek with the back of his hand.

"Adams said he's waiting for the paperwork. He's organizing a SWAT team. No idea how long that will take."

Tanya glanced at the officers by their squad cars.

"Have you seen Madden or Hatchet yet?"

"No sign of them, but everyone seemed shocked to see their vehicles here."

Tanya looked back at the castle. It was eerie to not see or hear anyone. It was like everyone was huddled inside, preparing for a raid.

She turned back to Fox. "I don't doubt what the girl said, but I can't help feeling there's something bigger at play here."

Fox squinted at her. "What on earth do you mean?"

Tanya glanced over at the sheriff, who was pacing by his cruiser. He was speaking into his phone, gesturing wildly.

Probably still negotiating the search warrant with a local judge.

The officers behind him had their heads down, reading something on their phones. In the backseat of her squad car, Deputy Yarrow talked to the victim in a low voice, as if she was reassuring her.

Tanya straightened up.

She lowered her voice. "We're going in."

Fox jumped to his feet, but Tanya grabbed his arm.

"Quietly."

He nodded.

"This way," whispered Tanya.

She walked casually toward the castle with Max at her heels. She slipped behind the buttress closest to the small side door.

It was still open, but there was no sign of life inside.

She flattened herself against the wall and drew her weapon.

Fox slipped behind the pillar next to her. He pulled out his handgun and gave her an inquiring look.

Tanya stepped up to the door and peeked inside.

"Now," she whispered.

Chapter Sixty-eight

T he foyer was empty.

Tanya slinked through the open doorway. Max darted inside ahead of her, like he knew they were on an urgent mission. Fox gave a nervous glance at the deputies before sliding in after them.

Tanya crossed the room and checked all four corridors that branched out from the foyer.

The strange hum they'd heard earlier had stopped.

"Which one?" whispered Fox.

"We need to stay undercover," said Tanya, keeping her voice low. "Linda could be near the entrance to the first hallway. That leaves three."

"Where do these corridors end up?" said Fox, a visible shudder going through him. "At the top floors or in the dungeons?"

"This is the ground floor of the castle. If there are dungeons, they should be accessible from here."

Tanya's eyes fell on her pup.

Max was already trotting through the second corridor, either following his nose or his intuition. He stopped and glanced over his shoulder as if to say, *You coming, Mom?*

"He's caught a scent," she said, stepping into the corridor where Max was. "Keep going, bud. Let's find out what this castle is hiding."

She and Fox walked side by side with Max leading the way. They soon came to a closed door at the end of the stone corridor.

"No cameras here," said Fox as he scanned the ceiling and the walls.

"Stand by," whispered Tanya as she reached for the handle.

Fox positioned himself behind her and aimed his weapon at the door.

The wooden door opened silently in Tanya's hand.

She peeked through the narrow opening to see a small staircase that went up to the first floor. The stairway was illuminated from up above, but she couldn't see all the way. She listened in, but all she could hear was a ghostly silence.

"Where's security?" whispered Fox from behind her.

"Maybe they don't have any inside the castle," whispered Tanya. "Or, they're busy someplace else in the building."

Tanya pushed the door open and climbed the steps slowly, her Glock at the ready. Her eyes and ears were alert, prepared for an attack.

Max trotted up the stairs by her heels, and Fox followed her from behind like a shadow.

When Tanya emerged to the top step, she stopped and stared, mouth open. She had time traveled five hundred years back.

"Unbelievable," whispered Fox, peeking over her shoulder.

If the exterior of the building had promised a medieval setting, it didn't disappoint.

HER LAST LIE

They were in a large hall with high ceilings. The exit on the other end was framed in an archway made of stone.

Intricately designed tapestries adorned the walls. The yellow light from the old-fashioned lamps cast uncanny shadows across the room. The immense fireplace in the corner, complete with an iron cauldron, looked like it had come straight from an old English castle.

Tanya felt the prickle of goose bumps on her arms. She gazed around the immense space, thinking it was the perfect setup for a medieval dinner party where royal couturiers ate wild boar and drank warm wine.

But the hall was empty.

She couldn't explain why the hair on the back of her neck was standing up.

Someone's watching us.

She whirled around, her gun aimed forward. But there was no one in the vicinity.

Fox clutched her arm.

"Who's that?"

Tanya spun around.

She gawked at the silent figure standing next to the fireplace. He was staring right at them.

Chapter Sixty-nine

I t was a man in a metallic knight's armor. He was holding a long
sword with an ornately carved hilt.

He was staring their way.

The figure was life-sized and looked very real, but Tanya shook
her head. "Empty armor."

Fox put a hand over his heart. "Geez. Almost gave me a heart
attack."

She nudged him with her elbow. "If he miraculously comes alive,
remember we have superior firepower."

She spun around, her heart skipping a beat, her eyes scanning
the hall.

"Where's Max?"

"By the doorway," said Fox, pointing at the stone archway.

Max was sniffing the carpet by the entrance.

Tanya walked over and bent down to examine what had caught
his interest. She checked the rug but couldn't see or smell anything.
Before she could say a word, Max padded through the doorway
and entered what looked like the main hallway.

She scrambled after him. "Slow down, bud."

"Are we just going to follow him?" whispered Fox, catching up to them.

"He's picked up a scent and I want to know what it is," said Tanya, watching her pup smell something on the floor again as if to make sure he was on the right path.

Fox scurried next to Tanya, frowning. "What's he trained for? Drugs? Explosives?"

"Human remains."

He shot her an alarmed look. Tanya realized what she had just inferred.

"He can also track injured people, lost kids, and such," she added quickly.

"You taught him that?"

Tanya didn't answer.

The bureau did, but I'm happy to take the credit.

They passed a series of stately medieval rooms. A gentleman's study, an old library, and a drawing room. There was not a soul to be seen, not even staff.

Tanya kept swiveling her head, her eyes darting back and forth to make sure no one would surprise them.

"Where are those people from the parking lot?" whispered Fox as they hurried along the hallway. "They couldn't have disappeared into thin air."

"Wherever they are, they're having a ball."

"A ball?"

"Massive party. Did you see Linda's fancy getup?"

Tanya searched the corridor, her brow furrowed.

"Wait. Where did Max go?"

She dashed to the end of the hallway, her heart racing. *I can't lose him again.*

But Max had turned a corner and was trotting along, his nose stuck to the ground.

"What's that smell?" said Fox, sniffing the air.

"Chlorine," said Tanya as she noticed it too. "There must be a swimming pool nearby."

Up ahead, she spotted a double glass doorway through which the late afternoon light streamed.

A courtyard?

Max was investigating something along the bottom of the doors. He pawed at the glass, like he wanted to get inside.

Tanya and Fox stepped up to him.

Through the patio doors, they could see a kidney-shaped aquamarine pool surrounded by beach chairs. The water in the pool was completely still. There was no one inside the courtyard.

"Not very medieval," said Fox. "But I can see why Camilla would have added this modern feature."

Tanya reached over to the door and pulled down the handle.

"Let's see what you've picked up, bud."

She had opened it only a few inches when Max squeezed through the narrow opening and darted in.

Tanya stepped inside and treaded quietly around the outdoor pool, taking in the empty chairs, the flower boxes, and the natural light that streamed from up above.

She stared at the castle walls surrounding them. All the windows looking out into the courtyard were covered in curtains. But someone had to only peek out of those windows to spot them down here.

"Hey, why's Max going there?" said Fox, pointing to the sign at the end of the courtyard.

Just as Tanya turned to look, Max crept under a set of swinging wooden doors and vanished from view.

She ran after him.

"Wait up, Max."

The hot humid air of the castle's sauna hit her as she stepped through the wooden doors.

"How many private sauna rooms do you need?" said Fox, coming from behind her.

"I don't know, but the one we want is that one." Tanya walked over to the door where Max was sitting with his head cocked to the side.

He looked up as she approached and wagged his tail.

"What's inside, bud?" said Tanya, reaching for the door.

She pushed it an inch and jerked back as a torrid blast of air slammed against her face. She peered through the narrow gap into a smoky mist. Max whined but didn't make a move to enter the sauna.

It took a second for Tanya to realize what she was looking at.

A lone female was sitting on a stone slab in the back of the sauna room, covered in a veneer of water beads or sweat. She was leaning against the wall, but had her head down and her hands on her lap, like she had fallen asleep. The woman was completely naked.

Tanya recognized her instantly. She knocked on the door.

"Camilla?"

The woman didn't look up.

"Madame Camilla?"

She still didn't look up.

An icy chill went through Tanya as she realized what had happened. She let go of the door and stepped inside, ignoring the heat swirling around her.

She stepped over to the naked figure and bent down.

There was a thin line of blood across the woman's neck.

Someone had slashed Camilla's throat.

Chapter Seventy

T anya turned back to Fox, who was standing by the threshold.

"Our killer's been busy," she said.

Fox grabbed the doorframe like he was trying to stop himself from collapsing.

"How...?" he whispered. "Why does this keep happening?"

Camilla was the sixth murder victim they had come across within the twenty-four-hour period they had been at Crescent Bay.

The little Tanya had known about Camilla had been distasteful. Still, a sliver of sorrow crossed her heart. Another human life had been cut short.

Why is this happening?

She pointed at the fresh blood splatters on the sauna floor. "This was recent." She leaned over and touched the dead woman's wrist. "Rigor mortis hasn't set in yet."

"We...," stammered Fox. "We were wrong. It's not her."

"I still think this is the work of a group," said Tanya, getting on her haunches to examine the cut on Camilla's neck. "She could have been part of it, got into a disagreement, and got... expelled, so to speak."

She turned to Fox.

"Everybody in this town is a suspect as far as I'm concerned."

"Even Adams?"

Tanya opened her mouth to answer, then closed it.

Only a half hour ago, she had been so petrified by the thought of finding an injured or dying Max, that Adams had taken the charge and led her to her pup.

Was that because he knew exactly where he had been caged? Or had he been sincere in his attempts to help?

She turned back to Camilla, wishing she had a blanket to cover the woman's body. It would be the decent thing to do. But she also knew that would be tampering with evidence.

She got to her feet with a sigh.

Something fluttered on the dead woman's lap. Tanya bent over her, squinting. Camilla was clasping something small and white in her hands.

Tanya looked around for a towel.

"What is it?" hissed Fox from the doorway, his voice tinged with anxiety.

"Gloves." Tanya scanned the sauna for a substitute, but there was nothing on the benches or on the racks. "Remind me to pack a box next time I go on a trip."

"Here you go."

She swiveled around to see Fox holding out a long, thin object.

"A whip?"

"A sauna whisk," he said, stepping in to hand it to her. "It was leaning against the wall outside."

Tanya took it, wondering about the kooky things people do inside saunas.

She stepped back toward Camilla and kneeled in front of her. Pushing the whisk's edge in between the dead woman's hands, she gently pried them apart.

The paper fluttered in the air, but it remained stuck to her skin.

Using her makeshift tool, Tanya raised Camilla's right hand a few more inches and loosened the object. Then, with a twist of the whisk, she dislodged the small sheet from Camilla's hand.

It fell gently to the floor.

Tanya squinted at the scraggly words on the note. They were faint, almost indecipherable on the soggy paper. But she didn't need to see the words. One glance told her she had seen this before.

"What is it?" came Fox's nervous voice from behind her.

"Last witness still alive," she said.

"Oh, my God."

Tanya knew what was going through his troubled mind. The killer was taunting them. It wouldn't be long before they found Eva, and it wouldn't be pretty.

"I'd bet the killer's still in the castle," she said.

Fox looked at her in alarm like he had just realized something.

"Maybe Linda's the killer. And we let her go."

Tanya nodded. "She's the only person we've seen in this part of the—"

A loud bang stopped her in mid-sentence.

Fox whirled around. Max growled, his heckles up. Tanya shushed him.

"Someone's outside," whispered Fox.

"Hold on to him," said Tanya. "We don't know if these people are armed."

Fox leaned over and grabbed Max's collar before he could dart out.

Tanya drew her weapon and stepped toward the wooden doors of the sauna.

Suddenly, a blood-curdling scream cut through the castle.

Tanya jumped. Max barked and lurched, trying to wiggle out of Fox's grasp.

"What in heaven's name was that?" said Fox, pulling the dog back. "Heel, Max."

Tanya peeked through the doorway. The courtyard was empty. She scanned the windows along the castle walls, but the curtains were still drawn.

She stepped out to the open courtyard, her Glock at the ready.

Staying close to the walls, she inched toward the glass doors, her eyes alert to movement from the windows above. She thought she saw a flash of a curtain, but wasn't sure if it was her imagination.

It was only when she got to the courtyard's entrance, she realized what had happened. Someone had thrust a long wooden bar across the double doors.

She yanked the handle down and rattled the glass doors.

They were locked inside.

Chapter Seventy-one

Outside, the castle hallway was empty.

A rustle made Tanya turn. Fox was creeping along the wall toward her, one hand on Max's collar.

"Who was that?" he said as he got close.

Tanya pointed at the wooden bar.

"Someone who doesn't want us out and about."

Her eyes flittered to the walls above them and back toward the sauna where Camilla's dead body sat. Max growled.

"Get to the other side of the pool," Tanya whispered hoarsely.

She waited for Fox to pull Max to safety before she aimed her weapon at the door's lock.

She took a deep breath in to steady herself. This was going to be loud. She would be calling attention to their presence, if the castle's security didn't already know they were here.

Tanya fired.

She threw her hands over her face, as the glass splintered all around her.

Max barked, his voice bouncing off the stone walls, sounding like a dozen German Shepherds were raging inside the building.

"The whole world knows we're here now," said Fox, coming over.

"Too late for that."

She surveyed the windows. No one seemed to be bothered by a gunshot echoing in the courtyard or a dog barking like mad.

Where is everyone?

Max pulled and huffed as Fox held on to his collar. Every muscle in his doggy body rippled like he couldn't wait to sink his fangs into the next person he saw.

Tanya turned her attention back to the door. The wooden bar was still in place, holding the doors closed. She reached through the broken glass and pushed the bar, but it was wedged on to something on the other side.

She holstered her weapon and picked up the closest beach chair. She slammed it against the glass panels.

Once.

Twice.

Three times.

The wooden bar fell to the ground with a thump. Tanya gave the doors a kick.

They swung open.

"Hold him," she called, as she pushed the shattered glass away with her boot.

She knew Max would dash out as soon as Fox let go. The last thing she wanted was for his soft paws to crunch on the broken glass. She grabbed a handful of thick beach towels from a deck chair and threw them over the remaining shards.

"Let's go!"

She jumped into the corridor, her weapon aimed in front.

Max barreled out of the courtyard, leaping over the towels, barking like mad. He headed straight down the hallway, in the opposite direction of where they had come.

Tanya dashed after him.

Her heart almost stopped as she spotted the silhouette in the shadows. They, whoever they were, were peeking out from behind a partially open door down the corridor.

"Hey, there!" she called out.

Max darted toward the person, with Tanya right behind him. But the door snapped shut before they could get to it. Whoever had been watching them had vanished.

Fox caught up to them, panting.

Max was pacing up and down the corridor, his hackles up, growling. Fox stared at the stone wall Tanya was scrutinizing.

"What are you looking at?" said Fox, his brow furrowed.

Tanya reached over and touched the wall. It felt solid to her fingers.

"I swear there was a door here."

Chapter Seventy-two

"It's a secret door."

Tanya felt silly as soon as those words left her mouth.

"I would have thought I imagined it, if Max wasn't acting up like this."

Fox glanced down at the dog. Max's pointy face was turned toward the wall, a low growl emanating from his throat. His ears were pricked, and his back was hunched like he was ready to lunge at something.

Or someone.

Fox got closer so his face was inches from the surface. He knocked on the stone slabs.

"I don't see a door."

"I swear there was someone behind there. They disappeared as soon as we ran over." Tanya felt the wall again. "Maybe there's a hidden entrance to the rest of the castle where all those people are."

Fox turned to her, his eyes scrunched.

"Did you see who it was?"

"They moved too fast." Tanya sighed. "That scream we heard could have come from behind this wall too."

Fox shuddered visibly.

"The creep factor's high here. Where's everyone?"

He swiveled around, scanning the hallway, and gasped.

"A camera."

Tanya followed his finger to see the bulbous electronic device above their heads. Goose bumps sprung up on her arms.

"They're probably watching us right now."

"Who are *they*?" said Fox.

"Your guess is as good as mine."

"Where's Eva?" Fox rubbed his face. "Who killed Camilla? Where are all those people who are parked in the back? And who screamed just now?"

Tanya pointed at the wall with her chin.

"I feel like all the answers are beyond this secret door."

She reached over and felt the slabs again.

"What's this?" she murmured, as her fingers crossed a crack on the surface.

She ran her hand along it, feeling the outline of a small door. Her heart raced. It was a perfectly camouflaged entrance. Camouflaged by a thin stone veneer designed in the same brown pattern as the wall.

"Synthetic stone," she muttered as she swept her hands across the facade. She gasped as she felt something circular and smooth, right where the doorknob would be. It was so well embedded into the wall, she hadn't noticed it at first.

"Found it."

Fox peered at the spot. Tanya pushed the knob, but it didn't budge. She poked it and thumped it, but nothing worked.

What do we need to get this door open? A magic spell?

She bent over and peered at the knob.

I knew it.

"There's a hidden keyhole here."

"Remember that huge key chain Linda had?" said Fox, stepping away from her. "I'll check the rooms nearby."

"If Linda has it, she won't give it up without a fight."

Fox lifted his sidearm as if to say, *but I have a gun.*

"She could be armed."

But he kept walking down the corridor, poking his head into each room. Tanya turned and stared at the secret entrance, wondering if there was another solution.

She gently nudged Max to the side.

"Out of the way, bud."

Taking a fighting stance to balance herself, she gave a swift kick at the door. The sting of the impact rushed up her calf and she doubled over in pain.

This door wasn't made of the same flimsy material as the entrances in the basement.

With a loud curse, she raised her weapon and aimed it at the doorknob.

"Tanya!"

She spun around to see Fox on the other side of the pool courtyard. He waved at her urgently.

With a quick glance at the door to make sure it hadn't miraculously opened by itself, Tanya stepped away and walked over.

Fox was standing by an entrance to a room along the hallway, slack jawed. He had his weapon, but it lay limp in his hand.

Tanya stepped up to him, with Max at her heels.

"That scream we heard," whispered Fox hoarsely.

Tanya followed his eyes. It was an old-fashioned library. It was dark inside, but the recessed antique fixtures shone a soft light into the corners.

The walls were lined with bookcases holding leather-bound tomes. On one end of the room was a mahogany desk with a bankers lamp and a box of tissue. The soft light cast so many shadows everywhere that she had almost missed Linda.

Linda was seated in a plush leather chair beside the desk.

She was in her purple ballgown, but her arms hung limp by her sides. Her head was turned toward the ceiling, and her mouth was open in a hideous but silent scream.

Someone had rammed a long sword right through her upper body.

It jut out grotesquely from her bleeding chest. The heavy hilt of the weapon was bent from the force of gravity and looked alarmingly like it would slice through her at a moment's notice.

"Oh, my goodness," said Tanya in a horrified whisper.

She stepped toward the macabre scene, like Linda's ghost was calling to her. As she got closer, the ornate hilt of the sword winked at her.

It was the same sword the medieval knight had held in the first room they had entered.

Chapter Seventy-three

F ox shut his eyes.

"What a way to die," he whispered.

Tanya reached toward Linda's neck and felt for her pulse.

Fox shook his head. "She couldn't have survived that."

Tanya pulled her hand back with a sigh. "I hope it was a quick death."

"This is getting insane." Fox stared at the body. "We just saw her an hour ago."

"The killer's on the prowl," said Tanya, circling Linda's chair, looking for clues that might indicate who committed the crime.

She bent down to examine the tablet that lay on the dead woman's lap. It was placed neatly in her hands.

"Odd."

A violent thrust of the sword into Linda would have propelled that device out of her hands and across the room.

"We were meant to find this," she said, pointing at the device.

Fox scrunched his forehead. "Is this a setup?"

"A message from the killer, I'd say."

Tanya glanced around the room for something to pick up the tablet with.

"Do you think it's the person you saw disappearing into the wall?" said Fox, strain in his voice.

Tanya shrugged. "We have to be careful. There could be more than one person working here."

He frowned. "Why didn't they try to kill us? They had us cornered in the courtyard sauna, didn't they? Easy targets."

"We're armed and we're hunting them."

"So they're afraid of us?"

Tanya's brow furrowed. "No. We're too much trouble." She paused. "Besides, I don't think we're their target."

"What do you mean?"

"These aren't random incidents. The killer or killers are selectively choosing their victims."

Fox gestured at Linda.

"But none of the vics have anything in common. The mayor, her husband, Julie Steele, Felipe Fernando, Camilla and now—"

"You're forgetting the MLM organization, or whatever it's a front for. Each of the victims was a club member. That's the connection."

Max, who had been busily investigating all corners of the library, came over to join them. He passed Linda's armchair and brushed against the dead woman's skirt. The skirt's hem sprang up and down as he trotted on the dress.

Fox clutched his heart. "Geez, I thought she'd come alive for a sec." He turned to the pup. "You're making me nervous."

Something small and shiny glinted from under Linda's skirt, but Tanya had more urgent matters to attend to.

"Stand guard by the door, Max," she said, pointing. "There's a good boy."

She pulled two tissues out of the tissue box on the desk. Using them as makeshift gloves, she picked up Linda's right hand and placed it on the tablet.

"Don't touch!" said Fox.

"I'll ask forgiveness from Dr. Chen later."

Tanya struggled to position the dead woman's thumb on the home button of the tablet.

"Watch out for the sword," said Fox as Tanya leaned too close to the corpse. "That blade could pop out at any moment."

Tanya grimaced, but pressed Linda's finger on the button until the screen came to life.

"That's a first," said Fox, shaking his head. "I don't think I've seen a dead person access their tablet before."

Using the tissues, Tanya picked up the device and placed it under the banker's light on the desk. She crossed her fingers, hoping the forensic lab wouldn't ream her out for tampering with evidence.

"Let's see what we're supposed to see."

She didn't have to search far as the video app was already open.

"This is what she was watching last," said Tanya, clicking play. "Or it's what the killer wants us to see."

Fox peered over her shoulder.

The video panned around an immense ballroom.

The hall was decorated in an elaborate flower arrangement, like a wedding was about to take place. Tanya and Fox watched quietly as the camera recorded the stained-glass windows, ornate sculptures, and the crystal chandeliers that dropped from the high ceiling.

A half a dozen people dressed in Victorian ballgowns and black tuxedos were scattered around in small groups, wine glasses in hand, chatting in muted tones.

"Where *is* this place?" whispered Fox.

"There's Camilla and Linda," said Tanya as the camera caught their smiling faces. The two women raised their wineglasses at whoever was behind the camera.

"You're right. It's a ball," said Fox. "Like some eighteenth-century shindig."

The camera moved to their left and focused on a group congregated nearby. They twirled around and waved at the camera.

Tanya paused the video and scrutinized their faces.

"That's Julie Steele." She pointed at the laughing young woman in the middle. "That's Felipe Fernando with his arm around her. They look like a couple. And that's Julie's mother and father next to him."

Fox stared, his eyes bulging.

"They were all murdered within the past twenty-four hours." He turned to Tanya. "Someone took revenge on the mayor and her entire family. Maybe this is a family affair, after all."

Tanya sighed. He was trying to rule out Eva from danger, but the evidence was still inconclusive.

She shook her head. "That doesn't explain the murders of Camilla, Linda, the girl who died in the explosion, or why Valerie was targeted."

She clicked play again.

The camera panned to a raised platform at the end of the hall. It zoomed in. Two large pillars flanked the stage. Strings of little white lights adorned the pillars, giving a festive feel to the platform.

But what was on top of the stage was anything but festive.

Tanya's stomach dropped.

"This is sick! What are they doing to her?" cried Fox. "Is this some fake Halloween game?"

Tanya stared at the wooden cross on the platform, her gut churning.

A young naked woman had been tied to the cross. She hung limp, like her life had been sucked right out of her.

No, this wasn't fake.

Chapter Seventy-four

The girl on the cross was alive.

Her chest heaved, like she was gasping for life.

Tanya stared at the barbaric image.

Why would anyone do this?

The woman's hair covered part of her face so it was hard to see what she looked like. Her body was sickly and scrawny, like she hadn't eaten for days. But it wasn't Eva.

Thank goodness it isn't Eva.

But then came the most disturbing part.

Julie Steele skipped up to the platform, wineglass in hand. Giggling giddily, she stepped over to the girl, tilted her head coyly, and flashed a bright smile. It was like she was taking a picture in front of a Christmas tree with lots of presents.

"This is psychopathic," said Fox, reaching over and punching the fast-forward button. "I can't watch this."

But Tanya knew what he was looking for.

Eva.

He stopped the video as the camera panned to the side of the stage. Tanya leaned in.

Camilla was ushering four young girls dressed in cute Victorian gowns onto the platform, like a teacher urging her students toward something fun. The girls ran up to pose near the girl on the cross, giggling like Julie had.

"What are these *kids* doing here?" Fox's mouth scrunched in disgust.

"They look barely twelve years old." Tanya scanned their faces. "Wait. We know her. That's Valerie. I'd bet these other girls are her friends. The ones we met by Patel's residence."

"This is so disturbing." Fox rubbed his eyes. "This looks like a cult."

The camera zoomed back to the young woman tied to the cross. Suddenly, she lifted her head.

Fox and Tanya jerked back. The girl stared at the camera, a haunted expression on her face. It was like she could see right through their souls.

"Hold on," said Tanya, her heart racing. She paused the video and zoomed in. "I know this face."

Fox blinked. Then, his face cleared. "My goodness."

He brought his phone out and scrolled through the images he had shown her the night before. He stopped at one photo and tapped on it.

"Madden's daughter." Fox's face darkened. "He sacrificed his own child? What a lunatic, and to think I felt sorry for him. He lied to us."

A shiver went through Tanya. Her heart ticked faster.

"Madden's daughter disappeared six years ago, didn't she?"

"That's what he said." Fox nodded. "Newspaper articles confirmed it."

"These girls are around eighteen or so now," said Tanya, pointing at the four kids on the stage. "Do you realize what this means?"

Fox rubbed his tired face.

"I don't know and I don't care. I just want to find Eva."

"The killer's targeting these girls. Valerie was—"

"Valerie is safe in Dr. Chen's clinic," said Fox, frustration laced in his voice, "but we still don't know where Eva is."

He stared at the paused video, his face contorted in disgust. He punched the play button, like he wanted to get it over with.

Tanya swiveled around and stared at Linda's dead body. Her brain whirred.

"I missed all the clues," she muttered to herself.

The puzzle pieces were getting clearer. They still didn't fit into a neat picture, but she could almost make out the outline.

What if I'm wrong?

"Eva!" cried Fox.

Tanya spun back around.

The camera had panned to a corner of the stage that hadn't been visible before.

Leaning against the podium was Eva Fox, dressed in a beautiful beige lace gown. She was alone, her head down, and her hands together, like she was praying. On her wrist was the diamond bracelet with the red vial.

The video stopped abruptly, and a still frame popped up.

Fox let out a cry.

The words that flashed across the screen made Tanya's blood go cold.

Last witness to die.

Chapter Seventy-five

F ox sunk his face into his palms.

His back convulsed as he sobbed silently. All the stress and torture from not knowing where his sister was, or if she was even alive, had finally overwhelmed him.

Tanya pushed the tablet aside.

Think, girl, think.

"Where's Adams?" she said to herself. "Still waiting for the warrant?"

She drummed her fingers on the desk.

"I'd bet everything Eva's behind that wall."

She yanked the desk drawer open, but all it contained was a blank notepad and a fountain pen.

Tanya stepped around Fox, and searched the coffee table, the armchairs, and the side tables. She walked up to the nearest bookshelf and examined the contents.

They were mostly historical tomes on medieval costumes, food, and norms. She pulled one out, half hoping to find a set of keys inside a hollowed book. She had discovered a hidden key that way during a previous case.

She flipped through the pages in vain, then threw the book down in frustration.

Where is the key to that door on the wall?

She shook her head as she tried to think.

Did the killer take the keys? Is Eva next? Is that what's happening behind that secret door?

"Eva," Fox cried through his tears. "Oh, Eva. Did they crucify you too?"

Tanya spun around to him.

"Do you want to find her alive?"

Fox lifted his chin and turned his tear-filled, bloodshot eyes to her. "What are you talking about? Of course, I do."

She walked over to him, put a hand on his shoulder, and softened her voice.

"We need to think clearly and be quick on our feet, okay?"

He gave her a miserable look.

"We'll find Eva," said Tanya. "We'll get through that door. I'll shoot it down if I have to."

Fox struggled to his feet.

"Let's go," said Tanya.

Max, who had been obediently guarding the entrance to the study, whipped around. He knew those last two words. *Let's go* meant action. He got up, tongue hanging, and tail wagging.

Tanya whirled around as she remembered something she'd thought had been insignificant. There had been a strange glint under Linda's skirt when Max's tail brushed past the dead body.

She bent down and pushed Linda's gown to the side. With a triumphant cry, she scooped the keychain from under the chair.

She flipped through them one by one, from ancient keys made of heavy iron to the smaller and modern brass-cut keys. A tiny flat key in the middle of the bunch caught her eye. It was in the shape of a dagger, paper thin but hard as steel.

She held it up.

"Open Sesame."

With a nod to Fox, she stepped toward the door, her gun aimed in front.

Tanya stepped out of the library and started walking toward the secret door, her eyes darting back and forth, her gun at the ready. Max trotted at her heels, happy to be back in action. Fox followed them quietly, his face scrunched in anguish.

The hallway was empty. And deadly quiet.

Even that peculiar hum was gone.

In the short time they had been inside the castle, two women had been murdered, Tanya had fired her weapon, Max had barked his head off, and they had broken down the courtyard doors. But no one had come to inquire or see what was going on.

It was like they had entered Sleeping Beauty's palace and all the residents were in deep slumber.

Tanya stepped up to the hidden door. She peered at the stone slabs, searching for the small split of a keyhole she had spotted earlier.

There.

As soon as she slipped the key in, the door moved.

She pulled back in surprise.

Fox stepped around her and thrust his hand out to open the door.

Tanya grabbed his arm. "This could be a trap," she whispered.

She peeked through the narrow opening, but it was too dark to see what was on the other side.

"Weapons out," she said. "Watch my back."

Fox flattened himself against the wall, his sidearm in his hands. Tanya peered into the yawning gap. There was an eerie quiet inside. She shone her flashlight into the darkness.

"A passageway."

The hum came again, louder this time and distinctive enough to be identified.

"Chanting," whispered Fox. "Like at a church."

"The only church that chants like that is a cult," said Tanya.

Chapter Seventy-six

They had entered an underground cave.

The air was stale and musty, like not much circulated through this tunnel. The walls were made of ochre stone, and the rough-hewn slabs on the floor were covered in a thin yellow dust.

Tanya shone her light on the ground and stopped.

"Shoe markings." She kneeled down to investigate. "Working boots. Size eleven or larger. I only see one pair."

"It's the shadow you spotted through the secret doorway," said Fox, peeking over her shoulder. "The killer. We'll have to be ready for him."

"I never said it was a man—" She stopped as she realized something. "Whoever it was, it had to be the person who kidnapped Max. I have never seen him run so fast in attack mode."

"Could it have been Hatchet?" said Fox.

"She's on the top of my list. She went AWOL around the same time you got beat up in your room and Max got dog-napped."

"What about Adams? We think he's outside with his team, waiting for a search warrant, but how do we know he didn't come inside?"

Tanya frowned. "He couldn't have taken Max because he was at Dr. Chen's clinic the whole time."

"I still don't trust the guy," said Fox. "They could be working together."

"We'll find out soon." Tanya got up and stepped away from the boot markings. "Stick to the side."

They walked in single file, hugging the wall to avoid interfering with any evidence.

Tanya could hear Fox's raspy breathing behind her. He was treading slowly, his back and shoulders hunched like he was expecting the worst.

He hadn't had the chance to recover from the many injuries he'd been subjected to over the past two days. Tanya was sure he was operating on pure adrenaline.

And hope.

"This thing is solid," she said, shining her light around to assure him. "It's modeled after an old-fashioned escape route. Whoever designed this castle didn't spare any expense to build it to spec."

Fox didn't reply, but his breathing got raspier.

If Tanya closed her eyes, she could imagine having time-traveled five hundred years back. A terrified prisoner trying to escape their royal captors. A shiver went through her, wondering what made Camilla build this creepy castle up the hill.

"We're on an elevation," she said as she felt the tunnel ramp upward. "This is taking us to a floor above. We're not going to the dungeons."

They kept hiking. The chanting got louder, the deeper they walked into the passageway.

Suddenly, the singing stopped.

Tanya and Fox froze.

"What's going on up there?" whispered Fox.

"Keep moving," whispered Tanya back.

The passageway snaked around like a maze and got even steeper the farther they climbed.

It took them four minutes to reach the end. The tunnel opened into a cul-de-sac with two exits, one large wooden door in front of them, and a small one to the side.

Tanya rotated her flashlight, but whoever she had spotted earlier had disappeared into the bowels of the building. She felt that strange sensation again, like there were people nearby, watching, waiting.

She reached for the small door and turned the handle gently, but the door didn't budge.

She put her hand on the larger entrance when the chanting started again. She jumped back, shock going through her like a lightning strike.

The singing was coming from just beyond the door. The chanting was loud but melodic, and it seemed like a harp was playing in the background.

Tanya remained stock-still, trying to guess the number of people and the size of the space behind the door.

"Sounds like a large hall," she whispered.

Fox put his ear to the door.

"There must be a hundred people inside," he whispered. He stared at Tanya. "Is this the ballroom we saw in the video?"

The chanting grew louder and louder until Tanya felt like she was in the room with them. It was almost hypnotic.

She looked down at her pup.

"Sit, Max."

Max sat down and thumped his tail.

"Good boy. Don't move till I come back, okay?"

He whined but remained in place.

"But we need him," whispered Fox.

Tanya shook her head. "We don't know what's on the other side. It could be dangerous. I'll call him if I need his help."

She reached toward the large door and tried the handle.

"You too. Stay here until I give the all clear. Got it?"

Fox shot her an exasperated look.

Tanya thrust the handle down and pushed the door open.

To her surprise, it slid quietly, like someone had recently oiled the hinges.

Chapter Seventy-seven

Tanya gawked at the bizarre sight.

The large door opened straight onto the stage.

Midway on the raised platform was the wooden cross. A white curtain shielded it from the hall and her, but Tanya got a glimpse of the occupant behind it.

Tied to the cross was a naked woman, her head hung so low that her hair had fallen across her face. Her skin was sallow, and her body was gaunt.

Tanya's heart jumped to her mouth.

Eva?

She didn't have time to get a closer look.

Gathered in front of the platform were about fifty people, frozen in their spots like an alien had just landed in their midst.

Tanya stared at them. They stared right back.

The women were in Victorian ballgowns and the men wore black tuxedos with white ties. Precious gems, gold, and silver twinkled under the chandelier lights, and the scent of luxury perfume lay heavily in the air.

In the middle of the room was a plush velvet throne from a fairytale book. A beautiful young woman in a royal blue gown was seated in it.

She was glaring at Tanya.

Who's that?

A golden-haired harpist was perched on a stool by the stage. She gaped at Tanya. Next to the musician was a familiar figure in a black gown with a dark scowl on her face.

Tanya gave a start.

Hatchet?

The acting sheriff looked livid at her intrusion. But to Tanya's surprise, she didn't make a move. Tanya hoped she didn't have her sidearm on her.

She reached back to shut the stage door behind her to make sure Max wouldn't bound out. But, Fox pushed her aside and stepped onto the platform.

"*Eva!*" he cried.

Tanya turned to the girl on the cross. She was completely immobile. Her skin was so pale and lucid, it was like she had been drained of blood.

Her heart sank.

She's dead. We're too late.

Tanya frowned.

Wait.

Fox wasn't looking at the girl on the cross. He was addressing the young woman on the throne.

Fox let his gun fall to the stage floor and stumbled toward the edge of the platform like a zombie.

"Eva!" he cried, his voice echoing through the now quietened hall. "Oh, my god, Eva. I thought you were dead!"

"What are you doing here?" snarled the crowned woman.

Tanya did a double take.

Eva Fox had been unrecognizable in her floor-length, royal blue gown of velvet and crystals. Her face was heavily made up and the gold tiara on her head shimmered. A diamond bracelet glittered around her wrist.

Eva rose from her throne, her eyes blazing in fury. She lifted her arm and pointed an angry finger at the stage.

"I told you not to come looking for me."

Her voice was hard and guttural.

Tanya's mind reeled.

What's going on here?

That was when she noticed the three black-suited men who stepped toward the throne.

Bodyguards.

They stood at attention behind Eva, like soldiers waiting for their command.

A brief nod from Eva was all it took. All three men drew their weapons at once.

Tanya was ready.

She had her gun aimed at them in an instant.

A shocked gasp rippled across the hall, but Tanya kept her aim steady. So did the men, their muzzles pointed at Fox and her.

Tanya knew the risk she was taking. A shootout would lead to panic and chaos. That would mean only one thing. A bloodbath in the ballroom.

"Put that away," cried Fox, turning to her. "Eva's here. She's okay."

"Get behind me," she whispered hoarsely. "She's going to kill you."

Chapter Seventy-eight

Fox's attention was on his long-lost, baby sister.

"Eva... you look so... different. What are you doing here with all these people?"

His voice was plaintive, almost pitiful. It was like he couldn't comprehend what he was seeing.

"I've been looking for you for days." He extended his arms toward her. "I thought... I thought..."

"You thought wrong," growled Eva.

If Fox hadn't been on a raised platform, he would have rushed over to embrace her. Tanya knew that would be the fastest way to get killed, but he didn't seem to realize he was staring death in the face.

Her brain raced.

I was wrong. So wrong.

Tanya was now sure the trafficking ring was a side gig. Those girls might have been lured for Patel, Felipe, and others, but this was really a cult.

A cult headed by Fox's sister.

Did Eva kill Camilla, Linda, Felipe, and the others?
Why?
Was this a fight for power gone horribly wrong?

Her mind whirled as the video they'd just watched in the library flashed to mind.

What about Madden's daughter? Was I wrong about that too?

She scanned the hall, but Deputy Madden was nowhere to be seen.

"We missed you so much," Fox was saying, tears running down his cheeks. "Zoe cleaned the spare room for you. Please come home."

Eva threw her head back and laughed. It was a mirthless laugh that made Tanya's blood go cold.

"If you think I'm coming home with you, you're seriously messed up." Eva's eyes turned hard. "I only said I'd visit you to keep you away from here. But I see you came, anyway."

Tanya kept her aim on the three guards. They could fire in an instant, and neither she nor Fox were wearing their Kevlar vests.

They were sitting ducks.

Behind the closed door of the passageway, Tanya could hear Max barking. He never liked being left out of the action. She wished she could grab Fox and force him inside the tunnel too, but making a sudden move now could mean life or death.

She straightened up and turned toward Eva.

It was time to take over.

"He's your only brother." Tanya projected her voice so everybody could hear. "He never meant any harm. Let him go. Let him return home to Zoe."

Eva glared at Tanya.

"How dare you barge into our sacred hall like this?" she spat out.

"Your brother went through hell to find you."

"I never asked him to."

Fox took a step forward and teetered at the edge of the stage. The three armed guards took a step closer to the platform.

"Watch it," Tanya hissed at Fox.

"Why... why w... would you say something like that, Eva?" stammered Fox, as he tried to grasp the truth.

Eva narrowed her eyes.

"You're so simple and naïve. You always were. You didn't even realize what was going on when we were kids. I went through hell, but you were too blind to see."

"I swear on everything holy that if I'd known what was happening to you, I would have stopped him."

"But you didn't, did you?" cried Eva. "No one stopped him. No one cared."

"I cared! Believe me!"

His heartbroken voice rang through the hall.

"I've found good people who care for me now." Eva's voice turned even colder. "Queen Camilla is always there for me. She's my family now."

Tanya raised a brow. Eva was speaking of Camilla in the present tense, like she was still alive.

Maybe Eva didn't murder Camilla.

A movement at the bottom of the platform caught Tanya's eyes. Her heart quickened.

Deputy Madden?

What's he up to?

Madden was crouched behind the pillar to her left. He was still in his crumpled uniform with the stains of the spilled drink from the night before.

Everyone's attention was on Eva and Fox. No one had noticed the dark shadow behind the concrete column.

How did Madden get here? Was it him I saw through the secret door on the wall?

Tanya wanted to confront the deputy, but she couldn't remove her focus from the three guards.

Something gleamed under the light behind the pillar. A quick side glance told her what was going to happen.

Madden had his semi-automatic rifle in his hands. The same weapon Tanya had seen in the backseat of his squad car.

This time, it was pointed at Eva Fox.

Chapter Seventy-nine

"Open up!"

The shout came from outside the ballroom.

Tanya's eyes fell on the main doors at the far end.

Adams?

More pounding came on the doors.

"This is the Sheriff's Department."

The guests, who had been staring immobile as the drama between Eva and Fox had played out, whirled around, clutching their hearts and gasping loudly.

It was like Sleeping Beauty's castle had finally woken up from a spell.

"I said open up!" hollered Adams.

Eva Fox stood erect by her throne, seemingly unperturbed by the disturbance. The only gesture she made was a subdued wave at her guards. If Tanya hadn't been watching her, she would have missed it.

On cue, the three men spun on their heels and marched toward the main entrance.

Tanya grabbed Fox by the arm.

"We have to leave. *Now.*"

"I need to talk to Eva."

Tanya wanted to shake him.

She's prepared to kill you.

"She's not the sister you know," she said in between gritted teeth.

With an angry hiss, Fox pulled his arm out of her grasp.

Suddenly, the sound of rapid gunfire came from outside the main doors. People fled in all directions, shrieking. Tanya dove to the stage floor, pulling Fox down with her.

The double doors crashed open. Adams and his deputies spilled into the hall, their weapons drawn.

"Police!"

"Everybody back!"

"Stay down!"

Tanya braced for a shootout.

A guard fired.

Deputy Yarrow, the female officer who had been comforting the girl outside, fell with a surprised yell.

Adams and his officers jumped on the three guards, snapping the weapons out of their hands and slamming them to the floor.

Tanya wanted to back them up, but if she let go of Fox, he'd jump straight into danger.

Her heart hammered as she watched the scene. To see a fellow officer get shot boiled her blood. She clutched Fox's arm even more tightly.

While two deputies watched over the handcuffed guards on the floor, the rest stepped through the crowd, as if searching for someone. The guests scattered to all corners of the hall in confusion, screaming. It was like watching someone pick up a stone in the woods to discover a swarm of insects running for cover.

Adams was the first to get through the manic crowd to the throne in the middle. Eva Fox stood silently, like she was invincible. Like she had been expecting him.

Her face was cool, and her hands lay casually by her side. But her mouth was slowly curving into a condescending smirk. *Go ahead, arrest me,* her expression challenged.

Adams spotted Hatchet standing behind the throne and stopped in his tracks, his eyes bulging.

"Hatchet!" he barked. "What the hell's going on?"

The acting sheriff opened her mouth to reply, but one discreet gesture from Eva and she obediently closed it. Hatchet stepped back, her head bowed.

"An officer is down!" shouted Adams. "We found Camilla and Linda dead in the building! There may be more victims. What do you know about this?"

Hatchet didn't reply, her eyes on Eva, waiting for instructions.

Adams swiveled around to Eva.

"Felipe, Julie, Mayor Steele, her husband, all of them. You're behind their deaths, aren't you?"

Tanya expected Eva to sneer, but instead, her face turned a dangerous shade of dark.

"Why didn't you do anything about it?" Her shrill voice rang through the hall, rising above the pandemonium.

The room fell silent.

The guests turned toward her from all corners of the hall, like they had been called.

"My people are being killed one by one, and you just sat there and did nothing!" screeched Eva, her face red with fury. "Why did they all have to die? Why didn't you stop it!"

Adams stared at her like he didn't understand.

Tanya watched the sheriff, wishing she had trusted him from the beginning.

The puzzle pieces were finally locking in. The picture was getting clear. She knew who was behind the serial murders now.

It wasn't Camilla, Linda, Patel, or even Eva who had gone on that killing spree. It was someone else in this room. But it was too late to tell Adams.

"Eva!" cried Fox from the platform. He tried to squirm out of Tanya's grasp, but she held on tightly.

"Do you want to get killed?" she hissed.

"Let me go!" Fox pushed her. "I need to help her!"

Tanya held on.

Fox twisted around to Adams. "That's my sister! She's innocent! Leave her out of this!"

Tanya heart raced as she noticed the pistol in Eva's hand. It had been buried in the skirt folds of her velvet gown.

Eva raised her arm and pointed her gun at the sheriff. Three deputies rushed in, but Adams put a hand up to stop them.

Tanya understood why he didn't jump on her. While the guards' intentions had been clear, Eva was unpredictable. She would take everyone in this hall down with her.

Eva smiled. She knew she held all the cards.

She cocked her gun.

Chapter Eighty

S heriff Adams glowered at Eva Fox.

"I didn't come here for games."

Tanya fervently hoped he was wearing a Kevlar vest underneath his uniform.

"I don't play games, Sheriff," said Eva.

"You're under arrest, Eva Fox. You will have multiple murder charges to contemplate. Hand over your firearm to my officers. Now!"

He turned to his deputies when the gunshots came in rapid succession.

"No!" shrieked Fox.

Eva was firing indiscriminately at the wall, the ceiling, the furniture. That didn't stop people from screaming in panic and stumbling over each other to rush out of the hall.

The deputies whirled around, shoving the guests roughly, trying to get a straight line of fire at Eva.

"Hold your fire!" shouted Adams. "Everybody down!"

"Eeny meeny miny moe," laughed Eva, whirling in a circle, faster and faster, like a dervish gone mad. "Who has the biggest death wish of 'em all!"

Tanya suddenly realized the best place to get an aim on Eva was from the stage.

She would risk getting shot in the head, but it was a risk she was willing to take. Rather her than Fox who was struggling with a dying wife, or the local deputies, or any of the guests in the hall.

She let go of Fox and scrambled on her stomach to the edge of the platform. Lying on the stage floor, Tanya aimed her Glock at Eva.

She put her finger on the trigger when a male voice rang through the hall.

"Stop! It wasn't her! I killed them all. It was me."

Eva stopped shooting.

All eyes turned toward the platform. Adams gazed at the stage, then around it, searching for the owner of the voice.

Deputy Madden stepped out from behind the pillar with his high-powered rifle in his hands.

A shocked hush fell in the room.

Tanya knew one pull of that automatic trigger would mean a massacre.

The officers turn their aim from Eva to Madden and back again, confusion clouding their faces.

Adams stared at his deputy.

"What on heaven's name are you doing, Madden?"

"I won't last very long," said Madden, ignoring him, his eyes on Eva.

"Stop right there!" hollered Adams. "Put that gun away."

But Madden kept advancing toward the throne. Toward Eva.

"Might as well take credit for what I did."

A gasp went through the ballroom.

"What the heck are you talking about?" bellowed Adams.

The scornful mask Eva had been wearing vanished. She stared at Madden, her eyes wide in shock.

Tanya watched her. *So she didn't know either.*

Madden kept advancing.

They were seconds away from a complete carnage.

Chapter Eighty-one

Tanya jumped to her feet.

"Deputy Madden!"

Madden turned his haggard face to the stage, like he knew she had been there all along.

His eyes were sorrowful. He was a man with nothing to lose, and men like that were the most dangerous of them all.

"You got rid of the evil in this town," said Tanya, gripping her Glock. "It was for good reason. I understand your motivation."

Madden jerked his head back, like he hadn't expected to hear that.

"You did it for Lila," said Tanya.

Madden waved his weapon at the guests, who threw their hands in the air in shock.

"They bled her dry." His voice cracked. "These people killed her."

"What on earth are you talking about?" said Adams.

"They were all here that day," said Madden, turning to the sheriff. "They tortured my baby girl. She cried for help, but they didn't care. They laughed while they murdered her."

He glanced behind Tanya, his eyes flitting toward the white curtain in the background.

"They killed her like they killed this girl today."

Adams and the deputies turned to the stage, their brows furrowed. All they could see was a white curtain on the platform.

Tanya stepped over to the cross and ripped the cloth away.

Fox gasped out loud. Adams and his deputies stared open-mouthed. The guests averted their eyes, like they didn't want to be reminded of their dirty deeds.

Tanya pointed at the murdered girl on the cross.

"Lila was strung up just like this, wasn't she?"

Madden's face scrunched up, like he was about to cry.

"She was only sixteen." His voice trembled. "They said they would make her famous, an influencer, but instead they.... they...."

"They recruited her into a cult." Tanya turned to Eva and her voice turned hard as stone.

"A cult that gifts special members diamond bracelets. A sign they could be used and abused by the pedophiles in the crowd. And if you're very special, they will bleed you to death."

"My lord," said Adams, putting a hand on his face as if he couldn't believe his ears.

"How dare you!" screamed Eva. "I did nothing wrong!"

Tanya scowled at the woman gesticulating wildly on the floor.

That will be her last lie.

"Leave her out of this!" shouted Fox at Tanya. "She's the victim here. Can't you see?"

"That's what you think," said Madden, his face pinched and flushed. "Your sister was Camilla's understudy. Camilla was grooming her to be the next queen. Look at her!"

"That's not true!" cried Fox. "Eva, tell them the truth!"

Eva straightened her shoulders. She swung around and pointed her gun at the stage.

At Fox.

"This is all your fault. You ruined everything. If you hadn't interfered, they would have never found me."

Tanya saw her finger go to the trigger.

She slammed Fox down to the floor just as the gunshot rang across the room.

Fox screamed.

"Eva!"

Then came the thundering rat-a-tat of the assault rifle.

People shrieked and shoved each other as they stampeded toward the exit.

It was like an earthquake had struck the ballroom. The pungent odor of gunpowder saturated the air. The wall behind the throne was streaked with blood splatters.

Her heart pounding, Tanya lifted her chin. Adams was shooting in Madden's direction, but the deputy had jumped behind the pillar.

Eva was on the floor by the throne, writhing under two deputies who were trying to pin her down. But with every burst of gunfire from Madden's rifle, they let go and slammed to the floor to save themselves.

Tanya soldier-crawled to the side of the stage. She had a good line of sight to Madden's back. He was ready to discharge his weapon again.

Tanya took aim and pulled the trigger.

Madden fell to the ground with a surprised cry, his rifle sliding through the marble floor. Adams pounced on it.

Tanya turned around to see Eva was standing up.

"Adams!" screamed Tanya. "Get down!"

He whirled around, but it was too late.

Eva fired.

Adams fell to his knees.

Fox leaped off the stage.

"Get back, Fox!" hollered Tanya, but he was heading straight to his sister.

"Stop it, Eva!" cried Fox, as he scurried toward her. "What are you doing? Stop it!"

Eva whipped around, her face red in fury. Her weapon was aimed at her brother now. With a chill, Tanya realized what she was about to do.

She turned her Glock on Eva and fired.

Eva fell to her knees, clutching her heart.

"Eva!" screamed Fox as he caught his sister in his arms.

Day Three

Chapter Eighty-two

L *ast witness dead.*

The words roiled through Tanya's troubled mind. She knew Fox would never forgive her for what she did. But if she had to do it again, she would still protect him.

Fox had a heart of gold. Eva had been evil. Tanya couldn't have lived with herself if she had let Eva kill her brother.

Max licked her hand.

Tanya looked down and stroked his ears.

"Don't know what I would do without you, bud."

He thumped his tail on the cold floor and whined.

Tanya put a finger to her lips. "Shh..."

She looked up to see if Sheriff Adams had woken up. He had spent the night in intensive care and had just got transferred to the regular ward.

Tanya slumped over in the hospital chair and rubbed her face. The incident in the ballroom was still a blur. The events of the past few days had been so out-of-the-world she was unsure whether she had imagined some of it.

"Hey."

She looked up.

Adams was awake.

Max trotted over and slid his wet nose into the sheriff's hand, tail wagging. Adams gave him a weak smile and scratched his head.

"Hey there, good boy."

"Good to see you up," said Tanya.

Adams turned to her.

"Thanks for saving my life."

Tanya shrugged.

"All I said was watch out."

"If you hadn't warned me, she'd have got me in the back." Adams sat up and coughed. He took a shaky breath in and let it out. "I'll take a bullet in the arm any day if the alternative is getting my vital organs smashed."

His face turned dark.

"How bad is it? Give it to me straight."

"Seven fatalities out of sixty." Tanya sighed. "About a dozen were brought here with major injuries, but the doctors say they haven't seen anything life threatening, so far."

"Seven gone." Adams shook his head. "From all the blood and guts in the hall, I thought there would be more victims."

He swallowed hard.

"Deputy Yarrow?"

"Bruised, but she'll live," said Tanya. "The guard's bullet hit her vest."

Adams let his head fall to the pillow. He let out a sigh of relief.

"And Madden?"

"He survived," said Tanya. "They finished operating on him the same time as they did you. Madden's in the corner ward, under watch by your deputies."

Adams sighed. "I'm to blame for all this. He worked under me for years. I should have seen this coming."

Tanya shook her head.

"No one, except for the cult members, knew what really happened to Lila. And Madden kept his feelings close to his chest."

"Until it blew up in our faces."

"You can't put that on your shoulders."

Adams patted Max's head absentmindedly.

Tanya got up from her chair. "I came to say goodbye."

Adams raised his head.

"Leaving so soon? What about all the paperwork? I thought you were going to help me with that too."

Tanya smiled a small smile.

How Susan Cross would love that.

"Duty calls. I've got to be back in Black Rock for Monday morning. Otherwise, I turn into a mouse or pumpkin or something."

"Well, we can't have that. How am I going to contact you the next time a cult is running my county?"

"I don't give my time to just anyone, but when I find decent folk who want to do the right thing...," Tanya paused. "I'll be there."

Adams nodded.

"Jack's lucky to have you on his team. Thank you, Stone. I still owe you that drink."

"Visit us in Black Rock when you're feeling better. We can have a beer on the pier."

"I'm holding you to it."

Tanya whistled to Max and slipped out of Adams' room.

Her stomach lurched as she trod down the hospital corridor with Max at her heels. She had one more thing to do that day, but she felt like throwing up every time she thought of it.

Go on. Do it. I owe it to him.

Her mouth went dry and her hands started shaking.

She hastened her pace.

She stepped up to the room six doors down from Adams. Low murmurs were coming from inside.

She peeked in.

Zoe had driven down that morning to Crescent Bay. She was sitting by Fox's bed, holding his hand. Her head was shaved, and she looked thinner than the last time Tanya had seen her.

Her heart jumped to her mouth.

I gave them another reason to grieve.

She was about to knock, when Max slipped by her legs and rushed toward Zoe, his tail wagging furiously.

"Max!" cried Zoe as she bent down to nuzzle him.

Tanya stayed by the doorway, unsure if she would be welcome. Her eyes flitted over to Fox. He stared at her.

Tanya cleared her throat.

"How are you feeling?"

His eyes filled with tears, but she knew those weren't shed for her. Or even for himself. Seeing her had reminded him of how his sister had died.

Max dashed over to Tanya, licked her hand, and zoomed back to Zoe, as if he was so happy to be among friends. Little did he know the turmoil going through everyone's minds.

Tanya stepped up to the foot of the bed, unsure where to start.

"I'm not here to ask for your forgiveness...." She stopped as something caught in her throat. "I just want to say I'm sorry for your loss. I'm sorry for the heartache I put you through."

She looked down.

What do you say to the man whose sister you killed?

Tanya felt a tear roll down her cheek.

The scrape of a metal chair made her look up. Zoe had got to her feet and was trudging toward her.

"Come here," said Zoe in a low, raspy voice.

Tanya froze.

If a grief-stricken woman fighting cancer wants to get her anger out on me, so be it.

She took a tentative step toward Zoe.

Zoe clutched her arm and pulled her close. She looked up at Tanya, her pale blue eyes filled with tears.

"Thank you for saving my husband's life," she whispered.

Before Tanya could reply, Zoe pulled her in for a hug.

Tanya didn't know how long they held each other, crying. What she did know was she was finally forgiven for doing the unthinkable. At least by Zoe.

When she pulled back and wiped her eyes, she noticed Fox was crying too.

"I'm so sorry, Fox."

"I was so... I was so wrapped up in finding my baby sister...," he whispered through his tears, "I didn't realize..."

Tanya nodded.

"I didn't imagine how much she'd changed," croaked Fox. "That wasn't what I.... I never thought in a million years she'd...."

He slumped back in his pillow and stared at the ceiling silently. It was like he was praying for an explanation for why his sister would end up the way she had.

Tanya reached out and squeezed his arm. She didn't have any answers for him. Nothing she could say would heal the hurt in his heart.

All she knew was she would never get over taking Eva's life. It would be a dark nightmare that would haunt her for the rest of her days.

But in her heart she knew she would do it again.

She would do anything to protect the good and decent folk in her life.

To be continued...

⬩――――⬩

I hope you enjoyed this story.

Would you like to know what happened to Deputy Madden in the end?

Four months later, Sheriff Adams visits Tanya Stone and Chief Jack Bold in Black Rock to share some news. Read the final twist to this story that no one, not even Tanya, expected....

....And learn why Camilla had initiated the blood-letting, killing ritual in her cult in the first place.

Download the twisty epilogue story for free, here.
Revelation on the Pier
https://tikiriherath.com/fbi-revelation-on-the-pier

⬩――――⬩

Dive into the next spine-tingling, pulse-pounding thriller in this series.
HER SECRET CRIME

Don't miss out on another fast-paced and spine-tingling murder mystery thriller with Special Agent Stone, Max, Chief Bold, and the eccentric characters of this small seaside town, each of whom holds a secret they'd rather you not find out....

The killer could be anyone. He could be standing right behind you...

Start reading HER SECRET CRIME next!
https://tikiriherath.com/fbi-book4

Continue the adventure with Her Secret Crime

An Excerpt – A Death in the Family

"I invited you tonight to witness a death."

Honoree's voice echoed through the dining hall of Kensington Manor.

No one knew she had a gun hidden in the folds of her red Prada skirt.

Confused murmurs rippled around the table. The family had just finished their six-course gourmet meal and had been waiting for the birthday cake. They had been ready to sing a birthday song. Not this.

The Kensington matriarch's eyes blazed.

"You're all liars, swindlers, and leeches!"

Shocked gasps swept across the dining table.

Honoree glared at each of her family members, one by one, as if to challenge them. One brave young man sat up and looked his grandmother in the eye.

Honoree Kensington was a tall, lithe woman, an imposing figure who turned heads wherever she went. Her posture was always as straight as a soldier, and her head was always held high like she knew the power she held.

"I know why you all came tonight." Her eyes turned cold and flinty. "You're here because you want the money. My money!"

Her small but captive audience shifted uncomfortably in their seats. The young man who had dared to glare back at Honoree leaned across the table. His mother, seated next to him, pulled at his elbow to say, *Don't do it.*

But he had already opened his mouth.

"We came here for your birthday, Grandmother, not to get beaten up like we're criminals."

The others whirled around, their eyes widened, incredulous he had said out aloud what they had been thinking.

Honoree's face flushed a deep red.

"But you are criminals!" She glowered around the table. "Each and every one of you. You have made my life miserable, after all I have done for you. So now, it's my turn to make your life hell."

Gasps rose from the table.

"What exactly have we done?" said a man in a wheelchair.

"We're family," said the young man. "Not some strangers in your boardroom."

"We have always loved you," a meek female voice said from across the table.

"You've always loved me?" Honoree threw her head back in mock laughter.

The family watched their clan's grand matriarch with their mouths open.

With her gray hair pulled back into an elegant swirl, and in her hand-tailored silk Prada gown and ten-carat diamond necklace, she looked like she was about to visit the Buckingham Palace for tea. But everybody around the table knew her handsome looks and immaculate dress were clever disguises of her true, dark personality.

I thought she had gone funny in the head before....
She's completely lost her mind now.
Dementia. That's what it is.
Probably Alzheimer's too.

A lone voice spoke up from the other end of the table.

"I'm your blood sister, Honoree. We stuck up for each other. We have always protected each other. You can't treat us like—"

Honoree snapped her head toward the blonde woman in the pretty floral dress.

"How dare you?" Her lips curled back into a snarl. "You lying, cheating, whore. I disowned you twenty-three years ago."

Her sister stared at her, stunned.

The sound of an ominous click made everyone jump, except for Honoree. Relief flooded their faces when they realized who it was.

The Kensington Manor's housekeeper and her husband were standing at the open doorway, holding a large silver tray. On it was a two-tiered Belgium chocolate cake decorated with 24-carat gold leaves and exquisite rose garlands.

It had taken the chef all day to make those sugar roses. It was too much dessert for a party of seven, but it was what Honoree had ordered.

Mariposa and Rafael walked into the hall gingerly, like they sensed the hostility in the air. The housekeeper turned to the matriarch with a nervous bow.

"Your cake, Madame."

"Take that back to the kitchen." Honoree's voice was as hard as steel. "Eat it. Give it away. Throw it in the dumpster. This party is over."

Rafael raised an eyebrow, but he quickly rearranged his expression to his usual impassive butler look.

"Yes, ma'am."

With their heads bowed in respect or fear, the couple stepped backward through the entrance and gently shut the hall doors behind them.

All guests turned back to Honoree Kensington, their faces scrunched in confusion, anxiety, or anger.

This was supposed to be a family affair, an occasion to celebrate the matriarch's seventieth birthday. Honoree's sister pushed her chair back and rose like she'd had enough.

But one look from the woman at the head of the table and she sat back down.

"I have made a will," said Honoree.

It was like she had slammed a sledgehammer on the table. The air suddenly felt thicker and heavier. No one dared to breathe.

A wry smile cut across Honoree's face.

"Whoever finds my will gets everything." Her smile widened, like she was mocking them. "All you other fools get nothing."

The horrified gasps around the table were louder this time.

Honoree raised her chin.

"But the winner, if there will be one, will soon find out they won nothing at all."

A few faces went pale.

Honoree smirked.

"Idiots! That's what you all are."

A woman wearing a sky-blue Channel suit with a pearl choker glowered at the matriarch, her perfectly manicured nails digging into the antique wood of her armrests.

"This is madness, Honoree," she spat out. "Are you feeling all right?"

Honoree slammed her fist on the table.

The crystal glass by her elbow crashed, spilling vintage Dom Pérignon over the pristine tablecloth.

Those who had been sitting nearest to her pulled their chairs back in alarm. The thousand-dollar-a-bottle champagne spilled over the edge of the table and onto the red Persian rug.

A babble of confused voices broke out.

"Is this some sick game?"

"Why are you playing us like this?"

"You can't do this to us!"

"What in heaven's name—"

Honoree raised her hand to silence them. She scraped her chair back and unfurled herself to her full height. Everybody shrank back in horror.

The chandelier's light glinted off the black pistol in her hand.

Everybody recognized the weapon.

It was Honoree's husband's gun, the one he used at the firing range on weekends. That was before he had died from cancer.

Honoree raised her pistol and whirled around the table.

Panicked shrieks filled the hall.

People scrambled under the table. A few peeked over the edge as if to check they had really seen what they had seen. A shaky sob came from behind a curtain.

The man in the wheelchair whimpered. "Please don't kill us. Please don't kill us."

The young man who'd dared stand up to his grandmother shouted from under the table. "Put that thing away! Put it away right now! You're going to hurt yourself!"

Honoree didn't even glance his way.

"You will start tonight. I wish you all a bloodied fight till the end."

With one last glare at her family, she put the gun to her forehead and pulled the trigger.

To be continued....

Continue HER SECRET CRIME right here:
https://tikiriherath.com/fbi-book4

HER SECRET CRIME: A gripping Tanya Stone FBI K9 crime thriller with a jaw-dropping twist.

A cruel inheritance game. A killer thirsting for blood. Sometimes, it's your own family who wants you dead....

It's midnight. FBI Special Agent Tanya Stone arrives at a private island with her K9 partner to investigate a suspicious suicide.

The matriarch of the wealthy Kensington family has just shot herself in the head.

Her blood-soaked face lies immobile on her gold-rimmed plate, red splatters on the sterling silver and pristine tablecloth. It was her seventieth birthday party, but the celebration is over.

Soon, Tanya realizes a deadly danger is lurking in the shadows.

A new terror rips through the mansion as a calculating killer starts targeting the remaining family members. One by one.

Tanya fights off disturbing memories of her own mother's brutal death to hunt the mysterious murderer.

She'll have to confront the liars, swindlers, and impostors first, because everyone in this twisted house is hiding a dark secret. But one truth remains chillingly clear.

Someone wants to protect a horrific family past by any means necessary. And their next targets are Tanya and her loyal K9, Max....

Pick up HER SECRET CRIME and get your thriller fix today!
https://tikiriherath.com/fbi-book4

There is no graphic violence, heavy cursing, or explicit sex in these books. No dog is harmed in this story, but the villains are.

Available in e-book, paperback, and hardback editions on all good bookstores. Also available for free in libraries everywhere. Just ask your friendly local librarian to order a copy via Ingram Spark.

A Note from Tikiri

D ear Friend,

      Thank you for reading this book. Did you enjoy the story?

My promise is to give you an exciting escape with every book I write, and I sure hope I have done so.

If you enjoyed HER LAST LIE, I would love it if you'd let your reader friends know, so they can experience Tanya and Max's thrilling adventures on the West Coast too.

You can leave your honest review on Goodreads, Bookbub, or the online bookstore from which you purchased the book. Just one sentence would do.

Thank you so much.

Hey, have you heard of the Rebel Reader Club?

This is my exclusive reader community where you can get early access to my new mystery thrillers before anyone else in the world.

You can also receive bonus true crime and real-life K9 stories, and snag fun bookish swag—from postcards, reader stickers, bookmarks, to personalized paperbacks and more.

You can join the club as a Detective, a Special Agent, or an FBI Director.

The choice is yours.

Or you can just follow the club for free and see if it's something you'd like to become part of. Hit the follow button and you're on.

https://tikiriherath.com/thrillers

(You might have to do a bit of sleuthing to find the door to the exclusive club from my site, but it's there. Prove you're a detective!)

See you on the inside.
My very best wishes,
Tikiri
Vancouver, Canada

PS/ Don't forget! Download the twisty epilogue story here.

Four months later, Sheriff Adams visits Tanya Stone and Chief Jack Bold in Black Rock to share some news. Read the final twist to this story that no one, not even Tanya, expected....

....And learn why Camilla had initiated the blood-letting, killing ritual in her cult.

Get your personal copy of **Revelation on the Pier** for free, right here:

https://tikiriherath.com/fbi-revelation-on-the-pier

PPS/ If you didn't enjoy the story or spotted typos, would you drop a line and let me know? Or just write to say hello.

I love to hear from you and personally reply to every email I receive. My email address is: Tikiri@TikiriHerath.com

The Reading List

T he Red Heeled Rebels universe of mystery thrillers, featuring your favorite kick-ass female characters:

—•—••—•

Tanya Stone FBI K9 Mystery Thrillers

NEW FBI thriller series starring Tetyana from the Red Heeled Rebels as Special Agent Tanya Stone, and Max, her loyal German Shepherd. These are serial killer thrillers set in Black Rock, a small upscale resort town on the coast of Washington state.

Her Deadly End
Her Cold Blood
Her Last Lie
Her Secret Crime
Her Perfect Murder
Her Grisly Grave

www.TikiriHerath.com/Thrillers

Asha Kade Private Detective Murder Mysteries

Each book is a standalone murder mystery thriller, featuring the Red Heeled Rebels, Asha Kade and Katy McCafferty. Asha and Katy receive one million dollars for their favorite children's charity from a secret benefactor's estate every time they solve a cold case.

Merciless Legacy
Merciless Games
Merciless Crimes
Merciless Lies
Merciless Past
Merciless Deaths
www.TikiriHerath.com/Mysteries

Red Heeled Rebels International Mystery & Crime - The Origin Story

The award-winning origin story of the Red Heeled Rebels characters. Learn how a rag-tag group of trafficked orphans from different places united to fight for their freedom and their lives and became a found family.

The Girl Who Crossed the Line
The Girl Who Ran Away
The Girl Who Made Them Pay
The Girl Who Fought to Kill
The Girl Who Broke Free
The Girl Who Knew Their Names
The Girl Who Never Forgot
www.TikiriHerath.com/RedHeeledRebels
This series is now complete.

+———••——+

The Accidental Traveler

An anthology of personal short stories based on the author's sojourns around the world.

+———••——+

The Rebel Diva Nonfiction Series

Your Rebel Dreams: 6 simple steps to take back control of your life in uncertain times.

Your Rebel Plans: 4 simple steps to getting unstuck and making progress today.

Your Rebel Life: Easy habit hacks to enhance happiness in the 10 key areas of your life.

Bust Your Fears: 3 simple tools to crush your anxieties and squash your stress.

◆━━━━◆

Collaborations
   The Boss Chick's Bodacious Destiny Nonfiction Bundle
   Dark Shadows 2: Voodoo and Black Magic of New Orleans

◆━━━━◆

Tikiri's novels and nonfiction books are available in e-book, paperback, and hardback editions, on all good bookstores around the world.

   These books are also available in libraries everywhere. Just ask your friendly local librarian or your local bookstore to order a copy via Ingram Spark.

   www.TikiriHerath.com

   Happy reading.

Debate This Dozen

T welve Book Club Questions

1. Who was your favorite character?

2. Which characters did you dislike?

3. Which scene has stuck with you the most? Why?

4. What scenes surprised you?

5. What was your favorite part of the book?

6. What was your least favorite part?

7. Did any part of this book strike a particular emotion in you? Which part and what emotion did the book make you feel?

8. Did you know the author has written an underlying message in this story? What theme or life lesson do you think this story tells?

9. What did you think of the author's writing?

10. How would you adapt this book into a movie? Who would you cast in the leading roles?

11. On a scale of one to ten, how would you rate this story?

12. Would you read another book by this author?

Tanya Stone FBI K9 Mystery Thrillers

*S*ome small-town secrets will haunt your nightmares. Escape if you can...

The Books:

Her Deadly End
Her Cold Blood
Her Last Lie
Her Secret Crime
Her Perfect Murder
Her Grisly Grave

A brand-new FBI K9 serial killer thriller series for a pulse-pounding, bone-chilling adventure from the comfort and warmth of your favorite reading chair at home.

Can you find the killer before Agent Tanya Stone?

www.TikiriHerath.com/thrillers

FBI Special Agent Tanya Stone has a new assignment. Hunt down the serial killers prowling the idyllic West Coast resort towns.

An unspeakable and bone-chilling darkness seethes underneath these picturesque seaside suburbs. A string of violent abductions and gruesome murders wreak hysteria among the perfect lives of the towns' families.

But nothing is what it seems. The monsters wear masks and mingle with the townsfolk, spreading vicious lies.

With her K9 German Shepherd, Agent Stone goes on the warpath. She will fight her own demons as a trafficked survivor to make the perverted psychopaths pay.

But now, they're after her.

Small towns have dark deceptions and sealed lips. If they know you know the truth, they'll never let you leave...

Each book is a standalone murder mystery thriller, featuring Tetyana from the Red Heeled Rebels as Agent Tanya Stone, and Max, her loyal German Shepherd. Red Heeled Rebels Asha Kade and Katy McCafferty and their found family make guest appearances when Tanya needs help.

There is no graphic violence, heavy cursing, or explicit sex in these books.

The dogs featured in this series are never harmed, but the villains are.

To learn more about this exciting new series and find out how to get early access to all the books in the Tanya Stone FBI K9 series, go to www.TikiriHerath.com/thrillers

Sign up to Tikiri's Rebel Reader Club to get the chance to win personalized paperback books, chat with the author and more.

Available in e-book, paperback, and hardback editions on all good bookstores around the world. Print books are available for free in libraries everywhere. Just ask your friendly local librarian or your local bookstore to order a copy via Ingram Spark.

Asha Kade Private Detective Murder Mysteries

How far would you go for a million-dollar payout?

The Books:

Merciless Legacy

Merciless Games

Merciless Crimes

Merciless Lies

Merciless Past

Merciless Deaths

◆━━━◆

Each book is a standalone murder mystery thriller featuring the Red Heeled Rebel, Asha Kade, and her best friend Katy

McCafferty, as private detectives on the hunt for serial killers in small towns USA.

There is no graphic violence, heavy cursing, or explicit sex in these books. What you will find are a series of suspicious deaths, a closed circle of suspects, twists and turns, fast-paced action, and nail-biting suspense.

www.TikiriHerath.com/mysteries

A newly minted private investigator, Asha Kade, gets a million dollars from an eccentric client's estate every time she solves a cold case. Asha Kade accepts this bizarre challenge, but what she doesn't bargain for is to be drawn into the dark underworld of her past again.

The only thing that propels her forward now is a burning desire for justice.

What readers are saying on Amazon and Goodreads:
"My new favorite series!"
"Thrilling twists, unputdownable!"
"I was hooked right from the start!"
"A twisted whodunnit! Edge of your seat thriller that kept me up late, to finish it, unputdownable!! More, please!"
"Buckle up for a roller coaster of a ride. This one will keep you on the edge of your seat."
"A must read! A macabre start to an excellent book. It had me totally gripped from the start and just got better!""

A brand-new murder mystery series for a pulse-pounding, bone-chilling adventure from the comfort and warmth of your favorite reading chair at home.

Can you find the killer before Asha Kade does?

To learn more about this exciting series, go to www.TikiriHerath.com/mysteries.

Sign up to Tikiri's Rebel Reader Club to get the chance to win personalized paperback books, chat with the author and more.

Available in e-book, paperback, and hardback editions on all good bookstores around the world. Print books are available for free in libraries everywhere. Just ask your friendly local librarian or your local bookstore to order a copy via Ingram Spark.

The Red Heeled Rebels International Mystery & Crime

The Origin Story

Would you like to know the origin story of your favorite characters in the Tanya Stone FBI K9 mystery thrillers and the Asha Kade Merciless murder mysteries?

In the award-winning Red Heeled Rebels international mystery & crime series—the origin story—you'll find out how Asha, Katy, and Tetyana (Tanya) banded together in their troubled youths to fight for freedom against all odds.

The complete Red Heeled Rebels international crime collection:

Prequel Novella: The Girl Who Crossed the Line

Book One: The Girl Who Ran Away
Book Two: The Girl Who Made Them Pay
Book Three: The Girl Who Fought to Kill
Book Four: The Girl Who Broke Free
Book Five: The Girl Who Knew Their Names
Book Six: The Girl Who Never Forgot
The series is now complete!

An epic, pulse-pounding, international crime thriller series that spans four continents featuring a group of spunky, sassy young misfits who have only each other for family.

A multiple-award-winning series which would be best read in order. There is no graphic violence, heavy cursing, or explicit sex in these books.

www.TikiriHerath.com/RedHeeledRebels

In a world where justice no longer prevails, six iron-willed young women rally to seek vengeance on those who stole their humanity.

If you like gripping thrillers with flawed but strong female leads, vigilante action in exotic locales and twists that leave you at the edge of your seat, you'll love these books by multiple award-winning Canadian novelist, Tikiri Herath.

Go on a heart-pounding international adventure without having to get a passport or even buy an airline ticket!

What readers are saying on Amazon and Goodreads:

"Fast-paced and exciting!"

"An exciting and thought-provoking book."

"A wonderful story! I didn't want to leave the characters."

"I couldn't put down this exciting road trip adventure with a powerful message."

"Another award-worthy adventure novel that keeps you on the edge of your seat."

"A heart-stopping adventure. I just couldn't put the book down till I finished reading it."

—•———•—

Literary Awards & Praise for The Red Heeled Rebels books:

- Grand Prize Award Finalist - 2019 Eric Hoffer Award, USA

- First Horizon Award Finalist - 2019 Eric Hoffer Award, USA

- Honorable Mention General Fiction - 2019 Eric Hoffer Award, USA

- Winner First-In-Category - 2019 Chanticleer Somerset Award, USA

- Semi-Finalist - 2020 Chanticleer Somerset Award, USA

- Winner in 2019 Readers' Favorite Book Awards, USA

- Winner of 2019 Silver Medal - Excellence E-Lit Award, USA

- Winner in Suspense Category - 2018 New York Big Book

Award, USA

- Finalist in Suspense Category - 2018 & 2019 Silver Falchion Awards, USA

- Honorable Mention - 2018-19 Reader Views Literary Classics Award, USA

- Publisher's Weekly Booklife Prize - 2018, USA

＊━━━━＊

To learn more about this addictive series, go to **www.TikiriHerath.com/RedHeeledRebels** and receive the prequel novella - **The Girl Who Crossed The Line** - as a gift.

Sign up to Tikiri's Rebel Reader club and get bonus stories, exotic recipes, the chance to win paperbacks, chat with the author and more.

＊━━━━＊

Available in e-book, paperback, and hardback editions on all good bookstores around the world. Print books are available for free in libraries everywhere. Just ask your friendly local librarian or your local bookstore to order a copy via Ingram Spark.

Acknowledgments

To my amazing, talented, superstar editor, Stephanie Parent (USA), thank you, as always, for coming on this literary journey with me and for helping make these books the best they can be.

❦───◦───❦

To my international club of beta readers who gave me their feedback, thank you. I truly value your thoughts.

In alphabetical order of first name:

Michele Kapugi, USA

Kim Schup, USA

And a special thanks to my Rebel Reader Team

Dar Myers, USA

Sheila Cottingham, USA

Ruth Frank, USA

Barbara Fiedler, USA

Arto Raukunen, Finland

To all the kind and generous readers who take the time to review my novels and share their honest feedback, thank you so much. Your support is invaluable.

I'm immensely grateful to you all for your kind and generous support, and would love to invite you for a glass of British Columbian wine or a cup of Ceylon tea with chocolates when you come to Vancouver next!

About the Author

T ikiri Herath is the multiple-award-winning author of international thriller and mystery novels and the Rebel Diva books.

━━━◆━━━◆━━━

Tikiri worked in risk management in the intelligence and defense sectors, including in the Canadian Federal Government and at NATO. She has a bachelor's degree from the University of Victoria, British Columbia, and a master's degree from the Solvay Business School in Brussels.

Born in Sri Lanka, Tikiri grew up in East Africa and has studied, worked, and lived in Europe, Southeast Asia, and North America throughout her adult life. An international nomad and fifth-culture kid, she now calls Canada home.

She's an adrenaline junkie who has rock climbed, bungee jumped, rode on the back of a motorcycle across Quebec, flown in an acrobatic airplane upside down, and parachuted solo.

When she's not plotting another thriller scene or planning another adrenaline-filled trip, you'll find her baking in her kitchen with a glass of red Shiraz in hand and vintage jazz playing in the background.

◆——◆——◆

To say hello and get travel stories from around the world, go to **www.TikiriHerath.com**